PLEDGED TO THE
HIGHBORN WARRIOR

BROTHERS OF THE SCARRED PLANET SERIES

TRINITY BLAISE

This book contains descriptions of many sexual practices, but this is a work of fiction and, as such, should not be seen in any way as a guide. The author will not be responsible for any loss, harm, injury, or death resulting from use of the information contained within.

Cover design by Romance Cover Designs

Dedicated to my alien romance cheerleader friends

Liz, Robyn, Ang, Emma and Tamsin

ONE

Kate

Rough fingers trail up my thighs as lips press hard against the throbbing vein in my neck. I place my palm against a muscled chest and watch the skin beneath it oscillate red then purple. Something latches on to the most intimate part of me, and a strange pulsing begins. I lean my head back and moan, the view of Earth through the vessel's window disappearing as I close my eyes.

I wake with a gasp at the sound of frantic knocking. The numbers on my clock beat red in the dark. Not even five in the morning. I moan and close my eyes again. Maybe if I just ignore the noise, I can return to that delicious dream again…

More knocking.

"Damn it." I force myself out of bed, and go to my window see my neighbor Robyn looking up at me, beckoning me to come down. Maybe she's still drunk from her barbecue the night before? Maybe *I* am? Those Mojitos were lethal. I groan as I feel the inevitable headache buzz at my temples. I still need to mark half my class's assignments before school tomorrow and tidy the whole damn house. I pad out into the hallway, quickly checking on my daughter, Isla, who seems oblivious to the racket Robyn's making.

I jog downstairs, nearly tripping over the basket of clothes I forgot to put in the washing machine yesterday. Will I *ever* have a tidy house? It was bad enough when I was still with Richard, my ex. He wasn't exactly dad of the year to Isla, but at least he did the washing occasionally—if he needed a shirt for the next day, that is. Speaking of which, there's the blouse I was hoping to wear to work tomorrow, the massive ketchup stain still there. I was supposed to soak that overnight. Well, there are a million things I was *supposed* to do, but I've learnt life doesn't quite work out like that, *especially* when you're a single mom.

I sigh and open the front door a sliver. Yep, there's Robyn. She's standing in her Snoopy pajamas with the kind of shocked expression I usually see from my students when I tell them crazy science facts, like how there are more stars in the universe than grains of sand on Earth.

"What's with the early morning door drumming?" I ask her, yawning. "You still drunk?"

"Haven't you seen it?"

"Seen what?"

"Look up!'

"This better not be that harvest moon you've been going on about. Have you noticed the time?"

She grabs my chin and makes me look up.

"Ouch!" I go to bat her hand away and then freeze. A huge globe hovers above our street. At first glance, it seems to be made from some kind of metal, but as I squint, I realize whatever material it's made out of is undulating in the moon-light, like ripples in golden silk. A loud humming noise is coming from it too that beats to the same rhythm as the hum I just felt throbbing against me in my dreams.

Maybe I'm still dreaming?

"What the hell?" I whisper.

"Michael's refusing to come look," Robyn says. "He doesn't believe there's a spaceship above our house. He says I'm still drunk. But it's there, right? I'm not going mad."

I continue staring at it, not believing my eyes.

"Jesus, say something, Kate!" Robyn shouts.

"Pinch me."

"What?"

"This is a dream. It has to be. *Pinch* me." She pinches my arm, and I flinch, rubbing my skin. "Okay, so I'm definitely awake."

More neighbors have come out of their houses, dressing gowns wrapped around their bodies as they stare up at the sky. The elderly couple from across the road have even set deckchairs up on their lawns and are sipping coffee in the moonlight as they watch the golden globe above.

"I always said this would happen," the elderly man calls across to us. "All the trillions of planets out there, we can't be the only intelligent beings."

"You're a science teacher, Kate," Robyn says. "Is he right? Is it aliens?"

"Unlikely," I say firmly, more to myself than Robyn, because this simply can't be possible. "The circumstances that led to humans cropping up here were super rare as it is," I explain. "Even if a planet has water sources, the chances of the microbes needed for intelligent life eventually bubbling out of the primordial soup is super low. Not to mention the fact the universe has been around for billions of years, plenty of time for aliens to show up. Why wait until now?"

"God, I love it when you talk dirty to me," Robyn jokes.

"Oh, I've got more where that came from. I haven't even told you about single-cell eukaryotes and—" I feel movement behind me. It's Isla, rubbing at her tired eyes.

"What's happening, Mom?" she asks. Then she stares up

7

at the sky, her green eyes alight with fascination. "Wow! Is it aliens?"

"Of course not, darling. It's probably some elaborate marketing ploy for a new movie," I say. Yeah, that's what it must be. A marketing ploy. Because it can't be aliens. It just can't be.

"Or a crazy government experiment?" Robyn suggests.

Isla frowns. I think she'd prefer aliens.

Robyn's husband, Michael, runs out then, a tablet in his hands. "You were right. It's all over the news."

We all turn to his screen. It's showing a familiar channel with a breaking-news ticker running along the bottom announcing in capitals: UNIDENTIFIED SPHERE-LIKE FLYING OBJECTS APPEAR IN SKIES AROUND THE WORLD. There's a satellite map of the world with icons representing the vessels, one over each country.

"Looks like we got America's one then," Robyn says.

The screen changes to show a live stream revealing a mammoth golden sphere hovering above a vast desert in Africa.

"The mothership," Michael says in an awe-filled voice.

Robyn and I exchange shocked looks. I swallow, putting my arm around Isla's shoulders. *This can't be happening.* The live feed disappears, and a news anchor takes its place. She puts her slim fingers to her ear and then nods. "Okay, this transmission has just come in."

"Something's happening!" Michael shouts out to our neighbors, holding the tablet up. Everyone gets their phones out, and faces all down our long street are illuminated by the lights from their screens.

"Is it the president?" Robyn asks.

"Yeah, probably," Michael says.

But the man who comes into view looks nothing like the president. In fact, he doesn't look like *any* man I've seen.

And yet he somehow feels eerily familiar to me. He's dressed in golden robes covered with swirling and moving geometric shapes. His white hair falls to his shoulders, and he has a neat white beard. His eyes are a vivid, otherworldly green. Most shocking of all, his skin seems to be oscillating like the material of the sphere above us... and like the man from my dreams. Not purple and red, but blues and greens. At a guess, I'd say he's in his sixties, maybe seventies, but who knows?

Floating in the air above him is a hologram of a female form sitting cross-legged against a psychedelic background with geometric shapes swirling all around her. A drum-like tune thrums with a rhythm that strikes familiar fear and—oh God—*desire* into my heart. I know that tune. But why? How? I take a deep, shuddery breath, pulling Isla even closer.

The music stops, and the being stares confidently into the camera. "Greetings. I'm the Grand Sovran of the Skarsdon region of the planet Obrothea," he says in a strange, almost mechanic voice. "Obrothea is the exoplanet your scientists identified last year as 75 Sisri."

"I remember that," Isla says excitely. "We learnt about it in school. The Kepler Space Telescope saw it. It's in a completely different solar system." I remember it too. The images the powerful telescope had taken were out of focus, but it was still clear to see the neon-green scars over the planet's surface, like earthquake cracks. I remember teaching it to my class of fourteen-year-olds. Of course, I know the chances of life there were deemed possible, but still...

"Ten years ago," the Grand Sovran continues, "we selected Skarsdonian warriors and human women—who we call Pledged—to conceive one hybrid child from each country on Earth. These children are the Sacred."

"Okay, that confirms it," I say, laughing as I shake my head. "This has *got* to be a prank."

"You sure?" Robyn asks, taking in the object above us with fearful eyes.

"Shhh, he's still talking," her husband says. We both go quiet and turn back to the screen.

"Now we have come to claim our Sacred," the Grand Sovran states, "and our Pledged too."

Gasps ring out around the street. Isla peers up at me with worried eyes. "It's okay, darling," I quickly say, stroking her long dark hair so like mine. "This isn't real."

"We understand the alarm this might raise," the Grand Sovran continues. "But it is important to understand two things. First, our Pledged and our Sacred children will always be treated with the upmost respect, receiving all the care and necessities they desire. Two, any resistance will be futile."

The camera pans out to reveal a being dressed in golden armor on the other side of the Grand Sovran. He's absolutely huge, standing even taller than the older man, and the muscles in his mammoth bare arms ripple with stark reds and deep blues. He stares into the camera with vivid green eyes framed by long lashes. Golden stubble caresses his cheeks and skims his tight jaw, and his hair falls in blond waves to his shoulders.

As I look at him, recognition punches me in the gut with a whirlwind of emotions I can't quite get a grasp on. One of those emotions is fear. A hot poker of pure fear, enhanced by the sight of his huge hand resting on the hilt of his sword and the war-like expression on his otherworldly face. But the other emotion racing through me is desire. Desire so hard and so true it's like this man is reaching through the screen and pressing his bronzed oscillating finger against my clit.

Robyn takes a deep breath, licking her lips. It's difficult not to. It's a visceral reaction. I close my eyes, trying to drive the desire away, but another image comes to me, one of this very being standing over me naked, every perfect muscle rippling with color as my hand reaches out for him. I quickly snap my eyes open and look back at the warrior on the screen.

Who are you?

"We will be making collections soon," the Grand Sovran says. "Thank you for your cooperation." And just like that, the broadcast abruptly ends.

"Collections?" Robyn shakes her head in disgust. "Like women and children are objects. Honestly, if this is a publicity stunt, they need to come back into the twenty-first century, right?"

I hear her, but I'm still thinking of the warrior. *Why* is he so familiar?

"Right, Kate?" Robyn asks, jogging my arm with her elbow.

"Sure," I whisper.

Michael peers up at the undulating sphere above. "Pretty elaborate prank though. Can you imagine what a kid fathered by those dudes would be like though?"

I look down into Isla's vivid green eyes, fear zigzagging through my heart.

They are eyes just like those beings on screen.

TWO

Kate

I quickly usher Isla inside, my mind whirring with all the possibilities. Why did it all feel so familiar and real, despite every rational part of me saying it can't possibly be? As though in response, the hum of the ship above thrums even louder in my ears, calling for me. Calling for Isla?

No. No, no, no, no. That's ridiculous.

"Is it real?" Isla asks, her voice cutting through my panicked thoughts. She's at the living room window, staring up at the object in fascination. Dawn will be breaking soon, and already it's a little lighter outside, making the sphere above look even more surreal and out of place. I would have loved a sight like this at her age, but life has since taught me not to yearn for the unknown. It can be *dangerous*.

"I don't think so, darling," I reply, pulling her into a hug. As I do, my phone rings. I pick it up and see it's my ex, Richard. I still get that sinking feeling whenever I see his name on my phone. It's been six months since our big break up, but the pain is still sharp. If only I could just cut him out of my life. But he's Isla's dad…At least, I'm almost positive he is. The thing that's always bothered me about her conception is not only the fact I was on the contraceptive pill at the time, but also that the dates never quite matched up. I met Richard at my twentieth birthday celebration and we didn't do the deed until a few weeks later, *after* I'd already missed my period. But I didn't hook up with anyone else during that time, so why would I question that Richard was the father? It was a shock when I told him I was pregnant, but he stepped up, and we'd both tried to make it work. Unfortunately, he was away too much with his job as a financial advisor to be a present father, and as I discovered a few months ago, too busy with his various mistresses too.

I sigh, putting my phone to my ear. "Hi, Richard."

"You've seen it?" Always the same with him. No greeting, no asking how we're doing. Straight in with his questions and demands.

"Yep, bit hard to miss."

"It's a prank. It has to be. Those dudes were clearly actors, especially the big one, the Thor lookalike."

I swallow down my desire at the memory of the warrior on screen. "Yeah, maybe."

"You don't sound so sure," Richard says, sensing my doubt.

I walk into the hallway, shutting the living room door behind me so Isla can't hear. "It's difficult not to take it seriously when one of those things is right above my house,'" I whisper. "I mean, *literally* right above my house, Richard."

"Our house," Richard reminds me. He's right. We do both own it. But soon neither of us will once it's sold. "You want me to come over?"

"No, we're fine," I quickly say. Last thing I need is Richard suddenly pretending he's some great protector and family man, like he wasn't the one I caught screwing my hairdresser on Isla's ninth birthday. I hesitate a moment as I look at the photo of Isla on the hallway wall, my gaze catching on her green eyes. "The weird thing is," I say, almost to myself, "it all feels so…familiar."

"Familiar? What do you mean?"

I close my eyes, the humming sound pulsing in my ears. "Remember I told you about the weird dreams I had about being on a spaceship? The anthem they played during the broadcast… I swear I recognize it from those dreams. And the big soldier, the Thor look-a-like. I *recognize* him."

"You're starting to sound like your dad, Kate," Richard says in a warning tone.

"I'm nothing like my dad!"

"Hmmm. I'm coming over. Isla needs a bit of Thompson family realism when stuff like this happens." It will only take him a couple of minutes to get here. He's been renting an apartment around the corner since I kicked him out.

"No!" I say. "We're fine. Isla's fine. I—" But it's too late. He's ended the call. I clench my fists in anger. Damn Richard. This is perfect for him, a chance to show he's in charge. I start pacing the hallway. What if he's right though? *Am* I letting my imagination run wild like my dad once did? His imagination had ripped my mom and I away from our secure lives and moved us to a commune filled with people determined to live an off-the-grid adventure. That had ended so badly, I'd promised myself I'd let go of all the dreams of adventure I'd once had. And yet now here I am with a spaceship hovering above my house.

What if this whole thing *is* real? Even worse, what if Isla *is* one of the kids these beings want to claim as their own? Those green eyes of hers have always been a talking point, especially considering Richard and I both have brown eyes.

Where *did* she get those green eyes?

I think of that insanely hot alien warrior and his intense green gaze.

"No, Kate," I snap at myself and clench my hands into fists. "Pull yourself together." As I say that, there's a loud knock on the door. I frown. Richard was quick. Maybe he ran? I open the front door and freeze.

It's one of them. One of the beings.

THREE

Tharin

I watch Kate's house, anxiety a fist around my heart. It's been many years since I was here on Earth. Already the memories of that first night I saw her ten years ago assault me. I'd never seen anything so beautiful as I watched her sleeping. Strands of dark hair across her pillow, red lips partly open, and lashes long against soft cheeks. I remember thinking to myself that here lay the mother of my future child.

It is strange to think how naive I was back then. Ruled by my curiosity about the human race and its exquisite-looking females. Curiosity that was eventually sated by nights spent exploring every part of Kate, my assigned Pledged, nights that surprised me again and again by how easily she responded to my fingers, my tongue, my cock. I had no idea how hard I would fall in love with her…and what that love would take away from me.

When our father announced last month it was time to claim our Pledged and the Sacred children we conceived with them, there were great celebrations through Skarsdon. But I didn't celebrate. How could I after what happened? Of course, Kate knows nothing of the tragic events that blighted our final night together. She remembers nothing of *any* of the nights we shared thanks to the memory-blurring drugs all the women were given. To her, those nights should be vague dreams. But they remain intrenched in my memories like the most exquisite and most deadly of weeds.

I watch Adin now, my most trusted defender, stride towards Kate's door. I stay in the shadows, away from sight. She must not see me. Not yet. I have to endure this first sighting alone and from a distance. That way, I can control my emotions before I must endure her presence properly for I am not sure if I will want to kiss her or kill her.

The door opens, and I hold my breath. There she is, just as I remember. That dark hair, a storm cloud around her pretty human face. Her tiny form. Her strange unwavering skin. There are changes, like the dark circles beneath her eyes. Her beautiful face is fuller, her body too. It only serves to make my yearning greater. My skin pulses purple, every sinew and fiber pulling me towards her. My arcism, unignited for so long, throbs at the mere sight of my Pledged, desperate to latch onto that fascinating part of her human anatomy they call the clitoris.

I pull my sword from its sheath and press its sharp blade into the soft skin of my palm, wincing as I draw blood. My father's words echo in my mind. *"She is just a means to an end, Tharin. A way to secure your future power and Skarsdon's fate. Forget the past. Focus on our future."*

"A means to an end," I hiss to myself. "She is just a means to an end."

Kate

I look up at the being standing before me in horror. He's like a gladiator and is at least seven foot tall with a stature so huge he fills the whole doorway. He's wearing the same chest armor as the warrior we saw on the broadcast, except his armor is more bronze than gold. There's a long, colorful sword latched to his waist. His skin up close is astounding, a whirlwind of light blues battling reds and purples. My curiosity fights with fear as I take all of him in.

Fear wins.

I stumble away from him. Sirens ring out in the distance, and behind him, neighbors appear at their windows, alarmed.

"I am Adin, your defender," the gladiator alien says. 'I do not mean you any harm. It's now time for you and Isla to come with us."

Isla appears from the living room, mouth dropping open when she notices the warrior at our door. I pull her behind me, shielding her just as Richard runs around the corner, stopping to catch his breath as he notices the warrior too.

"Daddy!" Isla shouts to him. "They've come to take us!"

"What's going on?" Richard says as he jogs over.

"We are here to claim our Pledged and our Sacred children," Adin tells him matter-of-factly.

"Stop him, Daddy," Isla shouts.

Richard hesitates a moment then curls his hands into fists and strides towards the being. He goes to grab the giant's arm, but it's no use. Even at nearly six foot tall, Richard looks like a child next to this creature. As if to prove the point, the alien warrior sweeps his arm around like he's batting an insect away, and Richard flies through the air and falls to the ground in the distance. Two other beings approach as several police cars screech into our street, their red and blue lights bouncing off the walls.

A memory darts through me then of bright lights bouncing off the dusty road outside the commune I'd called home for a while, of my mother being carried on a stretcher towards an ambulance. The memory disappears as quickly as it came as the two beings remove their swords from their sheaths and face the police cars. Oh God, this is really happening, isn't it? Have they really come to collect us?

"Run!" I hear my mother's voice echo in my head.

I grab Isla's hand, slip under the being's raised arm with her, and run down the side of the house. If I can keep up the pace, we'll get to a maze of alleyways behind the block in a moment. Even aliens—oh my God, that's really what they are, aren't they?—can't guess which turns we'll take, which entrances and exits we'll choose, right? They can't possibly know this neighborhood like we do. I can hear Richard shouting behind me. Are they hurting him? Maybe I shouldn't have left him. But Isla has to come first. She *always* has to come first.

I hear footsteps behind us. Thunderous. Threatening.

"Where are we going?" Isla asks. "What about Daddy?"

"He'll be okay," I lie. There's a hidden gap in the next set of hedges. It's the same gap we use most days for our shortcut to school. Another set of alleyways stand before it though, perfect for getting lost in. I duck through the gap and into the first alleyway, navigating it like I do every day until the field comes into view. If I can just get us across that field, we'll be at the subway, and we can disappear.

There's a swooshing sound above us, and we both freeze as a long shadow is cast over us. The scent hits me first. A musky otherworldly scent that makes a delicious, intense warmth whirl inside my body without warning.

I look up to see a giant figure standing on a shed in the yard next to us, his undulating, colorful skin breathtaking against the dawning skies above. *The warrior from the broadcast.* He's even taller and even more vast than the defender who was just at our house. His golden hair is tied back, the rising sun above making it shine. His thigh muscles ripple beneath the black leather-style pants he is wearing, and the skin of his powerful arms gleams purple and red. I feel that sucker punch of recognition and desire again, and my breath quickens. He holds my gaze, his green eyes so intense and scorching I have to look away.

Pull it together, Kate!

I go to run in the opposite direction, but it's too late. He jumps down in one swift movement. Everything seems to go still as he lands before us, a giant statue so tall my face barely reaches his chest. The wind stops. The birds above quieten. Even the clouds appear to still in their early morning drift. All I see is him, looking down at me with those green eyes, that scent of his filling every part of me. His whole presence seems to press into me, dominating me with a cacophony of sensation.

Isla clasps my hand, whimpering as the being lifts a small golden vial and pops open the lid with his huge thumb. An acrid stench fills my nostrils and then darkness descends. The last thing I remember is falling into the being's huge arms, Isla calling out my name.

FOUR

Kate

The hum wakes me, throbbing at the core of me, filling me. I moan and turn over. Whatever I'm lying on moves with me, my elbow sinking into some soft substance I can't place. Then I remember what just happened. I sit up, instantly reaching out for Isla.

"Mommy!" Isla is sitting beside me, her hand on my shoulder. I pull her into my arms in relief.

"Isla, darling." I search her face for any sign of injury. "A-are you okay?"

"Yes, I'm fine," she says with a yawn. "I fell asleep when I smelt that weird thing the soldier was holding. Where are we?"

I look around. We're in a large, perfectly circular room with golden curved walls and nothing else apart from the bed we woke on which sits in the middle of the room. Or at least I think it's a bed. It's round and king-size, but there are no duvets, no sheets. Instead, we're sitting in a warm, multi-colored mist. It feels lovely, luxurious, as though I'm lying on a cloud.

A cloud.

A thought instantly comes to me. Are we on a spaceship? Childish curiosity and fascination battles with fear and doubt.

"Is this the spaceship?" Isla asks, repeating my thoughts, a hint of fear mixed with fascination in her voice too.

"I don't know." Fear darts across her face. "But we're not hurt, are we?" I quickly add to reassure her. "We're okay, and we're together."

She nods. "Will Daddy be here? Do you think he's okay?" I recall the shouts I heard before I lost consciousness. I very much doubt they brought Richard here. Didn't the Grand Sovran announce he was reclaiming the children and the mothers of those children? No mention of any fathers.

"I don't know, darling," I admit.

"I want to go home."

"Me too. Let me see if there's a way out." There's no sign of a door, so I stand and walk around the room with my palm against the wall. It suddenly ripples beneath my skin, and I snatch my hand away. I hesitate a moment and then press both palms against the wall. It feels just as it looks, like metal, and yet it's warm and… Yes, it's definitely moving, like water rippling beneath a golden sheet. It suddenly shifts beneath my hands, and a door-shaped part of the wall shimmers and turns translucent before disappearing all together. A large living area is revealed. There are two golden chairs, a round golden table, and shelves filled with books along some of the curved walls. Isla goes to run into the room, but I grab her wrist to stop her. "Wait, me first."

I walk in as Isla stays close behind me. I place my palms on the walls again and walk around until the wall ripples again, revealing a wardrobe with golden clothes hanging inside.

"There are no hangers," Isla says. "How are the clothes even hanging?"

She's right. They're all floating in mid-air with nothing supporting them. I reach my hand into the wardrobe, and the air around it pulsates. I snatch my hand away, and the wall solidifies again. That's it confirmed then. We *are* on a spaceship. What other explanation can there be for this kind of technology? I continue my circuit of the room with Isla following me, both of us gliding our palms flat against the walls. As I reach the wall across from the wardrobe, the spot in front of me suddenly softens. Another wardrobe? As it turns translucent, I can see the outline of someone behind it. A very *big* someone. I step back, gasping as the wall completely disappears to reveal the being who first came to the house—the one with the cropped dark hair. What did he call himself? Adin, that's right.

I explore the area behind him. It looks like a golden tunnel. I consider running down it with Isla, away from this creature, but what good did that do me last time? Isla stares at the being's fluctuating skin tone with curiosity. Up close, under this light, it's really quite something to behold. I want to say it's like a rainbow, but that would suggest an almost child-like quality. This being is anything *but* childlike. No, his skin is like the swirling colors of the screensaver on my laptop. Or the Northern Lights.

"Where are we?" I ask, trying to keep my voice strong and steady.

"We're onboard the *Iressent*, our main learning vessel," Adin replies, "the same vessel you were brought to ten years ago."

I've *been* here before? How is that possible? I have no memories of it. And yet, what about the dreams I have?

"I'm your designated defender," Adin continues. "Anything you need, you ask me."

"Are we on a spaceship?" Isla asks.

"That's how humans refer to them, yes," Adin answers.

Isla frowns. "Is it the thing that was above our house?"

He smiles down at Isla. "No, that was a different vessel, Isla. Their purpose was to transport you here, to the *Iressent*." I think of the vast sphere sitting above the Sahara desert. Then I think of the words the Grand Sovran uttered in that broadcast. *Fathered. Claim. Collections.*

"Why are we here?" I ask. "Is this what the dude on TV meant about collecting human women and children?"

"Oh, no," Isla whispers, moving even closer to me as she squeezes my hand.

"Don't worry," Adin says to her. "We're on our way to Obrothea, our planet. Many exciting adventures await you there."

Adventures. My father had said the same about us moving to the commune. I will *not* allow Isla to go through the same thing I did.

"Look," I say, crossing my arms as I look this mammoth soldier up and down. "I don't know how it works on Obrothea, but you can't just force women and kids out of their homes and make them go somewhere else. That's *kidnapping.*"

"All will be well. You'll see." He frowns as he looks us both up and down. "You're still in your sleepwear. New clothes were provided in your wardrobe."

"We're fine as we are, thanks," I say.

"You must wear them."

"I don't like dresses," Isla calls out from behind me.

"You will have to change," Adin says kindly. "I will give you a few moments to put them on. Only the items in the wardrobe may be worn. No earthly clothes can remain on you. Now get changed. " He steps out of our room, and the wall reappears.

I curl my hands into fists, ready to pummel the unexplainable wall with them. How dare these beings make us wear these outfits? I pause, thinking of Isla. My mother used to say I needed to pick my battles. It's just a dress, after all. I go to the wardrobe and open it again, putting my hand on what I presume is Isla's dress. It's soft, high necked and glossy. I notice there's a swimsuit-type item to go under it.

"Yuck," she says as she looks the dress up and down. "*So* not me."

"I know, darling, but we have to."

Isla sighs and takes the dress reluctantly. As she changes, I examine my own dress. It's super slinky, floor length, and ridiculously low cut. Absolutely *not* the kind of thing I'd wear. Well, not now, anyway. Maybe ten years ago when I was twenty. Will it even fit me? I search inside for some underwear like Isla's, but there's nothing.

"I think there's a mistake," I call through the wall. "There's no, erm, underwear."

"That's correct," Adin shouts back.

"You're kidding me, right?"

"No, I do not *kid*," he replies in a serious voice. "Please hurry, Kate. The Grand Sovran is not a fan of tardiness."

Pick your battles, I remind myself. *Pick your battles.*

I quickly undress and pull the dress over my head. It shimmies down my body, caressing my bare nipples and skimming my hips. I look at my discarded bra. It's bad enough not being able to wear knickers, but no bra? My breasts aren't exactly small. They need all the support they can get.

"I don't like it," Isla says as she peers down at her dress. I have to admit, she looks cute in it. But *cute* isn't Isla's idea of a good look. Usually, she prefers to wear black leggings and logo tops.

"It looks nice, sweetheart. I'm sure there will be other clothes. At least I *hope* so." I say as I look down at my own outfit.

She laughs. "You look like the Oscars trophy with more bumps and lumps."

"Wonderful. Okay, we're ready," I shout out.

The wall shimmers again, and Adin reappears. "Good," he says as he takes us both in with his strange, green eyes.

"This isn't exactly practical wear," I say through gritted teeth.

"It's not meant to be. Come." He gestures down the long, curved corridor.

I stay where I am. "Not until you tell us where you're taking us."

Adin sighs. "You really are stubborn. The Grand Sovran will be addressing you all. He'll make you understand."

"*Make* us understand," I say, shaking my head in disbelief and eyeing his sword. "That *really* fills me with confidence."

He looks very sad for a moment. "We would never hurt you or Isla. Never. Now please, come."

I hear voices in the distance. *Female* human voices. Children too. It would be good to see other people and not feel so damn alone in this god-awful situation, so I follow this huge defender down the corridor, listening as the metal of his armor clinks with each step.

"Will there be food?" Isla asks him. "I haven't had breakfast yet."

"Of course," Adin replies with a smile. "There will be a great celebration feast. You will always have all the food you desire."

I take the chance to search our surroundings, trying to find any possible way to escape, but it's just one endless stream of golden corridor. No vents. No visible doors. No windows. Are we still over the Sahara? Are we even on Earth? Maybe we're moving through space at this very moment. I can't help the unwanted shiver of excitement that runs through me. But this is no trip of discovery. We're here under duress.

I sigh at my reflection in the pulsing bronze of Adin's back armor. My brown eyes look tired and scared, and strands of my dark hair are sticking up on end. I have to admit, the dress fits my petite, curvy frame perfectly, though I *would* prefer if the whole thing were less revealing. I take Isla's hand, giving her a reassuring smile. She returns it hesitantly. When I look back up, I see we're heading right towards a wall at the end of the corridor. Adin puts his hand out, and the wall dissolves.

"It's like Harry Potter," Isla whispers.

"It is," I whisper back. *Let's just hope there are no dementors and dark wizards here.*

We step through into a new wider corridor, and the whole atmosphere changes. This area is filled with women and children, some hysterical, some deathly silent. There are about twenty women and children plus two defenders dressed like Adin at the front. I hear different accents, see different shades of skin. All mothers and children plucked from every country in the world.

How were we chosen?

All these women seem just like me, not particularly extraordinary. We're just scared and tired mothers. We're all wearing the same outfits too—the women in the slinky dresses, the girls in cute shift dresses, the boys in shorts and tops. I notice we're the only ones wearing gold though. The other women and children are all wearing a darker shade, more bronze like Adin's armor than gold. Why are *we* dressed differently?

Isla looks nervously ahead of her. This must be so daunting for her. "There are children here from every country in the world," I say to distract her, noting as I do that all the children have the same green eyes as her. They're all a similar age too, around nine. A feeling of nausea swirls inside my stomach as I look at all the children. These beings say they fathered "sacred children", and yet how is that possible? I would have remembered having sex with an alien, for God's sake. What I *do* remember are hazy dreams of being touched, dreams that still linger, and days feeling unutterably tired, as though I'd been up most of the night. Is that how they did it? Did they abduct us in the night and drug us to make us forget?

I notice Isla watching me and force myself to smile. "Do you remember how many countries there are in the world?" I ask her.

"195," a nearby boy says in a British accent. He's tall with blond hair and, of course, green eyes. He looks *incredibly* familiar.

"I knew that," Isla replies, giving him an eye roll.

The woman next to us turns, and I let out a gasp. Now I know where I recognize the boy from. The woman is Princess Helena, wife of future heir to the British throne, Prince Alex. Her face is streaked with tears, and her whole body is shaking. I'm used to seeing her strawberry blond hair all glossy and coiffed, with perfect makeup and beautiful dresses. If the boy is her son, that means he's Prince Henry.

"Excuse my nephew," another woman—a young, pretty blond woman—says. I think she may have been one of Princess Helena's bridesmaids from what I recall of the wedding that adorned magazine covers all those years ago. "He's a bit of a know-it-all."

"It's fine," I say.

"I'm Charlotte," she says. *Charlotte.* Yes, that's Princess Helena's younger sister. "I take it you're American? Brooklyn maybe? I can tell from your accent. Oh, and the fact Brooklyn was where the American version of those UFOs were according to the news." She leans in close to me and whispers, "I call them the Unexplained *Fucking* Objects.'

I smile. I have a feeling Charlotte and I are going to get on very well. "Hi, Charlotte. I'm Kate, and this is Isla.'

"Nice to meet you," she says. "From the shocked look on your face, I can tell you're aware know-it-all here is Henry, and this is Helena." Helena doesn't look at me, just continues staring ahead. "Sorry," Charlotte whispers, "she's still in shock."

"I get it. So where's your child?" I ask.

Charlotte laughs. "Oh, I have no child. I'm just the stupid one who insisted on accompanying my sister and nephew when the aliens came for us."

My mouth drops open "You volunteered? And they let you come?"

She nods. "How can they resist another fertile human?" She seems jokey when she says that, but I can see the fear in her eyes. "So where do you think we're going?" she asks as we all shuffle down the corridor.

"The Grand Sovran is supposedly going to address us," I whisper. "Somehow *make* us understand why we've been kidnapped and forced here." Fear flickers in Helena's eyes. "It'll be fine," I quickly say to the princess, wondering whether I should curtsy or something. "They won't hurt us. We're too important to them."

"She's right, Hels," Charlotte says.

"How can you be so sure?" Helena snaps in her cut-glass accent. "You saw the way those beasts took out our security team, Charlotte. And did you *see* the size of the warrior during the broadcast?" She shivers. "I pity any woman who has to deal with him."

"I wouldn't mind," a tall woman with an Australian accent and long, curly black hair says. "He was *beautiful.*"

"Ah, a *beautiful* kidnapping alien. How lovely," I can't help but say.

"Sarcasm is the lowest form of wit, you know," Helena drawls. I frown. She really is playing the snooty British princess down to a tee.

"But she's right," a nearby redhead says in an Irish accent as she fingers the cross hanging from her neck. "We mustn't speak of these beings in such ways. They *are* our kidnappers."

The Australian women rolls her eyes and turns away.

"So where are the other woman from your corridor?" Charlotte asks me.

"It was just us," I say. "Are all you guys in the same corridor?"

Charlotte nods. Different color dresses. One corridor to ourselves. One defender assigned to us two, when these women have two defenders for twenty of them. Why? What's so different about me and Isla?

We all go quiet as the women and children ahead of us begin to disappear through another wall. But Helena refuses when it's her turn. "Nope, I am not going in there," she says, shaking her head.

"You must," the large defender overseeing her corridor insists.

"Why?" she retorts. "Why must I?"

"You will get the chance to spend time with the man you are pledged to," he says in a tone that suggests she would be crazy not to relish such an opportunity.

"Why exactly would I want to do that?" Helena snaps back.

"Because you will have an opportunity to do your duty to Skarsdon," the defender replies. "Now go through. The Grand Sovran does not like tardiness."

Helena rolls her eyes and walks through the wall. I take a

deep breath as I prepare myself to do the same. What did the defender mean by 'duty to Skarsdon'? And who is the Pledged I'll be performing that duty with? The huge warrior who carried me away from my home?

Well, I guess I'll find out soon enough. I take a deep breath and walk through the wall.

FIVE

Kate

The hall we all walk into is a vast, golden globe with curved stained glass windows featuring creatures similar to the psychedelic hologram from the TV broadcast. On the fringes of the globe are trees and plants of all shapes, sizes, and colors. Some I recognize as pink-hued rose bushes and flame-colored lilies. Others look like nothing I've ever seen before. There are purple and green cactus-like plants stretching into the air and blankets of pulsing baby-blue fur balls stretched across the ground. There are colors I don't even recognize and scents I've never encountered. A mini waterfall explodes at the side of the room, multi-colored water splashing down into a small lake. In the middle of it all are several long shimmering tables and benches that stretch across the width of the room. In front is a raised area with another table. Hovering above it is that strange hologram I saw in the broadcast.

The whole thing is quite spectacular, and for a moment, the hundreds of women and children who have emerged from all parts of the hall just stare, open-mouthed. Defenders begin leading us to our tables, which, as it turns out, float in the air just as our dresses did in that wardrobe.

I'm pleased when I'm asked to sit at Charlotte's table, which is in the middle of the room. From the accents at this table, we all speak English—British and American, plus Australian, South African, and a few others. I hear Eastern European accents from the table in front of us, and African accents behind us, with many more around the huge hall. Somehow, we all seem to be speaking English though despite the multitude of accents. In fact, now that I think of it, how it is possible I understood Adin? Surely a whole different alien species would have a different language?

I watch as the defenders take their places at the ends of each table. Adin stands closest to our end of the table, his green eyes never leaving us. Isla presses close to me, and I put my arm around her.

"What's happening, Mommy?" she whispers.

It's hard to hear her over the wailing of some of the children. With 195 kids in one space in the most insane situation, of course some of them are upset and misbehaving.

"I don't know," I say to Isla. "Don't worry though. I'm here. It's very beautiful, isn't it?" I don't want to gloss over the truth of our predicament, but I don't want to scare her either. If I can highlight the good points, this experience doesn't have to be all negative...right? She looks around and nods, but I can see the worry in her eyes. A hush falls over the room as there's movement at the front of the hall. One after another, seven giant beings walk in, all male and all looking to be in their twenties. They're all inexplicably tall too, at least seven foot. Each one is golden haired and green eyed, with that same swirling, prismatic skin. Four of them are wearing robes, like the Grand Sovran, and three are dressed in golden gladiator-style gear. I notice two among them are almost identical but one of them is robed, and the

36

other is in warrior gear and has a jagged scar down his hand-some face.

Among them is the Thor-like warrior who kidnapped me and Isla. The one from the broadcast. I have to catch my breath as I stare at him. He's mesmerizing, and frankly, the effect he's having on me is unreal. Uninvited desire builds up inside me. I curl my hands into fists, trying to stamp it down. I do not want to feel this way about the being who stole me and my daughter from our home. I suddenly get a vague memory of him carrying me down my street as neighbors watched, Adin in front with Isla in his arms. I remember the sound of sirens, gunshots too. What was that strange spray he used to make us faint? And why was he there at my house? Was he present for every mother and child this race was claiming as their own?

Is he Isla's biological father? As quickly as that thought comes to me, I sweep it away. It's all nonsense. As though sensing my gaze on him, he turns to me, somehow picking my face out among the crowds. A powerful jolt shoots through me as our eyes meet. My head fills with the sound of breathing, deep and hot. I feel hard skin pressed against mine, large fingers pressing into the soft skin of my neck as I arch backwards—

"You okay?" Charlotte whispers. "You seemed to disappear for a moment."

My face flushes with embarrassment. "I'm fine."

I look back at the otherworldly warrior who feels so familiar to me, and part of me has to wonder again if I'm pledged to him, as they call it? It would explain the special treatment.

Before I can truly think about it, the Grand Sovran takes his seat at a large, bronze throne in the middle of the high table, the large warrior on one side, one of the men in robes on the other.

"On behalf of my Highborn sons and I," he says, gesturing to the other men at the table, "and Skarsdonian's most fearless warriors and sages," he adds, gesturing to a viewing platform above I hadn't even noticed yet filled with over a hundred similar-looking beings dressed in golden armor and robes, "I wish to welcome all our Sacred children and Pledged human woman to our vessel, the *Iressent*."

"What do you want from us?" Helena suddenly shouts out in a shaky, hysterical voice. "Don't you know who I am?"

Charlotte grabs her sister's arm. "Helena, shush!"

"But they must understand, Charlotte," Helena says. "I'm married to the future King of England!" A murmur goes up around the hall as the other women crane their necks to look at her.

Charlotte puts her head in her hands. "Great, now everyone knows."

"Your previous status means nothing to us." The Grand Sovran's voice is inhumanly loud, the tone of it thrumming right through me, and right through every person in the hall judging from the silence that falls over us all. His skin swirls red and midnight blue. There seems to be something beneath their skin that reacts to emotion. Once again, as much as I *hate* this situation I find myself in, I can't help my fascination.

"The leaders you once knew are no longer your leaders. *I* am your leader now," he continues, "Your earthly status is gone. Whether you were a slave on Earth or the wife of a future king. A police officer or a prostitute. It makes no difference to how you will be treated here. What's important is that you are the mothers of our Sacred children. You are all as one to us."

Murmurings of protests rise and fall along the crowd.

"As for what we want from you," the Grand Sovran continues, "you know yourself what special children you have produced." He smiles. "It is these Sacred children who will secure the power and future of Skarsdon."

"Haven't you got your own women to have kids with?" a woman asks in a Scottish accent. "Are they infertile or something?"

"We do have our own women," the Grand Sovran replies. "And they are very fertile and very worthy. But the simple fact is, it is only with you human women that we can produce the kinds of children and heirs," he says, nodding at his huge warrior son, "who can help us continue Skarsdon's greatness."

"Let us go home," another woman shouts out. "We don't want to be your breeding mares!"

"We *are* taking you home," the robed man sitting on the other side of the Grand Sovran says in a cold, smooth voice. He is leaner than the other beings, with short golden hair sheared close to his scalp and high cheekbones. Like the other brothers, he is beautiful to look at, but I detect a coldness in his narrow green eyes as he surveys the room. "Our planet will be your new home. You and your child will live with your Primes in the kind of luxury even you," he says, eyes drilling into Helena's, "are not used to."

"Are we still on Earth?" a Japanese woman a few rows down asks.

"No, we're no longer on Earth," the being answers back. "We're currently in what we know as sector 7.88 of your solar system. We'll reach Obrothea in three days. In fact, we're already at a point in your solar system where humans are unable to reach us. So wipe any chance of return from your minds."

Women start sobbing, children wailing. I feel it coming myself, the horror of it all. But I hold it all in and hug Isla close to me as her eyes fill with tears. She's never been one to cry, and it makes me feel worse to see her on the edge of doing so.

"Stop crying!" the robed being booms, red pulsing under his skin. Does the red represent anger? The Grand Sovran shoots him a look, and the robed being takes in a breath and closes his eyes. When he opens them, he seems calmer. "You should not be fearful. You will be treated well. *Very* well. You will never want for food, for entertainment, for friendship, for all the comforts you enjoyed while on Earth. You will never have to lift a finger to clean or to toil."

"Sounds *divine*," the Australian woman drawls, drawing disapproving looks from some of the other women.

"You are, after all," the robed being continues, "our most important commodity."

"Commodity," I say, shaking my head. "What a lovely way to refer to us." I must have said it louder than I thought, because people turn to look at me, including the huge warrior. He shoots me a hard look.

"Now, there are a few things that will be helpful for you to know," the robed being continues. "First, my name. I am Ethos. Remember it. It is thanks to me that your Sacred children are here. *My* experiment led to their conception." His voice is full of pride, but he just makes me sick. "Second, the reason you understand me, and each other, is that while you were unconscious, you were each injected with translator pods just behind your right ear. This means we can all communicate, regardless of language."

I reach behind my ear and feel a small bump there. I check behind Isla's ear and see she has a small red bump there. "This is insane," I whisper.

"Crazy," Charlotte says. Then her eyes widen as she looks to the front. "Oh my God, *what* is that woman doing?"

I follow her gaze to see a tall, athletic-looking woman leap onto her table, run down it, and jump onto the defender

40

closest to her. He stumbles backwards, taken by surprise as she wraps her arms around his neck and leans forward to bite his cheek. He finds his footing, grasps the woman around her waist, and flings her off him. She lands with a thud, her head rebounding off the table leg. The defender strolls up to her, letting out a roar as he removes his sword from its sheath and raises it above his head.

SIX

Kate

The colossal warrior who feels so familiar to me strides across the stage, his legs long and muscled, his golden hair lifting with each step. He jumps off the stage with the same feline reflexes I noticed in the alleyway, and without hesitation, thrusts his sword into the defender's side just before the defender has a chance to do the same to the woman. The defender collapses to the floor, his sword clattering from his hand as he looks up at the warrior with shock. I press Isla's face into my chest as the warrior stands over the woman.

"Healers!" he shouts, his voice booming around the hall. Two strange wispy beings with bald heads approach from the back of the hall dressed in silver jumpsuits. One approaches the fallen defender, and another goes to the injured woman. Both of the injured are lifted and carried away. The blood from the defender's wound leaves a trail on the floor, dripping onto our table as he is carried past us.

"Oh God," Charlotte whispers, shaking her head. "Oh God." I reach under the table and squeeze her hand.

The warrior turns to us all, his green eyes seeming to take

every single human face in as he continues to hold his sword, blood dripping down his leather-clad thigh. "As you can see," he says in a deep, strong voice, "we will not hesitate to protect you, *even* at the cost of our own people." He sighs as he places his bloody sword back into its sheath. "Please refrain from rebelling in the way you just witnessed. We understand human women and children are strong willed. It is both a curiosity and a fascination for us." Is it my imagination, or do his eyes alight on me as he says that? "But I prefer not to see the blood of my own defenders on my sword as a result of that stubbornness. Now let's focus on filling our bellies."

He returns to the table and sits down. I didn't expect him to speak so eloquently. He looks more like the kind of men back on Earth who spend their lives in the gym, preferring to express themselves in monosyllabic sentences. He looks troubled by what he just had to do as well. His brow is creased, and his skin is swirling mournful blue and grey colors.

My attention is drawn away from him when dozens of new beings appear from all parts of the hall, both men and women. They are very tall, but their hair is dark and long, plaited neatly down their backs, their bodies adorned with green robes. They place an assortment of dishes on the tables featuring exotically shaped purple fruits and strange bubbling stews that smell of meat and herbs. I catch the eye of the female serving us. Like the men, she has very human features, but her height and the hint of oscillating skin beneath her robes proves she is anything but. She looks young, maybe late teens, and there is a sadness in her eyes. How does she feel about this all? I wish I could ask her, but she avoids my gaze.

As the plates are put down, I hear some of the children around us making ew sounds, and I can't help but smile. "These alien warriors don't know the true meaning of a challenge until they face a room of fussy eaters," I say as the other mothers down the table nod in agreement. But then more servers come out, bringing with them more recognizable dishes like breads and pastries of all shapes and sizes, plus trays of scrambled egg.

"Ah," Charlotte says, "maybe they *have* done their research?"

"Don't!" Helena snaps, stopping her son from reaching for a slab of bread. "What if it's poisoned?"

I stop Isla too and look around the hall, watching other mothers taking tentative bites of the bread. They seem fine, and before I know it, Isla is reaching for a large pastry and sinking her teeth into it.

"This is yummy," she declares.

"Well, I guess they wouldn't poison their most valuable *commodities*," I say with a shrug. I take a lump of bread and examine it. It looks like any other bread. I sink my teeth in and chew. It definitely has the same texture, but there are flavors in it I don't recognize, scents exuding from it too. It is delicious though. I can't deny that. As I eat, I turn my gaze to the raised table. The beings there are eating like ravenous beasts, teeth tearing into bread and the meat. Only the warrior is still, eyes cast down to the table's surface with that troubled look still on his handsome face. I stop my rising desire by sinking my nails into the soft skin of my palm. He looks up and catches my eye before quickly looking away again. I drag my gaze away too.

The rest of the meal is subdued, the image of the wounded defender and injured woman strong in our minds. After a while, Ethos stands, his golden robes swishing around his tall body.

"Now that you have eaten, I will explain some practicalities," he says. "You have all been divided into ten areas, with twenty mothers and their children in each area. Within these designated areas are facilities to make your stay as comfortable as possible. Each day, your rooms will be cleaned by our Fostinian attendants. If you need anything, ask your defender, and they will bring it to you." I look at the dark-haired girl who is filling up our glasses with water now. Fostinian. What does that mean?

"Meals take place here," Ethos continues, "in the grand hall at eight am, one pm, and six pm sharp. You will be escorted here by your allotted defenders. After breakfast, all children will attend school."

Murmurs of protest sound around the room. I look down at Isla, heart thumping in fear. No, I can't let her out of my sight.

"Mothers, please let me continue," Ethos shouts. The room goes quiet. "There is nothing to fear. Your children will be returned to your rooms at three pm."

I shake my head, pulling Isla even closer. Other women do the same, some of them crying out in protest while their children whimper.

"I don't want to leave you, Mommy," Isla says.

An idea then occurs to me, and I stand up. "I'm a teacher," I call out. The room goes silent. "Let me go with the children, and I can teach them."

"I teach yoga," a South African woman shouts out. Other mothers start shouting out how they can help teach the children.

"Tell me, do you know our history?" Ethos shouts over the din. "Do you know our customs and our ways? Our scribes are the best people to teach your children the ways of their new world." My shoulders slump. "Children," Ethos` continues, "please stand and await your scribes."

There are more protests around the hall.

"Mothers, quiet!" It's the Grand Sovran's turn to shout now, his voice booming. "Can you not see you are scaring our children?" He opens his hands, palms up, and smiles. "Children, do not be scared. I promise you that you will enjoy your day immensely. There are many toys to play with, books to read, and new friends to be made. Now I do not wish to ask this again. Please stand so you can meet your special scribes and ensure your return to your mothers later."

Ensure your return to your mothers. Is that a veiled threat?

Either way, it seems we have no choice. All I can do is make sure Isla isn't scared. So I turn to her and give her a shaky smile. "I know it'll be fine," I say firmly. "You mustn't worry about anything. They clearly worship the ground you kids walk on," I add, and the other kids on our table turn to look at me.

Charlotte nods as she hugs her nephew. "Kate's right, you'll probably have a whale of a time," she says. "What other prince has had the chance to learn about a whole new species?" Helena remains silent, eyes wide as she rocks back and forth. I can see why Charlotte insisted on coming with her. She obviously knew her sister wouldn't be able to cope. I see some other mothers also acting quiet, withdrawn, shocked. Then there are the angry ones. What about me? All I can be is the best version of myself, the one that reassures my daughter and makes this horrific experience as calm as it can be. The version that gives her some hope we'll find a way out of this. My mother was the same when things got scary in the commune. I have to follow her example.

I lean close to Isla. "We'll figure a way out of here," I whisper to her. Charlotte catches my eye and nods, obviously thinking the same thing. "For now, just go to school. I'll be waiting for you."

Dozens of beings file into the room. Some look like the golden-haired men, but others are darker, like the Fostinians who served us. They're dressed in practical pale-blue vests and pants. The being who stops at the end of our table smiles at me with a kind look on his face. He looks almost doll-like with big green eyes, plump lips, and impossibly high cheek bones. A long plait of black hair hangs down his back. Does that mean he's a Fostinian? An overwhelming feeling of familiarity and calmness fills me.

I stand with Isla and hold her hand as I lead her to this—what was it they called them? Scribe? The scribe squeezes Isla's shoulder as she goes to him. I can see she's trying not to cry, because her bottom lip wobbles. I force my own tears away and give her a reassuring smile. I can't let her see me upset. But the moment she's out of sight, I break down, sobbing into my hands as the other mothers do. Charlotte hugs her sister, crying too, but Helena just continues to stare ahead blankly.

I notice the warrior watching, a pained expression on his face.

"Mothers," Ethos shouts. The room goes quiet. "You will now meet those you were pledged to ten years ago. The fathers of our Sacred children. Now, please follow your defenders and do your duty to Skarsdon."

I look at the familiar warrior at the top table. Is he the being I'm about to meet? And exactly what will I have to do with him as part of my duty to Skarsdon?

SEVEN

Tharin

I storm from the great hall, conscious of the defender's blood upon my sword. It had to be done. The fool allowed his anger to take over. Maybe if I hadn't been so distracted by Kate and the way her dress hugged her curves, I could have stopped him before he drew his sword. Even now, I grow hard just thinking about her.

Weak, Tharin, weak.

I work my fingers into the wound on my palm. This is not the way it should be. Or maybe it is? If it is just mere lust I'm feeling, is that so wrong? I need to seed her again, after all. It's my duty, and lust will have a role to play in that. As long as it is no more than that.

"Well done," my brother Remus says as he pats my back. He wears the same robes as Ethos, but he is about as different from Ethos as the sun is to the moons. "It's important our defenders understand how sacred our Pledged are," he continues. "What possessed the fool to stand over the human woman with a drawn sword?"

"What possessed him was his ego," our youngest brother, Kiah, says as he joins us. "He couldn't take being so easily overwhelmed by a weak little human woman."

"How many times do I have to tell you, Kiah," I say, "human women are anything but weak."

"Yes, you certainly learnt that to your detriment," Ethos says with a raised eyebrow as he passes us. "I do not know why Father allowed your Pledged to board this ship. If it were up to me, I would have taken the child and left that betrayer to rot on Earth."

Anger as fierce as the Obrothean sun storms through me. I shove Ethos up against the wall, my thumb and forefinger circling his neck. "You have no proof she is a betrayer. And remember, she is the mother of my Sacred child," I growl into his face. "Do not speak of her that way."

Ethos laughs. "You still believe she didn't conspire with Ryker to cause the invasion which killed our mother and sister?"

I feel that same dart of pain I always do at their mention. "I know Kate didn't."

"Tharin, let your brother go," our father says with a warning tone as he places his cool hand on my shoulder. I release Ethos reluctantly. "You of all people should know why we allowed Tharin's Pledged onto the ship, Ethos. The combination of Kate and Tharin's DNA is particularly potent. We need her here to produce more children like Isla. We need her here," he adds as he squeezes my shoulder to ram home the point, "to produce our strongest ever royal lineage."

"As you keep reminding us, Father," Ethos hisses under his breath.

"I shouldn't have to remind you," Father says in a tone that tells Ethos he has gone too far. "Now leave, all of you. Tharin and I must talk." All my brothers leave, and I'm alone with our father in the long golden hallway. "How are you, son?" he asks me. "I know this must be difficult for you."

I go to press my fingers into my wound but then stop. My father will notice. He notices everything. "I am well," I lie.

"You know how important this is for Skarsdon?" he says, face deadly serious. "You know how important it is to produce more children like Isla?"

"Of course, Father." How can I not? It is rammed into us every day, how these Sacred children will be Skarsdon's saviors. It was the whole reason behind the experiment ten years ago. With rumors that ass canker of a prince from the Gatika region was engineering a powerful army of soldiers made impossibly strong with experimental hazes, we needed something to give us an edge. My brother Ethos had already been experimenting on samples taken during our expeditions to Earth over the centuries. Ten years ago, he had a break-through when he discovered that combining our DNA with humans could result in hybrid children of astounding strength and resilience. Obrothean children have always been strong but these human-Obrothean hybrids could possess the kind of strength and skill needed to defeat the Mad Prince's army. To defeat *any* army.

It was just a theory then though. Until we saw the children come of age this year, we couldn't be sure. The proof we saw last month though made it clear Ethos's theories are a reality. These Sacred children are even stronger and skilled than I was at that age, and that's saying something. Even better, Isla is the most powerful of them all, proof that I, the future heir to the throne, am worthy of the crown.

"You also know how important it is to seed your Pledged again as soon as possible," my father continues. He must notice the discomfort on my face for his sighs. "You have to put the past behind you, son. I know it is a challenge you will overcome for Skarsdon." He reaches into his pocket and pulls out a vial. "I hear how stubborn these human women can be. A drop of this vevatia and—"

I shake my head vehemently. "No. I have never needed that potion to make a woman want me. I did not need it ten years ago, and I will not need it now."

My father smiles. "Like father, like son." Then the smile disappears from his face. "But things are different now. Remember, Kate is not one of your fawning subjects, and you are not the same man you were ten years ago. I know how much of a challenge this will be. But all you need to do is remind yourself she is a means to an end. That this is all for Skarsdon."

"For Skarsdon," I repeat in a strong voice, placing my fist to my heart. My father is right. I have to be strong. Commanding. Emotionless. It's the only way to endure this.

Kate

"Mates? Pledged? Do you realize how outdated you all sound?" I ask Adin as I jog to keep up with him. We're back in my corridor now, all alone. He doesn't reply. "So where are you taking me? Why wasn't I taken with the other women?"

"You will find out soon enough."

"What about Isla? Where's this school they've taken her to? What will she learn?"

"Isla will be fine. I promise you that. Castian is Obrothea's very best scribe. He will look after her, and she will learn a great deal about her new home."

"Learning the facts isn't enough. Don't you understand that all the kids have been thrust into a new situation and—"

"Yes, we are aware of that. The mental wellbeing you humans are so obsessed with will be addressed as well," Adin says firmly. He comes to a stop at the end of the corridor. "Your Prime is through there."

Nerves dart through me.

"Go, Kate," Adin says, giving me a soft shove. "He is waiting."

"Don't you have to open the door with your hand?"

"You can. You're his Pledged, remember? You will always have access. It is your room now."

My room. I don't like the sound of that, and yet my body seems to as a thrill of desire shoots through me. Desire made even more keen by the possibility the being waiting for me might be the gorgeous First Defender, as he is known. *Damn body.* I peer behind me down the corridor, wondering if I can run away, but we're in the middle of space on a vast spaceship. Where would I go? And what about Isla? I pause a moment and then place my palm on the wall. It shimmers and dissolves.

The room is a complete contrast to the other places I've seen so far. It's large, yes, but it's made up of shadows and dark tones, the walls a throbbing mixture of deep blues, blacks, and dark reds. The colors of anger. There are tall columns around the room, and heavy curtains dominate one wall to the left of me. To the right is one of those strange beds —huge, dark, and swirling with mists.

I feel a stammer of apprehension. Are we in a bedroom for a specific purpose? Is this what this meeting is all about? Will the Primes assert their authority and force themselves upon us? *I'll die before I let him do that.* I back away, placing my hand against the wall to get out, but it doesn't budge. I search the dark corners of the room.

"Hello?" My voice echoes off the walls.

I take a breath and step farther into the room, my bare feet sinking into soft warm mists. We don't have a carpet like this in our room. The feel of it suddenly triggers a memory of my cheek being pressed into a similar carpet, long strong fingers digging into my buttocks as a tongue trails up my open thighs. I shake the images away. Did they lace our food with something to make me hallucinate? I ignore the small voice that reminds me I had these visions before I ever set foot on this spaceship.

To one side of the room there are several floating shelves filled with strange objects I don't recognize and books, lots of books that seem to change color as I watch. There's a shelf of photos as well, all of the same two women—one young with long, golden hair and an older woman with dark hair. Candles flicker around the photos, as though this shelf is a shrine to the dead.

A giant form steps out of the shadows then, casting dark shapes against the walls that seem to swirl in excitement in his presence. He takes another step into the center of the room, and I can hardly breathe. It's him. He's changed out of his golden armor and is wearing a loose tunic top spun from a fine gold material. Golden buttons lie open to reveal hints of a muscled chest, purples and reds swirling beneath bronze skin like ribbons. His tanned feet are bare now, pressed deep into the carpet of mists. The muscles of his legs are thick and defined beneath the leather material of his trousers.

It's his face that astounds me the most though. High cheekbones are shrouded in soft golden stubble. He has a straight nose, heavy golden eyebrows, and long lashes framing those green eyes. His hair is like blond silk to his shoulders, the front swept back off his face in a plait. His skin fluctuates with the dark colors swirling beneath—pools of ink one moment and then sparks of purple the next. Standing this close, I notice there's a deep wound on the flesh part of his palm that is still weeping blood. He is digging his thumb into it, over and over.

We stare at each other, and the space between us seems to

flex and pulse. Around us, the walls fluctuate like bloody ribbons, and the mist on the nearby bed undulates and throbs purple, reflecting the uninvited sensations rushing inside my own body at the sight of him. I close my eyes, trying to control the heady sensations and the way my pulse seems to be throbbing right between my thighs.

"Open your eyes," he commands in a voice that seems to thrum through me like the humming of the ship. I take a deep breath and open my eyes, looking right into those intense green orbs of his. I force myself to hold his gaze.

"I am Tharin, First Defender of Skarsdon," he says.

"And I'm Kate, head of science at the Vera Rubin Academy in New York." I grimace. Did I really just say that?

His lips twitch up slightly into a smile, but then he clenches his fists, and the serious expression returns. "Please, take a seat," he says, gesturing to two large misty armchairs in the corner of the room.

I cross my arms. "I'm fine standing, thanks."

He pauses a moment and then sighs. "Fine. Do as you wish."

"What am I doing here? Why are we *all* here?"

"You are here because our Sacred children have reached their full potential. It means they are ready to be trained in their rightful place, on Obrothea."

Fear bubbles inside me. "Trained? For *what*?"

"An assortment of roles, depending on their skills."

"What is this, a Victorian workhouse?"

He looks confused. "Excuse me?"

"They're kids, for Christ's sake. Not workhorses. And Earth is their rightful place because they are *human* kids. Isla is *my* human kid," I add, jabbing my finger against my chest.

"All these Sacred children are half Obrothean. So that makes Isla mine too," he counters, green eyes sparking with challenge.

I vehemently shake my head. "Not a chance you're Isla's father." Even as I say it, I know I can't say that for certain.

He crosses his own arms, looking down at me defiantly. "I can assure you, I am."

"No, her father is my husband, Richard Thompson." I don't add that he's now my ex.

His lip curls in disgust. "A man like him could never produce a child like Isla. Obrothean genes are superior to human genes. You will see that in time as Isla grows. Have you not already noticed her strength, her agility?"

I frown. Yes, her teachers have remarked on it in the past. I've noticed it too. She's always first in races, always able to endure intense physical activity better than others. But my father was a strong man. I just assumed she was growing to be more like him.

"How can you prove any of this?" I say. "And even if it is true, you can't just invade Earth and take us away. That's kidnapping. It's a horrendous crime. Heartless. You are evil, all of you, and I will *never be*lieve you're my daughter's father."

He closes his eyes, taking sharp intakes of breath. The colors under his skin swirl black and red, the walls too, and I can see he's digging his thumb into that wound on his hand again. I watch as he tries to control himself, taking some pleasure in the fact I'm aggravating my kidnapper so much. Eventually, the walls begin to turn pale blue and green.

"Fight the truth all you wish, Kate," he says in a calm voice. "But here are the facts. Ten years ago, I planted seed in you, and Isla was conceived. And now, I will plant seed again so you can birth more Sacred children like Isla."

My mouth drops open in shock, and I back away. "You're disgusting."

He matches my steps, moving towards me. "We will raise strong children, as is the Skarsdonian way. You will not have to see me apart from when I need to seed you. We can start now," he says, gesturing to the bed. "The sooner we do this, the less time we need to spend in one another's company. You are fertile. All the human Pledged my brother chose are highly fertile. We may only need to fuck a few times to produce as many children as my parents did."

"I will *never* allow you to fuck me," I shout.

"But you have already," he shouts back, his voice so loud it makes me wince.

"No, I don't believe you. There's no chance I'd have let you near me."

All of a sudden, he strides across the room, the walls frantically pulsating purple and red with each step. He stands before me, so tall my eyes are in line with the top of his hard abs, which I can glimpse through the thin material of his top. He grabs my shoulders, huge fingers digging painfully into my flesh. This close, his musky, intoxicating scent invades my nostrils, making me giddy. "How do you think Isla was conceived?" he hisses. "We have fucked, many times, over and over, and you loved it."

I try to push away from him, but he stands as still and as strong as an obelisk. "You're lying," I shout back. "I would never have allowed it."

"You more than allowed it. You *wanted* it. Let me remind you." He grasps me around the waist, lifts me so we are face-to-face, and slams his lips against mine. Though the movement is fierce and strong, his lips feel soft. Images whirl in my head of another time like this, our gazes locked as he moves against me, his beautiful face slick with sweat. I find my lips responding, moving against his as warmth spreads between my thighs.

Then I come to my senses and somehow find the strength to hammer my fists into his vast chest. I try to push away from him, kicking at his muscled thighs. "Let me down! I hate you! I hate all of you! You disgust me!"

He lets out a growl and lets me go. I fall to the ground with a thud, the mist gathering up to cushion my fall.

"Adin!" he calls out as he turns his back to me and retreats to the back of the room.

I shuffle back against the misty floor, watching as the skin of his broad, muscled back pulses an angry midnight blue beneath his tunic. Adin walks in and looks down at me, confused.

"Take her away," Tharin says without looking at us.

"But she has only been here a few moments, Tharin," Adin says, confused.

"Take. Her. Away!" Tharin's voice booms.

Adin sighs, disappointment in his eyes. "Come," he says to me.

I quickly stand and take one last look at Tharin as I leave the room with Adin. As I walk down the corridor, I hear him let out a roar.

———

Tharin

When Kate leaves, I let out a roar. It's impossible to be around her. Why did I kiss her? What a fool. It was as though my feet, my hands, and my lips all moved of their own accord. It was uncontrollable, the desire to touch her, painful even. It will only get worse. I will tell my father that I'll be there for the child, but I cannot see Kate again. If he wants his First Defender to function, this woman must be removed from my presence. He will simply have to accept I will not be producing more heirs with her. But even as I consider that as an option, pain darts through me at the very thought of not seeing Kate again. This is why she must be banished. I cannot control what I feel when it comes to this human.

I go to the photos of my mother and sister. "Why am I being punished like this?" I ask them as though they were here. I imagine my sister mimicking our father, telling me it is my duty, and that I must be strong for the sake of Skarsdon. But then she would swipe me around the head and laugh at me. Our mother would walk in, calling me her warrior boy, as she was known to do even when I was an adult. "Be strong, Tharin, my warrior boy. You have the power to overcome this."

I thought I had all the power in the world when I first met Kate ten years ago. I'd watched as she woke to the sight of me in the very same vessel we're on now as it hovered above Earth. Surely this human would take one look at me and want me instantly, as all the women I'd encountered in Skarsdon had? Instead, she'd jumped from the bed and started throwing my books at me as I ducked out of the way.

"Who are you?" she had screamed. "What the hell am I doing here?"

Castian had spent most of his life studying humans and had produced a booklet to help us navigate their confusing emotions. We were told that should we be met with any violence—and the dent in my forehead from the corner of the book suggested I had—we should sit calmly, as though to meditate. That only seemed to infuriate Kate more, and in the end, I'd had to grab her wrists to stop her.

"At least let me introduce myself without having a book thrown at me," I'd shouted as she'd struggled against me. "I am Tharin of the planet Obrothea, and you are on a trans-porter vessel above Earth. Look." I had gestured out of the window. She had turned and gasped at the view of her beloved Earth below. But then her fight had returned.

"Why am I here?" she'd asked again, backing away to the corner of the room.

"To understand us, and for us to understand you."

"What if I don't want to understand?" she'd replied. But I could see from the look in her eyes as she'd taken in my swirling skin, so different from human skin, that she was intrigued. "How did I get here?"

"Transporter beams," I had replied. "There is a direct link from your bed to this vessel, undetectable by human technology."

"Beams. Like…beam me up, Scotty?"

I'd frowned, unaware back then of the TV show the earthlings call *Star Trek*. "I don't know what you mean, but all you need to know is nobody on Earth is aware you are here."

Her eyes had widened in fear. "I *am* returning to Earth, aren't I?"

I'd smiled. "Of course. And you will remember nothing thanks to the liptus haze in your beam when you return. It will just seem like a dream."

Her gaze had travelled over me. "I'm dreaming now, aren't I?"

Castian had suggested we could pretend it was all a dream. That was how the memories of this experience would be left in the human women's minds anyway, just vague fragments of dreams. But I needed this to be real for my Pledged. I knew that the moment I laid eyes on her. "No, this is very real."

"I think it's a dream. It has to be." She'd shrugged. "Oh well, it's better than my usual dreams of sitting in a lecture hall naked listening to Professor Adams talk about cosmology in the Middle Ages. So you mentioned a planet Obrothea?" Over the next few hours, I gently began to share facts about our planet, our people. She was fascinated, lapping up the knowledge with an enthusiasm that had turned me on just as much as her beauty. Despite how hard she made my cock, I did not try to seed her that night. I knew we had six more nights and I did not wish to rush her on that first night. I needed her to *want* me. On the second night, I turned up the charm, greeting her without my chest armor so she could take in all of me. She woke, memories from the night before temporarily regained thanks to the stident haze in her beam. She'd smiled lazily up at me, eyes filled with desire as they traveled over my muscled chest, but then the desire was replaced by shock. "Jeez, put a shirt on," she'd shouted.

The rest of that second night, she would not let me near her, instead just wanting to talk. It was frustrating, but still, I enjoyed talking with her. I was as fascinated with Earth as she was with Obrothea, and she told me much that night, including the terrible tragedy that befell her mother. All the time, I could see the clear desire in her eyes, but she kept herself well away from me. It confused me. This had never happened to me before, and from what I'd heard from the other men on the vessel, they weren't all experiencing the same problems with their Pledged. Many had seeded their humans the first night. It was humiliating. I was the First Defender and heir to the throne. I had given pleasure to many, many willing women all over Obrothea. And yet this human woman was not letting me near her?

The next day, I found Castian. He had laughed when I told him of my troubles. "I warned you all it might take time to bend these human women to your charms," he'd said. "It seems Kate is more stubborn than others."

"But I don't understand," I'd replied. "It's clear she desires me, and I desire her. Why deny herself the pleasure?"

"Some human women are different from Obrothean women. They prize holding themselves back, especially more religious women. Why not use the vevatia potion to help loosen her inhibitions? Remus experienced the same problems with his woman, and he has decided to use the potion on her tonight."

"No."

He had laughed again. "Then your balls might explode, my friend. I can already see the toll the frustration is having on you." He was right. My balls were hard and painfully engorged with unreleased seed. I wasn't used to it. I seeded every day when on Obrothea. It kept me strong and focused. In the end, when Kate was returned to Earth after that second night, I had to resort to satisfying myself to stave off the painful frustrations.

And now I feel the same. The sight of Kate in that dress just now... The way her nipples poked through the thin material. The scent of her sweet secretions. Ethos knew what he was doing when he chose those dresses. He knew what that scent of hers would do to me. My brother loves to torture me.

I growl, sweeping my glass off the nearby table. It had taken all my control just now to stop myself from throwing her onto my bed and sinking my cock into her. I hate myself for even kissing her. I hate the fact she clearly remembers nothing. I want her to remember. I want her to feel that passion again...and feel the guilt, too, over what she did to me. I want to punish her with the guilt, to ram my cock into her so hard she cries. A reprimand for the lives she cost. But as much as I want to inflict pain, I want to make her moan in pleasure too.

I sink down onto the bed, putting my head in my hands. It is such a confusing, painful mixture of emotions. Oh Goddess Tsuki, what can I do? I want to taste her again. That taste that I have yearned for all these years. I want to lift her dress and part her thighs. Breathe in her scent. Press my tongue against her clitoris and sink my fingers into her. One, two. Just to hear her moan again. To feel her body convulsing around my knuckles as it did so many times ten years ago.

I let out a howl and tear open my breeches, freeing my pulsating cock. Pre-seed the color of my desire and anger squeezing out of me. I smooth it over my length and groan as I slide my palms up and down until I explode, my seed erupting from me.

After, I lie on my bed, spent. I promised myself I wouldn't allow this to happen. I promised myself there would be no emotions involved, no uncontrollable desire. I would seed her, and that would be that. Look how weak it is making me.

I force myself to stand and buckle myself up again, looking at the photos of my mother and sister, guilt coursing through me. How can I be with the woman who caused their deaths? I can't fall for her again. It will be my undoing. I just know it. I find my wound and work at it with my finger.

Stay strong, Tharin. Stay strong.

Kate

Adin grabs my wrist and yanks me down the corridor as I hear another loud roar from Tharin behind us. *Good.*

"You cannot say things like that to your Prime, let alone the First Defender," Adin says, clearly rattled.

"He cannot kidnap me and my child. But, hey, he still did it anyway."

Adin clenches his jaw. "You were supposed to be in there for several hours. This was your chance to ask questions. For Tharin to plant seed too, if you so wished."

I laugh, shaking my head. "Listen to yourself. As if I would ever let that beast 'plant seed'," I say, using my fingers to make quotation marks.

He shoots me a furious look. "You did before, quite willingly. And he is your Prime."

"I would never have willingly done that," I say, despite a voice deep inside me telling me I absolutely did. "Look, I know he's your prince or something, but he's a—" Adin gives me a warning glance. I pause. Maybe I need to be careful? In some countries back on Earth, you say one word to criticize a ruling family, and you can have your hand chopped off. I take a deep breath, calming myself. "It's difficult for me. This complete stranger—an *alien*—is claiming to be the father of my child and is trying to essentially force me to have another child."

"He would never force you. It's not the Skarsdonian way to force oneself upon a woman."

"He must have if he claims to be the father of my child. The whole thing is disgusting and perverted."

Adin looks taken aback. "Why would you say that? All mothers of our Sacred children were willing participants. Conception is scientifically impossible for Obrotheans if the woman is unwilling."

"Scientifically impossible? What do you mean by that?"

"If you had stayed long enough in Tharin's rooms, you may have gotten the answer to that question," he snaps. "It is not up to me to tell you our ways. It is up to your Prime."

"Well, I refuse to see him again." As I say that though, my gut unwittingly twists in protest at the idea of not seeing him again.

"You will have no choice," Adin says. "You do not realize what a privilege it is to have the First Defender and future Grand Sovran as your Prime."

I gulp. Tharin is the future king? "Well, that just makes him even more responsible for all this. Surely he had the power to say no?"

"Actually, he—" Adin pauses. "You must talk to Tharin

about all of this. It's a shame you didn't make the most of your time with him. Now you have a whole afternoon ahead of you with nothing but lunch to entertain you. At least you'll have books to read, I suppose." He puts his hand on the wall, and it disappears. "I will collect you for lunch. You need to hope Tharin will not be there. He will be very angry." Then he turns and walks away.

EIGHT

Kate

A few hours later, I file into the great hall with the other women for lunch. We all look around the dining room, hoping to see our children there too, but there is no sign of them. I notice there's a more positive buzz on the air, though, and some of the women are talking excitedly. Maybe they liked their Primes. *Lucky them.* Others are crying, though, silent and sad. Helena still looks completely shocked by the whole experience, staring ahead with her eyes wide as Charlotte rubs her back.

"Hey," Charlotte says to me as we sit down. "How'd meeting your Prime go?"

"He kicked me out after five minutes."

She laughs. "No way. So he's an A-hole then?"

"Yep. I promised myself no assholes after I caught my ex cheating on me, and now I get the prince of all assholes. What about you?" I ask Charlotte.

"Oh, I don't have a Prime. I'm the idiot who volunteered, remember? I think they're still trying to figure out what to do with me. I had to hang out in the communal area all on my own, *so* dull. I'm used to being outside, not stuck on some spaceship."

I frown. They have a communal area?

"At least there were books to read," Charlotte continues. "Did you get those weird glasses to read them with?"

"Yep." I was frustrated at first when I flicked through the array of books in my room. The text within had made no sense at all. It was just made up of strange symbols. But then I noticed some gold-rimmed glasses set to one side. When I put them on, I was shocked to see the strange text suddenly turn into English.

"The glasses are so handy, aren't they?" Louisa, the redheaded Irish woman from earlier says, joining our conversation.

"Sure," I reply. "Who *doesn't* want to read about the wars of Skarsdon and herbal plants of Obrothea while wearing crazy-looking glasses?"

Charlotte laughs. "Scintillating stuff. To be fair though, the war books are fascinating. Seems the Grand Sovran's family has experienced more drama than our British royal family, and that's saying something."

I peer at Helena. "Speaking of royals... How's your sister?"

"Fuming because her Prime, Persean, isn't one of the princes. If she had to be kidnapped by aliens, she at least wanted the very best kind of alien." She sighs. "He kept his hands off her though. That's something."

"Mine did too," Louisa says, fiddling with her cross. "I get the impression some of the other girls had a tougher time though." I follow her gaze to the Eastern European table, where one skinny, black-haired girl is being comforted by the other women. Her face is bruised, and her dress is torn.

"She won't have been forced, Louisa," Anaya, the

Australian woman calls over to her. "My Prime told me it's totally against their laws. Maybe she fell or something?"

"Just because something's law, doesn't mean it's abided by," I say.

"Kate is right," Helena says, finally talking. "And anyway, Persean told me their laws do not apply to those they call Highborns—the royals sitting up there." She gestures to the raised table. "Maybe she's pledged to one of the princes?"

"Wow, elitist much?" Charlotte says, shaking her head. "Poor girl."

We all turn to look at the girl and go silent. I shake my head in disgust as I regard the royal brothers. Which of them is she pledged to? Then something occurs to me. If the rules don't apply to the royals, why didn't Tharin just force himself on me earlier? *There's still time,* a voice inside me says.

"Oh, stop looking all gloomy," Anaya says. "We don't really know what happened. Anyway, who's to say we girls need forcing? I mean, you have to admit, these men are just gorgeous."

"If you're into muscly types," Louisa says, wrinkling her nose.

"Well, I am, and I was *very* willing," Anaya says. "Honestly, I can't even put it into words what my Prime did to me."

"Don't tell me you let him…" My voice trails off.

"When you're sitting across from a hulking chunk of goodness like that, can you really blame me?" Anaya says with a shrug.

"Have you forgot we've been kidnapped?" Louisa says. "You should have had more willpower. He has *forced* you from your home."

"Louisa, you really need to take that stick outta your ass," Anaya says. "Anyway, home was never a good place for me. At least here I get my place cleaned. Did anyone else notice how immaculate the rooms were when we got back from seeing our Primes?"

I think back to how it felt to walk into my room after being with Tharin to find a perfectly made-up bed and gleaming surfaces. Clearly, someone had been in to clean the place in the few minutes I'd been away. I've grown so used to coming home after a day at work to a trashed kitchen, bed covers unruly, and clothes all over the floor thanks to the manic rush in the morning to get Isla to school and me to work. I have to admit, it is nice to know that's one thing I don't have to worry about while being here. I mean, I really don't need to add to my current list of worries. Being kidnapped and forced to another planet are enough at the moment.

"At least you had choices on Earth," I say. "We don't seem to have any here."

"Did I have choices?" Anaya sighs. "Look, all I'm saying is these warriors are *gifted*." She licks her lips as she stares up at the viewing gallery. I follow her gaze to see the men up there watching us. The idea we're all being watched like cattle just makes it even worse.

"The things they can do," Anaya continues. "The extra bits they have." She leans in close to me and Charlotte, lowering her voice. "Turns out they have an extra belly button. They call it their arcism. It's just above their cocks. But that ain't no normal belly button, let me tell you. You ever tried one of those airflow suction vibrators that are all the rage?" We all shake our heads. "Well, let me just tell you, their arcisms are like that but *better*. When their arcism is pressed against your clit..." She takes in a breath. "I can't even describe the feeling. I came in, like, seconds."

"Anaya!" Charlotte says, unable to stop herself from laughing.

70

"Not just that," Anaya continues, "their come is like a friggin' rainbow. It comes out all multicolored."

I look at her in shock. "You're kidding, right?"

"Nope," Anaya says, biting her lip. "My Prime told me their come is so strong, it works its way into our DNA."

"Now that just sounds wrong," Charlotte says.

Anaya shrugs. "I kinda like it. There's even this thing called Fortification. In some couples, the man's come effects the woman's DNA and makes her develop this, like, super immunity to illnesses and stuff. My Prime said he told me all this ten years ago. I can't believe I forgot it all."

"Yep, that totally sucks," I say. "Essentially having our memories *stolen* from us."

The seven brothers enter the hall then, Tharin among them. I can't help it, my gaze lowers to his stomach, imagining this arcism hidden beneath the band of his pants.

"Now if *he* was my Prime," Anaya says, following my gaze, "he wouldn't have to wait too long before I was on my knees."

Louisa turns her face away in disgust. "Anaya, honestly."

"She *is* telling the truth though. He is rather appealing," Helena says.

"I thought you didn't like the look of him," I say.

Helena turns her glacial-blue eyes to me. "I never said he wasn't beautiful to look at."

Charlotte rolls her eyes. "It's because she's learned he's heir to the throne."

"It's not just that," Helena snaps back at her. "He's a true hero according to what Persean told me. Positively *brutal* on the battlefield."

"Yes, I read that in one of the war books," Louisa chimes in. "I can't believe he was just sixteen when he killed the King of Gatika."

"What happened?" I ask Louisa.

"He teamed up with his older brother, Ryker, to kill the king. Two teenage assassins."

I sneak a look at Tharin. He surveys the room. His gaze latches on mine, and his jaw tenses.

"Which one is Ryker?" I ask, looking at the other brothers.

"Oh, he's dead," Helena says nonchalantly. "Persean told me Ryker was behind an invasion ten years ago that led to the slaughter of the Grand Sovran's wife and daughter from his first marriage."

I think of the photos of the two women Tharin had in his room. Are they of his mother and sister? "But Louisa just said the two brothers fought together?"

"The whole Gatikan King assassination thing was four years before Ryker's invasion," Helena says. "Persean says Ryker had a big bust up with the Grand Sovran and was banished from Skarsdon after the Gatikan war. When Ryker came back to invade Skarsdon, it was a betrayal of biblical proportions. It was so bad that Tharin ended up killing him."

"He killed his own brother?" Anaya asks. "I mean, I guess if he caused the death of Tharin's mother and sister. But still…"

"He killed his half-brother," Louisa corrects her. "Ryker the Rebel—that's how he's known now—was the product of their mother's first marriage. You know she once lived in Fostinia, the very region that invaded Skarsdon ten years ago and caused her death? All so tragic really," she adds with a sigh. "In fact, Kate, your defender Adin is Ryker's brother, another son from that first marriage."

My eyes widen in surprise. "Why isn't Adin sitting with his brothers then?"

"He's the Grand Sovran's stepson. He doesn't have the royal blood running through his veins, does he?" Helena says it as though I'm stupid for asking.

"And despite all that, Adin remains loyal to the Grand Sovran and the man who executed his brother?" I say.

Anaya leans forward. "My Prime also said—"

"Can we stop calling them our Primes?" Louisa suddenly interrupts in a shaky voice. "Sorry, it just really grates on me as it gives them even more power over us."

"They already have all the power in the world," Helena snaps. "There is nothing we can do about it."

"But we *can* control the words we use, even if we can't control anything else," I say, giving Louisa a sympathetic smile.

Louisa nods. "It's something I always tell my boys." Her eyes fill with tears, and something occurs to me then. Many of these women have left other children behind, the siblings of their Sacred children. It makes me feel even angrier. I look up at Tharin and curl my hands into fists. I will not let these beasts take my freedom away.

Tharin

I watch Kate eat. Each time I catch her eye, she glares at me. Good. I do not want things between us to be congenial. I just need to seed her and be done with it. I grab a chunk of bread and bite into it. It tastes of nothing. I am rarely without appetite, but her presence is making me react in ways I do not like. It is making me weak.

I force myself to eat, even as it makes me feel sick. As I do, I notice my father leave the table. I follow him to the place he often retreats to after dinner, the Sacellum. It sits in the center of the vessel, a circular cathedral that mimics the one in the city of Skarsdon. It is rare to see me here in this place of worship. We have strict definitions. I am a defender.

Therefore, my place is fighting on the battlefield or honing my skills on the training ground. My father and four of my brothers are sages, their roles one of holy leadership and scientific learning. My father, in particular, spends most of his time in prayer, whether in the splendid Sacellum that dominates the center of our city, or here in this mammoth transporter vessel.

My father often tries to encourage me to visit these places of worship. Usually, the oldest child and heir to the throne trains to be a sage. It's seen as a preferable path for a future Grand Sovran. My father's firstborn, my half-sister Thesera, was a sage, one of the very best there was...until she died. When she was taken from us, I became the heir. There was talk of pushing me to be a sage, but my reputation as a defender was already too strong to justify it. So it is now accepted the next Grand Sovran will be a defender. I think it is right. There is much turmoil to come, and surely a warrior is best equipped to deal with that turmoil? Not everyone agrees though. I have heard whispers over the years from the sage community that the role would be better suited to Ethos, the second oldest son. But my father insists it must be me.

I walk towards my father now, the soles of my leather boots thumping on the white tiles below. The Sacellum on the ship is not as big as our planet's Sacellum, but it is still impressive with tall walls made from the finest acrenium— the unique rock we drill from our core. Its pulsing veins dance with color to reflect emotions, just like our skin, which has absorbed enough of the substance to do the same. The walls here usually drum a soft white and blue, reflecting the calmness within, but with my presence, it oscillates between black and red. It is a large room, but it feels small and oppressive to me right now, as though it is a tenth of the size. Faith has never sat comfortably with me.

I stop behind my father. He stands upright with his arms

stretched up, palms connected in the sacred prayer to our Goddess, Tsuki. "What is troubling you, son?" he asks, not needing to look my way to know my mood. The walls tell him enough.

"Kate," I say firmly. "She must go. I'm sorry, Father, I have tried, but it's impossible."

"You know I cannot agree to that. She is too important."

"Am I, your son and First Defender, not important?" I ask him. "It is torture having her here. It will affect my ability to battle."

My father's bitter laugh echoes around the great hall. "Our great warrior. The most lauded war hero in generations. And yet you are brought to your knees by her? Heed my advice, do not let her control you. She is just a weak human woman."

"Human women are stronger than you think, Father. Like Mother and Thesera, she—"

"Do not dare to compare a human to them," my father shouts. The walls turn ink black. "Even with all Kate possesses in her genetics, she is nothing like your mother and sister."

"Of course," I say, inclining my head. "I was not suggesting she is."

"You just need to seed her. That is all," he says dismissively. "It happened reasonably quickly before. You may only need to endure her company once a year to produce more heirs."

"It may not happen as quickly as you think," I say. "I cannot see her complying."

"Then use the vevatia on her."

"No, I will never use it. I'd rather find another like her," I suggest. "Ethos can send a scouting vessel back to Earth."

"Ethos has searched already. Do you not think your brother wants a human woman just like Kate for himself? It is the combination of your genetics with hers that makes your coupling so unique. Only the two of you can produce hybrids like Isla." He places his hand on my shoulder. "Son, you know the disease that ravishes my body."

I clench my jaw and try not to think of the disease that is weakening his heart. I see the results of it more and more each day, not just through the withering of his muscles, but also the way his colors are fading, so much so that paints are used to make him appear stronger than he is.

"I may not even see the year out," he continues. "If I can die knowing your position as future Grand Sovran has been strengthened even more with another child like Isla on the way, then I can take my place by the All Creator Tsuki without worry. "

Of course, he is right. As always with Obrothea, a position of strength is maintained with three things: a strong army of defenders, wealth to buy influence, and a powerful Grand Sovran with as many heirs as possible. What could be more impressive than heirs as genetically superior as Isla? That was why Kate was chosen for me. Ethos's tests had shown just how unique our children would be thanks to our combination of rare genetics.

It is a burden I must carry to ensure the future of the region I love. Though Skarsdon still remains the seat of power for all of Obrothea, our enemies are closing in. A great war between Skarsdon and Fostinia, maybe Gatika too, is sure to come. There are still regions who are undecided about which side they will fight on. By showing a position of strength when my father dies—and that may come sooner than we feared with his disease—I can convince more regions to join us in the battle. To achieve this, I must seed Kate, even if it half kills me to be with her.

I look at my father's pale face. I have to do this for him. For all of Skarsdon. "I understand, Father."

He smiles, relief flooding his face. "I knew you would, son."

I walk from the room, the burden of what I must endure weighing heavily upon me.

Tonight, I must see her again. Tonight, I will have to convince her to let me seed her and be done with it.

NINE

Kate

When Isla returns to our room at three on the dot, she's buzzing. Apparently, it was "so cool" and her scribe Castian is "the best teacher ever…apart from you, Mommy."

After she's had a snack from the array of delicious fruit that sits in a bowl within our room, we both sit down in the lounge area. "Do you want to ask me anything, darling?" I'm aware she must be curious about all this talk of the aliens being the children's fathers.

She bites into a fruit that looks like an apple but is bright purple inside. "Not really."

I sigh. Clearly, she wants to avoid the subject. "I know you've heard all the chatter about Sacred children and Pledged. You know, if you want to talk about anything—"

"It's fine, Mommy. I know the aliens think they're our dads or something. But I know who my real dad is. Richard Thompson."

I smile to myself. She sounds just like how I sounded with Tharin earlier. But I can also see some doubt written on her face. "Yes, that's right," I say. "Anyway, we've only been here a day. We know nothing."

"Exactly."

"But you know you can always talk to me and ask me any questions. I know how scary this must be."

"It's not scary," she replies. "Everyone's been super kind, and the other kids are *so* cool. There's this one kid in my class from a place called Nauru. Have you heard of it? It's the third smallest country in the world, and even though she speaks a totally different language from me, I understand *everything* she says."

I smile. Though part of me wants to shake her shoulders and remind her we've been abducted by aliens, and that's frigging awful, the other part is pleased she feels safe and is enjoying herself, despite how weird this situation is. If one of us is going to enjoy this all, I'm pleased it's her. Over the next couple of hours, I let her talk more about her new friends and all the things she's learnt.

Her enthusiasm wains somewhat when she sees yet another tunic dress waiting for her when we get ready for dinner. I have a new outfit waiting for me, a shorter version of what I wore earlier. They *really* need to up their fashion game. When Adin arrives, we follow him to the hall, and I think of all I've learnt about him. It's amazing how loyal he's remained to Tharin, despite the fact that Tharin killed his brother. But then that same brother instigated an invasion that led to their mother's and sister's deaths.

When we get to the hall, it looks different. The walls are darker, and candles flicker on the tables. The area by the waterfall has opened up too, revealing a separate hall with hundreds of seats gathered around a large stage. Then I realize another change. I can see through the windows into space. Gasps and excited chatter spread around the room as others realize this as well. Children run up to the windows as the defenders watch and smile. But I stay where I am, a truck-load of emotions smashing through me.

"Wow, will you look at that," Charlotte whispers as she joins me with Helena and Henry.

"It's… It's beautiful," I whisper. I walk towards the window as Isla darts ahead of me with Henry, taking in the blackness interspersed with bright sparks of silver and trails of moon dust beyond. "I once dreamed of seeing space from up here."

"I think she's having an orgasm over the sight of space," Anaya says.

I roll my eyes. "Come on, you can't deny what a sight it is. I don't recognize any of the star formations though."

"Does this mean we're in another solar system?" Henry asks me.

I smile down at the young prince. "Looks like it."

I really have always dreamt about seeing space up close. I was fascinated with the night sky at the commune. We arrived there when I was thirteen. The kids were all allowed to stay up as long as they wanted, and though my mother tried to insert some kind of bedtime routine, I'd invariable sneak out to stargaze with my father's old telescope. I began to map the skies.

We didn't have access to computers or TVs, and there were no astronomy books at the commune, so it had been up to me to outline the constellations for the other kids. Producing those beautiful maps became my passion. I began to formulate a plan for myself during the two years I was at the commune. I wanted to travel the world to map the skies when I grew up. It would be my own adventure. I knew my options would be limited since we didn't attend a formal school. We were all taught during the day by my mother and another woman. My mom wasn't even a qualified teacher. She just happened to know a lot about music.

After my mother died, all thoughts of adventure were driven from my mind. When I left the commune at fifteen and went to live with my aunt, I worked my butt off to graduate and then put myself through university, studying space sciences. After Isla was born, I finally trained to be a teacher. Watching excited kids learn about the universe was as close as I could get to traveling the world to find my own wonders.

It's amazing to think that I'm now up in space, seeing stars and planets firsthand. Except I'm doing it from an alien slave ship.

Charlotte nudges my arm as the royal brothers walk in. My eyes instantly seek Tharin out. He's wearing a beautiful gold tunic and dark gold breeches. I curl my hands into fists, pushing uninvited sensations away. He doesn't look at me. Instead, he seeks out Isla and smiles as she does a little jig of excitement at the sight of space. It gives me a jolt to see him actually smile. He notices me watching him, and the smile is instantly wiped from his face. Instead, he scowls and turns away.

At least the feeling's mutual.

The Grand Sovran joins his sons, his green eyes lighting up as he watches the excited children. As much as I despise this situation, it's clear these beings adore our Sacred children, as they call them. I'm not sure that takes away from the fact they've abducted and impregnated human women to create them.

Tharin's talk about training the kids for something also worries me. I need to find out more about that. Maybe I should be a little more congenial the next time I see him so I can find out what he meant?

When we get to our tables, dishes are already laid out. There are also large goblets of drink.

"Is it wine?" Charlotte asks, leaning over one and sniffing it.

"I hope so." Alana pours herself some and takes a sip. Her eyes light up. "Delicious. And I already feel a bit drunk, hurrah!"

I place my hand over my cup before she can give me some. "Not for me."

"Ah, come on, Teach," she says. "You need to loosen up. Even our resident bible basher is having some," she says, gesturing to Louisa, who takes a small sip of her drink.

"I don't really like that term, Anaya." Louisa turns to me. "The drink *is* very nice though, Kate. I read about it in one of the books. It's called pemelonian. It allows you to get a little bit tipsy without a hangover the next day."

I shake my head. "I need to have my wits about me."

"Oh, please," Helena says with an eye roll as she quickly drains her own cup. "This is our life now. We're not getting out of here. Might as well make the most of it."

"There's always hope," I say, helping Isla fill her plate with food as I fill my own.

Anaya's eyes go dark as she chews on some bread. "I've learnt the hard way that's not true." She peers up at the viewing area. "I wonder if my Prime is watching me? Did I tell you he's a kind of politician back in Obrothea? Me, having a politician as a Prime, isn't it hilarious?"

"*You* might like the idea of your Prime watching you," Charlotte says, "but others don't." She gestures to the young Eastern European woman who had seemed upset earlier. She doesn't look any happier.

"I heard she's a Russian ballerina," Helena says, taking a delicate sip of her pemelonian.

"Poor thing." I impulsively pour myself some of the drink and take a quick sip. I feel like I need it. The floral citrus flavor bursts on my tongue. "Wow, this is divine." I take another sip, savoring the taste and sensation, smiling as it winds its way down my throat.

Suddenly, the familiar anthem rings out. The room goes quiet, and we peer into the auditorium next door to see beings with colorful hair on the stage playing the anthem on large drums. Behind them, a huge screen bursts to life, and a beautiful animated film begins to play. The scribes file back in, beckoning for the children to join them. The scribe Isla is so enraptured with, Castian, stands at the end of the table and puts his slim hand out to her.

"No," I say, pulling Isla close to me, not wanting to let her out of my sight again. "Stay here."

I can see Isla wants to go with the other kids, but she remains close to me all the same. Tharin watches us, a small crease in his brow. Then he looks at Castian and jerks his chin up. Castian sighs and walks over to me. He really is very tall, and his skin oscillates green and blue. "I'm Castian," he says softly, putting his hand to his chest. "I'm your daughter's guardian and scribe. She will not leave my sight."

"No, *I* am her guardian," I say. "She's staying with me."

He smiles. "You have not changed, Kate. Stubborn as ever."

I frown. "You know me?"

"I was on the vessel you were brought to over Earth ten years ago. We spent many hours talking, when Tharin allowed it."

Allowed it. Lovely.

"I hate not remembering that time," I say. "Taking our memories is just one more awful thing you lot have done to us."

"Mommy, you're being rude. Castian is really kind. Please can I go? The other kids are."

"I will look after her," Castian says. "I promise."

I clench my jaw and then nod before I change my mind. Isla gives me a quick hug. Before they walk off, I grab Castian's wrist and look into his strange eyes. "Don't let her out of your sight."

"Never." He bows to me, takes Isla's hand, and leads her to the stage. I watch them, still brooding over the fact there are whole nights I've forgotten from ten years before. It feels just as much a violation as the idea of them impregnating us. To take our memories away like that is just cruel.

Charlotte seems to sense my mood. "It sucks, doesn't it?" she asks.

"Yep."

"The thing I can't quite wrap my head around," Charlotte says, "is how the hell did these aliens get hundreds of women to consent to sex with them?"

"Who says we consented?"

"Helena's Prime insists they did. She seems to believe him. He told her each woman only spent seven of their most fertile nights on the vessel during the month it was above Earth. Seven nights and all these women were happy to just roll over and open their legs, including the happily married ones? Nah, something doesn't add up."

"I hear you. I don't like it either. Even worse we remember nothing.'

"How *convenient*," Charlotte murmurs.

I sigh and take another sip of my drink, enjoying how quickly it makes me feel drunk. I ought to temper my drinking. I can get a bit silly when I'm drunk. But the truth is, it's good to be among other women, chatting and drinking like this nightmare isn't happening. I learn Charlotte works in an art gallery back in London but once tried out for the Olympic archery team. Louisa is a stay-at-home mom in a small town near Dublin, and Anaya works as a cashier in Melbourne.

"Most boring job in the world," she slurs as she tells me about it. "I mean, I have no idea what the hell's going on here, but at least I'm not working."

I realize I would probably be getting ready for work the next day by now. I would have marked all the kids' assignments and be ironing my clothes. Instead, I'm here getting drunk with a bunch of women trying to forget their fears, all while being observed by aliens.

Is this my life now? I worked so hard to qualify as a teacher, a feat made even more difficult considering I wasn't in school much as a kid. Is that all down the drain now? What sort of future lies ahead for me? I look over to the windows, feeling that thrill inside me again at seeing space up close. I suddenly want to get even closer, so I stand and weave between the tables, sensing Tharin's gaze on me as I do. I don't care. Let him stare.

When I get to the window, I place my palm against it and stare out at the stars. The window is cold and smooth beneath my touch, and I imagine it flexing and disappearing before me like the walls here do. It's so vast and so magnificent out there. I imagine being out there, free with Isla in my arms. *Escaping.*

I wish my mother had tried to escape the commune. She was clearly so desperate for release in those final months of her life. She had loved it on the commune at first. Mom had brought a heavily pregnant woman she'd found handing out leaflets in town into our home to get a cool drink. I still remember the way my father's eyes lit up as the woman began to talk of this sense she and the other commune members had that something big was on the horizon—alien invasion, Russian invasion. It didn't matter, it was *some* kind of invasion that we all needed to prepare for. My dad had the same sense, and a month later, we sold our house and moved into one of the ramshackle buildings on the old farm that made up the commune.

The first eighteen months was an adventure with lots of joy-filled dinners and non-stop fun. Sure, the adults gathered supplies and weapons, but it wasn't really too noticeable. Then the self-assigned leader, a stocky white-haired man in his sixties who we all called Azalah, began to talk of the invasion being imminent. Things took a serious turn then. More weapons were bought, more alcohol consumed. My mother could see it. She even casually mentioned leaving once, but I was all tangled up with one of the boys on the commune by then, and the last thing I wanted to do was leave.

One star-riddled night, Azalah gathered the men to practice their aim after they'd all been drinking way too much of his homemade brew. They didn't know my mother was taking a walk. No one knew who fired the shot that struck Mom in her chest and killed her. She may have survived if they hadn't taken so long to call an ambulance. Azalah had insisted she would be better off treated in the commune with his "prayer warriors" and herbal medicine rather than by those "lizard doctors." I begged them to call an ambulance, but my father was too deep into all the conspiracy theories by then. When it was clear all the prayers and herbs in the world wouldn't work, an ambulance was eventually called, but it was too late.

Oh Mom.

"It's beautiful, is it not?" I look up with a start to see Ethos standing beside me. "All this too," he adds, gesturing around him. "You do realize how very privileged you are, don't you?"

I can't help but laugh. "Privileged? I'm not sure that's how I'd describe myself right now."

His jaw clenches. "I know this is difficult for you all. It goes against your twenty-first century human beliefs."

"Seventeenth century too," I can't help but say. The drink I've consumed has made me even braver than normal.

"Are you not happy to be pledged with the First Defender and heir to the Skarsdonian throne?"

"Not if he's forced upon me."

"It will not feel like that if he administers you with the vevatia he has been given."

"Vevatia? What's that?"

"It is an ointment that helps women feel more sexually uninhabited."

My mouth drops open. "So a rape drug?"

"Rape?" He laughs. "You are being ridiculous."

"*You're* the ridiculous ones, kidnapping human women and using a *rape* drug on them."

He shakes his head. "As defiant as ever. You're lucky you're even here after what you did ten years ago."

I look at him in surprise. "What do you mean?"

"Ask Tharin." He storms off and anger swells inside me. How dare he say *I'm* the one who did something bad when *they're* the ones who dragged us from our homes and essentially used a rape drug on us?

Before I know it, I find myself following him, ready to give him a piece of my mind.

Tharin

I rise from my chair, unable to quell the storm of anger that surges through me as I watch Ethos talk to Kate. What is he saying to her? Remus puts his hand on my arm as he follows my gaze. "Sit back down, brother. You mustn't cause a scene."

Just as Remus he says that, Ethos storms off, skin pulsing red and black. Kate starts after him. I've seen her angry like this before. It clouds her judgment, especially if she's had some pemelonian. It takes me three strides to catch up to her. I grab her wrist and yank her into the shadows of the hall as she battles against me.

"Let go of me," she hisses, slamming her free hand point-lessly against my chest. "I know how you made us have sex with you. You *raped* us."

"Rape? You're being ridiculous."

That seems to infuriate her even more. Her pretty dark eyes turn wild as she tries to kick at my skins. This will not do. I carry her into the corridor as she continues to thrash against me. It's like holding a tiny tornado against my chest, and her moving against my cock makes me hard.

"Where are you taking me?" she says. "I will *not* let you give me any vevatia."

Vevatia. How does she know about vevatia? Ethos, clearly. That cock-juggling fool! I get to my room, press my palm against the wall, and stride through as it dissolves. I drop the human tornado to her feet, and she instantly runs to the door, but it's a solid wall again.

"Damn these stupid Harry Potter walls!" she screams. She turns to me, arms crossed. It pushes her breasts up, making me harden even more. "Take me back,' she says. "You will not touch me."

"Not until you calm down."

"I want to see my daughter."

"She's safe with Castian. She is *not* safe with her hyster-ical mother arguing with one of the Highborn."

"Oh, we wouldn't want to argue with a Highborn, would we?" she says in a mocking voice. "Highborn are above all laws, after all. Even rape, clearly."

"I did not rape you."

"Well someone clearly raped the Russian ballet dancer. Probably one of your brothers if he's been able to get away with it."

Now I'm very confused. "Russian ballet dancer? I don't understand."

"There are rumors she was raped, and considering Highborns are above the law, I bet it was one of your brothers."

Fury whirls deep inside me as I pace the room. "I know who the ballerina's Prime is. Loxley is not a Highborn." I pause before her. "He'll be punished, trust me."

I don't add I will take great joy in punishing him. I detest the man. I warned Ethos about including him among the chosen warriors ten years ago. There were rumors about his aggressive ways towards woman when we stormed Gatika, rumors he raped several women who were rounded up in a nearby village, something I had absolutely forbidden.

Nothing could be proven, so he remained in position thanks to his wealthy family. When I saw him board the vessel for Earth ten years ago, I was not happy. And now my concerns have been validated. He has taken his Pledged violently against her will, despite the proclamations against it.

"You say Loxley isn't a Highborn. What if he were one though?" Kate asks. "Would you punish him?"

I frown. She has a point. It would be difficult for me to justify any punishment if he were a Highborn, even for a crime as heinous as rape.

"Just what I thought," she says in disgust. "You're all so used to taking what you want. It's clearly what you did to me ten years ago."

"How many times do I have to tell you that I would never force you? As far as I know, none of the Pledged were."

"I don't believe you. There's no way this number of women would agree to have sex in such a short space of time. Clearly, we were coerced into it with this vevatia rape drug."

I look at her in shock. "I know of your rape drugs on Earth. Vevatia does not make you forget, nor does it constrict movement. It just heightens desire. And anyway, it was only used by a handful of the men."

"Nope, you're not convincing me."

I clench my jaw. Why must she persist with this? "The reason your inhibitions were loosened was probably because of the haze combination filtered into the beams. It can make women feel as though they are in a dream."

"Well, this time I know it's not a dream and I won't let you touch me."

"Fine," I shoot back. "I will not touch you unless you are begging for it."

She turns away and laughs. "As if!"

Her dress plunges low at the back as well as the front, and I can see her beautiful, olive skin, skin I once traced my lips down. The walls around us pulse red and purple with my anger and desire.

"You are so deluded," she says.

I clench my fists. It infuriates me to think she truly believes I'd forced her. It infuriates me she has forgotten all I taught her about us, including the fact that forcing a woman will not lead to what we all want—conception. I stride towards her, grab her arm, and pull her towards the back of the room. She batters her fists into me again, but it just makes me even more determined...and makes my cock even harder too. "Stop fighting me," I hiss at her. "I am about to teach you a valuable lesson."

TEN

Kate

"I don't want you teaching me any lessons," I shout, slamming my fists against Tharin as he lifts me and carries me to the other side of the room. At first, I think he's going to throw me onto his bed. Instead, he plonks me down onto one of two chairs and sits across from me. I go to jump up, but he pulls my chair towards him so his knees are blocking me.

"This is what you need to know," he says, his voice serious. "We Skarsdonians always aim to produce the strongest offspring possible. This can only happen when a woman orgasms."

My cheeks flush, and I try to avoid his intense gaze. "That's ridiculous."

"No, it is science. Not only do the contractions encourage the seed to progress, but they have a very specific impact on Obrothean seed. The contractions massage the individual gametes—sperm as you call them—igniting them in what we call the rousing."

"The rousing? What does *that* mean?"

I notice him shift in his seat, adjusting himself. I can see the outline of his hard-on—a huge hard-on that has been building from the moment I struggled against him earlier. My breath quickens, and I force my gaze away.

"The rousing," he continues, voice husky now as his glance travels over my breasts, "is what occurs when contractions and secretions combine in a particular way to ignite usually dormant enzymes in our seed, enzymes needed to produce our offspring." He leans even closer, and I can smell his heady, musky scent.

"Kate, you need to know it was always important to me that we reached the optimal conditions. We found that two orgasms, sometimes three would produce the best kind of..." He swallows, his Adam's apple bobbing up and down, "... secretions, the kind that would drip from your pussy and stretch between my fingers."

My mouth drops open. The way he's talking...

"You can't say things like that."

"I apologize. It's the only way I know how to explain it." He licks his lips, and I squeeze my thighs together, urging my body to calm down as my own—what did he just call it? —*secretions* ooze out of me. Damn my body. I quickly stand and smooth my dress down at the back, feeling a wet patch there. I look down at the chair, embarrassed to see the fabric is slightly wet too. Tharin follows my gaze, and his expression makes my clit throb. My breath stutters, warmth pumping and pooling at the core of me.

Two, sometimes three orgasms.

"I'd like to go please. I promise I have calmed down."

He stands, his bulge is even more pronounced now. "Are you sure? It's important for Isla that you are calm."

"Yes, very sure. Thank you. I get the message loud and clear." I back away, bumping into a table and knocking a drink over. It spills over the table's surface and drips to the floor.

Dripping. Juice.

Oh God.

"Fine," he says, going to the wall and pressing his huge palm against it. I feel him brush against me, and I have to hold my breath to calm myself. The wall dissolves, and I'm free. I can't go back into the hall right away. I *have* to pull myself together before I do. Tharin knew what he was doing back there. It was cruel. A form of torture. When I'm in the safety of my room, I lean against the wall and reach under my dress. My thighs are slick with the embodiment of my want. I trail my fingers over it and rub my wet fingertips over the nub of my most sensitive part. I close my eyes and imagine Tharin, his full lips and the intensity of his green gaze heavy with lust. Those muscles, and God, the outline of his desire.

"Oh God," I whisper, finger moving faster over my clit, stroking it. I imagine him sitting across from me in that huge chair, watching me as he moves his hand up and down his huge cock. Am I imagining it? Is it a memory from ten years ago? I moan now as the sensations build, swirling like the colors of the walls around me. Circles of sensation drawing closer and closer and closer until there's finally a release. I let out a cry, sliding down the wall with a sob.

I wake misty headed and stretch, feeling Isla sleeping soundly beside me. It took a while to get used to not having sheets and any sense of solid matter beneath me, but this bed is the most amazing one I've ever slept on.

My dreams didn't help me feel rested though. They slammed into me, uninvited, even more intense and hot now that I'm so damn sexually frustrated. I think all Tharin's talk of juices rubbed off on me, because my sleepy mind is filled with images of his huge head between my legs, his golden hair over my thighs as he laps his tongue against me.

Damn it, I need a cold shower, stat. I get up quietly, letting Isla sleep as I go to the large bathroom in the main living area of our suite. There's a huge shower in there, and a bath too. It's all voice controlled.

"Shower on," I say. "Cold."

I duck under the shower, feeling the icy cold on my skin. I stifle a gasp and force myself to stay put. Tharin is just a few meters away. I think of the words he spoke last night and the sight of his arousal. Was it true what he said? Did he make me orgasm over and over ten years ago?

Jesus, Kate!

"Colder," I shout out. The water responds, turning even icier. It's unbearable, much like this affect Tharin has on me. I turn the shower off and head back into the room, waking Isla and getting us both changed into the predictable golden dresses from the wardrobe. *Some variety would be nice.* Adin is waiting for us as we step outside, and we follow him down our corridor and into the next one with the other yawning mothers and children shuffling along. I can still smell the sweet sickly scent of pemelonian on them.

As we get to the hall, I notice people have stopped walking and gasps are ringing out around us. I follow everyone's gaze to see what has shocked them. There's a body hanging from the ceiling at the front of the hall.

ELEVEN

Kate

Tharin is standing in his golden armor next to the dangling body, his hair pulled back off his face. His unearthly beauty stands at odds with the dead body beside him. I quickly cover Isla's eyes. The defenders command us all to sit down at our usual tables. As we do, the other Highborn brothers walk onto the stage, looking up at the body in confusion. I notice the other Primes are all watching with surprise from the viewing platform above too.

Did they not know about this?

A hush falls over the hall as Tharin walks to the middle of the stage. I can see the effect he has on the women. Many of them watch him with adoring eyes despite the shocking spectacle before them.

"This is Loxley," he says, voice rebounding off the walls that pulse black and red in his presence. "I tied a noose around his neck and strung him up here to die because he forced himself upon his Pledged." His gaze settles on me. "That is not acceptable."

Is it the Russian girl's Prime?" Charlotte whispers to me.

"I think so.'"

"Any Obrothean who forces himself upon a woman here without her consent will be executed," Tharin continues. He pauses slightly and then nods to himself, as though he's only decided something right in that moment. "For the first time, this applies to all Highborns too."

His brothers exchange shocked looks, and I'm shocked myself. Clearly, they knew nothing of this change. His brother Ethos looks particularly angry, leaning towards his father to whisper furiously to him.

"As First Defender," Tharin says firmly, "this is my decree." He returns to his chair and picks up a large piece of bread, rips into it with his white teeth, and glares up at the dead man.

I notice the Russian girl is leaning her head on her friend's arm, looking relieved.

"Wow, that was some drama," Charlotte says.

"And highly unusual," Louisa adds. "From what I've read, the pronouncements haven't changed for centuries. Changing it so Highborns have to adhere to it too is really something."

I frown. Did Tharin change the pronouncement because of what I said the night before? What's he trying to prove? That he's inherently good? No. How can he be good when he kidnapped me and my daughter? I won't allow myself to think that.

After breakfast, I ask Adin about the laws as I follow to Tharin's rooms. "So is Tharin in charge of the laws then?"

"Yes," Adin says. "As First Defender, it is his right to change pronouncements. Of course, it hasn't been done for centuries," he adds with a frown, echoing what Louisa just said.

"Interesting," I murmur.

"This is why it is important for you to be patient with

Tharin. He is a good man. Together, there is much you can do."

"Together. Like king and queen?"

"Of course."

I swallow nervously. The thought has occurred to me. He is heir to the throne, after all. Unlike Helena, I have no ambitions for such a responsibility, *especially* if it's forced upon me. "You know him very well, don't you?" I ask Adin. "I mean, you *are* his half-brother?"

"That's right."

"And you had another brother, didn't you? Ryker?" He tenses up at the mention of Ryker's name. "How did you feel when he invaded Skarsdon? It must have been an awful time."

"I was angry." We stop at the end of the corridor, and he turns to me. "Go, Tharin is waiting."

I sigh and place my palm against the wall. It shimmers and fades. I don't think I'll ever get used to that. Tharin is next to his bed, his hair down now. It lies like a gold wave against his shoulders as he tries to unlatch his golden chest armor. He winces, rubbing at his huge hand, exposing the wound there. Why hasn't he gotten it treated by the healers yet?

I consider helping him for a moment but feel it would be a signal of compliance. A signal I do *not* wish to give. Just because he changed a law doesn't take away from the fact he was part of the mechanisms that allowed that poor Russian woman to be violated. That he allowed us all to be kidnapped. As one of the Highborn, a clearly influential and revered warrior *and* future Grand Sovran, he had the power to stop all this. But he didn't.

He notices I'm watching him, and his face hardens as he rips the armor off. He walks to the wall and places his huge hand on it to reveal a wardrobe filled with different garments.

I try not to be distracted by the sight of his bare back rippling with muscles and shifting colors.

"Another thing you Highborns get more of," I say.

He looks over his shoulder at me. "What do you mean?"

"Clothes. We get two dresses a day," I say, gesturing down at my gold dress. "Same one in the morning. Same one at night."

"Are they not cleansed?"

"Of course. But they're always the same. They're not very practical either, are they?"

"They are not comfortable?" he asks as he pulls a loose white shirt over his head.

"Actually, yes they are," I reluctantly agree. "But they're just not... They're not what I'd *choose* to wear. Nor what Isla wants. She's more of a tomboy really."

He gives me a confused look. "What do you mean by *tom boy*?"

"I mean when it comes to clothes, she's not a fan of dresses. I think she'd rather wear your armor, to be honest." I gesture to his chest plate on the bed.

I see a flicker of pride in his eyes. "That's good to hear. She'll be a great warrior someday."

"I don't think so. My daughter will not take part in any battles."

"Of course she will. It is a great honor."

I sigh. What's the point in arguing? We are so different. "So that was an interesting breakfast," I say, wandering around the room.

He sighs heavily. "Yes, I did not like your human bread. It is one of the earthly foods made to please you, but it's too dry for me."

I roll my eyes. "No, I mean the dead guy hanging over our heads as we ate."

"Ah, yes. He went against a proclamation. It had to be done."

"So publicly?"

He shrugs. "It's our way."

"But to have a dead body hanging there in front of the children."

"You humans do the same."

"Not in America. The last time we had public executions was centuries ago."

His brow creases. "I see. I'll keep that in mind in the future."

I stop at a photo I haven't noticed before of Tharin with his six brothers standing against a huge gold palace. "If it was one of your brothers who'd raped the ballerina, would you have punished them in the same way?"

He hesitates. "Maybe. It would of course depend on which one. Ethos and Magni, I would happily kill. However, Remus, Kiah and—"

I laugh. "Just what I thought. One rule for you Highborns, another for everyone else."

"But that's no longer the case. You heard me earlier. I have changed things."

"Are you sure about that? What if you learn Remus has broken a serious proclamation?"

"He wouldn't. He abides by all the rules, as do all the Highborns."

"But what if he did?"

He sighs. "This is a stupid conversation, Kate. Though the proclamations did not apply to us officially, we would never break them."

"Fine. It looks like we need to agree to disagree." I stop in front of a shelf filled with what looks like medals. They are strange glass-like structures that oscillate with color and I recognize Tharin's name on them. "There's something else that's bothering me."

Another long sigh. "Please, do share it with me," he says sarcastically.

I shoot him a look. "Did you gather any other evidence to prove Loxley raped the ballerina?"

"Why would I need to? You told me he did."

"I wasn't an actual witness though. The Russian didn't even tell me herself. I heard it from other women."

"And?"

"What I'm trying to say is you didn't prove beyond a reasonable doubt that Loxley was guilty. I mean, he was. But what if he didn't force himself on her? You might have killed an innocent man." I shrug. "Just playing devil's advocate for a moment."

He looks at me in alarm. "Why do you want to side with the devil, Kate?"

I can't help but smile. "It's just a saying on Earth. It means I'm testing the strength of an argument by expressing an opposite or contentious opinion."

I think I see a hint of a smile on his face. Was he being serious? Had he really not heard of the expression?

"I see," he says. "Well, we can question your sources and the girl, of course. If they are found to be lying, we will burn out their tongues."

My mouth drops open. "Are you being serious?"

"Yes, it is the ninth pronouncement. A lie will lead to fire of the tongue."

I throw my hands up in the air. "Seriously?"

He broods over it for a while, staring into the distance. "So you really don't think I did the right thing?"

"Maybe. But you can't be sure."

He shakes his head in frustration. "You human women always make things so complicated."

"Known lots of us, have you?"

"Just you, and that is enough. Trust me," he says, regarding me out of the corner of his eye.

I go to one of the shelves filled with all sorts of books. "You like to read?" I ask.

"When I have the time. It calms me."

I pick up a huge green book and leaf through it. I can't understand the strange text without my handy alien reading glasses, but I can see from the blood-filled battle scenes pictured within that's what it's about. "Yet another book on wars," I say with a sigh. "Is Obrothea ever *not* at war? It would be nice to read something about, I don't know, your solar system and geology."

"I cannot deny it is a very tumultuous planet."

"And now you're taking our children there?"

"Rest assured, our Sacred children—*especially* Isla—will be kept safe. Not to mention the fact that Skarsdon has not experienced a war for years now."

I peer over my shoulder at him. "But is it really safe being in such a war-hungry world? I appreciate not all countries on Earth are peaceful. But things are pretty damn stable in the United States. How do you *really* feel about bringing the girl you believe to be your child out of that safe world to live in an unstable world like Obrothea?"

He sighs. "Nothing is certain, Kate. Not even in the United States. What matters is that Isla is prepared for anything. The problem with Western society on Earth is it has turned people soft. There is nothing to fear, nothing to fight for."

I shake my head. "It's not as black and white as that. We have a lot to worry about, like climate change. But one thing I can say for my country is we're not at war. How can you guarantee the next Obrothean war isn't around the corner?" I gesture to his discarded armor. "I mean, you and your defenders are dressed as though it could be."

"Our Sacred children and you, our Pledged, will be the most protected assets in the whole of Obrothea. You and Isla will live with me in Skarsdon Palace in the city of Skarsdon, the most luxurious, most defended abode on the planet."

"On a planet ravished by violence and war? It doesn't matter how pretty your palace is if the planet you force us to live on is so battle scarred."

His jaw clenches. "Maybe it will help if you learn more of Obrothea. Come, let me show you something." He strides across the room to some other shelves lined with a variety of rocks. It reminds me of a shelf I have in my classroom with my own collection of rocks. I have mostly Earth rocks but there are a couple of meteor fragments too.

"Come," he says again, beckoning me over. I sigh and join him.

"These five rocks represent all five regions of Obrothea," he says, a glow of pride in his eyes. "Each one depicts a region's unique and beautiful landscape. Landscapes that will awe you when you see them. This is from the north," he says, gesturing to a smooth black rock shaped like an oval with a strike of neon green through it. "It's from the island regions of Gatika. That is where we won our great war twelve years ago. You should see the black and golden beaches there. It's quite something to behold."

"There are black beaches on Earth," I say with a shrug.

"But none like Gatika's. The sands are both black and golden and glow an iridescent hue at night. Combined with the purple skies and three moons, it is a sight to behold at dawn."

"Three moons?" I ask.

He nods. "You were always so fascinated to hear of that.

We spent hours talking of Obrothea's beauty and unique characteristics."

I roll my eyes. "Hours I don't remember. How did you take our memories, by the way?"

"You were given a very strong dose of liptus on your last night," Tharin explains. "It interfered with your memories, either blotting them completely or making you think they were mere dreams. Traces of the same potion were added to the beams that transported you back to Earth each night too, so you were not burdened with memories of the night before while going about your day-to-day life."

"But it did burden us with feeling absolutely exhausted with no idea why the next day," I say, remembering how tired I was at the time. "So what you're saying it, every night over that week was like meeting you for the first time again, like the movie *50 First Dates*?"

"That sounds like a strange movie. No, your memories from the previous nights were reignited when you arrived back on the vessel. A herb called stident was filtered into the bed mists on the vessel to help you remember again."

"Jesus, so complicated and so many herbs." I think about it. "So on the last night, our memories were taken and never returned?" Tharin nods. "Well, those memories weren't yours to take, you know."

"It was for your own good. Can you imagine how it would have felt the past ten years, to know you *willingly* conceived a child with an alien species?"

"Willingly," I repeat, rolling my eyes. He holds my gaze, and for a moment, I find I cannot look away. I force myself to and point at a dusty red rock. "Where's this from?

He comes to me, standing so close I can feel his breath on my cheek. "This is from the Yarabion desert region," he says. "It is very hot there. In contrast, on the south side of Obrothea, are the icy plains of Malrisia." He nods at a pink glowing rock. "Unlike your white snowy plains, ours are pink. It is very cold there, so cold your skin can freeze in minutes in certain conditions."

"Sounds lovely."

He looks at me with a frown, and I realize I'm being rude. He clearly loves his planet.

"I guess it's the same in some parts of Earth," I quickly say. "I imagine the snow looks very pretty all pink."

"It does." He gestures to a black and purple rock with a jagged green scar running through it. His eyes grow cold as he looks at it. "This rock is from the Fostinia region."

"Where your slaves and half-brothers come from? Your mother too?" I add more softly.

He goes stiff. "They are not slaves. This is from Skarsdon," he says, gesturing to a golden rock. He touches it softly with his large fingers, his fondness for his home region clear. It is beautiful with glistening sand-like hues.

"Can I touch it?" I ask. He nods, and I smooth my fingers over it. It feels grainy and sparkles under my skin. "So the landscape is golden in Skarsdon?"

"Yes," he replies. "It is very beautiful and mountainous with golden lakes."

"Wow."

"You will be able to explore the whole planet, if you wish," he murmurs, his mouth close to my ear. I try to control the sensations rushing through me and the desire to turn and touch him. "I know how much it will fascinate you," he continues. "You spent two years looking through your father's telescope at other planets and stars on the commune, and now you will have the chance to live on one."

I step away from him, frustration rushing through me. "You can't possibly understand how annoying it is to hear you mention my dad when I don't remember telling you about him or the commune."

He is quiet for a few moments and then nods. "Yes, I can imagine that's rather frustrating. I'm sorry." There is true sadness in his eyes, and I have to look away before I start thinking he's a decent guy.

I gesture to the neon-green scar in the Fostinia rock. "What are the green scars all about?"

"Acrenium scars. Acrenium was discovered many centuries ago when the Great War of Malrisia caused the ground to open up. There, beneath the ice, was a unique rock with veins that change in color to reflect emotions. We began to drill the rest of the planet and discovered even more. Acrenium scars began to open up across the landscapes. It is in all we build now, under our very skin too."

My eyes are unable to stop traveling over his oscillating skin. "How does it get into your skin?"

"Drilling over the centuries has exposed so much acrenium that it has seeped into our DNA. We are now an extension of it."

I step closer, curious to watch his skin oscillate a variety of colors. It does seem to pulse beneath his bronze skin, as though threading through his veins and lighting him up from within.

"You can touch me if you wish," Tharin says. "You can feel it through my skin."

I take a breath and place my hand on his biceps, feeling it throb sightly as his skin begin to glow purple. "Your skin is...vibrating."

Tharin nods. "It's the acrenium."

I can't help but wonder if all of him vibrates. "What do the colors mean?" I ask.

He holds my gaze. "Purple is desire."

I snatch my hand away. "Must be difficult having your feelings pasted all over your skin and the walls for all to see."

He gives me a crooked smile that makes my tummy stir. "Yes, it can be very difficult."

I smile slightly too. I can't help it. I walk away, trailing my fingers along the walls. "So this acrenium is pretty important then?"

"It is *everything*. Like gold and diamonds on Earth. Skarsdon has the highest concentration of acrenium, which has made us as powerful as we are today."

"Lucky you." I stop as I come to the shelves filled with photos of who I presume are his mother and sister. "Your mother and sister?"

He nods.

"I heard they died. I'm sorry to hear that." His green eyes fill with tears, and he looks away as he clutches the top of the chair. It's strange seeing such vulnerability in this huge warrior. I can't help but feel sorry for him, even though he's my captor. "Do you mind me asking what happened?"

His free hand curls into a fist. "Fostinia invaded Skarsdon ten years ago. My mother and sister were killed during the invasion."

"Ten years ago. Did it happen while you were above Earth?" I ask. He nods stiffly in response. "I heard your half-brother, Ryker, was involved. Surely he didn't kill his own mother and sister?"

His jaw tenses at the mention of Ryker's name. "Not directly, no, but his actions led to their deaths."

I shake my head. For Tharin to have lost his mother and sister like that... It would break any one's heart, even a seven-foot hulk of a person. I'm tempted to take his hand. Instead, I take the seat across from the one he's standing next to. "I'm sorry you had to go through all that. It must be even worse that it's your own brother who instigated it all. Why would he do that?"

He looks down at me with weary eyes. "Can we not talk about it, Kate? It weighs very heavily on my heart."

"Of course."

"Anyway, we have talked enough of me." He sits down across from me. "You lost your father two years ago, did you not?"

It's now my turn to clam up. "Ah-huh."

"To cancer?"

I nod, looking down at my hands.

"Were you with him?" he asks gently.

"I was in the end. I thought about not being there. We didn't have much contact after my mom died." I peer up at him. "Did I tell you about what happened to my mom too?"

He nods. "Yes."

"God, I really told you a lot, didn't I? It took me months to tell Richard all that."

"We grew close, despite the short amount of time we spent together. Very close." His voice is husky as he says that, his green eyes intense with emotion.

I can't bear the way he's looking at me. It's doing all sorts of things to me inside. I turn away and gesture to the rocks. "My parents would love all this. I mean, obviously they'd hate the whole kidnapping-their-daughter-and-granddaughter part," I add with a small laugh.

Tharin sighs. "I wish you would stop using that word."

"But it is kidnapping, Tharin. We've been taken by force from our homes."

"We had to for the sake of Skarsdon. Wouldn't you do the same to protect your country, your children?"

"But why is it best for Skarsdon? You and your father keep hinting at something the kids possess, and you mentioned some kind of training. What's it all about?"

He is quiet for a few moments. "Our hybrid children possess abnormal strength, speed, and intelligence. For Isla, and any child the two of us produce, that is even more pronounced."

"Why?"

"You and I share the same gene marker," Tharin explains. "It is very, very rare. Ethos discovered it when the genetic tests were carried out on your ancestors."

"Ancestors?"

"Yes, we have been observing humans for generations, bringing many onboard our learning vessels above Earth for centuries to discover more about you. Our sages found it particularly useful to monitor specific family lines."

"So members of my family may have been taken up in vessels? Even before ten years ago?"

Tharin nods. I think of my father and all his paranoias. Maybe he was taken onboard a vessel like this, and residues of those experiences remained in his memories? It would explain so much.

"It wasn't long before we realized the combination of your specific genes with mine would produce offspring of the highest quality," Tharin explains.

"Quality? Like some kind of meat."

His nostrils flare. "You know I don't mean it like that. Isla means the world to me."

I think about it for a moment. "So Isla is like some kind of super human Obrothean hybrid. How does this benefit Skarsdon exactly?"

"It is a show of strength for our enemies and those we need to join us when we seek to defeat those enemies."

"That's why you and your father are so desperate for us to produce more kids like Isla? It's all a power play." I examine his face. "How do you feel about the girl you call your daughter being used as part of that?"

He smoothes his large hand over the golden stubble on his cheeks. "This is not easy for me. I know it is the best way of strengthening Skarsdon's standing in the world, but I don't exactly relish the idea of all this either, you know, especially seeing *you* again."

I frown. "You didn't want to see me again?" It's ridiculous, but it almost hurts to hear him say that. "Why?"

He holds my gaze, and I see a heady mixture of pain and torment in his green eyes. He goes to open his mouth to say something, then he quickly shakes his head. "It's not important." I think of what his brother Ethos said about me doing something bad ten years ago. Is it related to that? "You must go now," Tharin says. "It will be your lunch soon, and I have to prepare for our return to Obrothea."

"But it's ages until lunch." Did I really just say that? It surprises the hell out of me that I actually want to stay and learn more about Obrothea and this huge, gorgeous warrior. He seems determined to send me on my way and gestures to the area of the wall where the door is. I hesitantly stand, sigh, and walk towards the exit. When I turn to look over my shoulder, I see the walls are dark red and blue, the color of anger.

Did something bad happen between Tharin and I ten years ago?

Tharin

Kate slips from my room. I would love her to stay. I can see she feels the same way, but this isn't how I want things to go. All those feelings I have for Kate—feelings I have worked so hard to trample down—are roaring to the surface unabated. I was a fool to think they would not. Part of me detests it. Fears it. The pain after discovering my mother and sister died as a result of what Kate did was extreme. I promised myself I would never risk such pain again. I presumed the role Kate unwittingly played in their deaths would ensure my old feelings for her would not return, but talking to her now felt exactly like those first nights we spent together all those years ago.

On our third night together, we continued to talk and get to know one another. I realized then that there was something deeper than the mere desire to thrust my cock into her. Though I had lain with many women, feelings had never come into it. Only the hardness of my cock and the throb of my arcism. This human woman was different though. Something grew between us, and I saw she felt the same when she woke to find me sitting on her bed, the stident haze on her pillow taking effect. She was happy to see me again.

It is the same now. Those feelings are reigniting, growing. But everything is so different now. Ten years ago, I knew nothing of true grief and torment.

My wall vibrates and pings, a signal somebody wishes to come in. I stand, heart thumping at the thought it might be Kate. "Come," I say. Instead of Kate though, it's Remus who walks in, his face etched with worry. "What's wrong, brother?" I ask him.

"It's father. He has collapsed."

TWELVE

Kate

I can't stop thinking of Tharin, especially when neither he nor his brothers and father are at the high table when I go for lunch. I'm disappointed and that completely annoys me. Why am I starting to feel something for this warrior? Talk about Stockholm syndrome.

I try to distract myself after lunch with some new books I find in my room. These ones are more focused on Obrothea's solar system and geology. Did Tharin arrange for them to be delivered after I moaned about the non-stop war books? I can't help but smile to myself as I flick through them with my strange reading glasses on, staring at the maps of unfamiliar star systems. Yes, they must be from him. I have to admit, that is kind of sweet.

There I am thinking of him again.

When Isla returns, she's full of excitement about her day. I happily listen to her as she talks about all she has learnt, pleased for the distraction. When it's time to get changed for dinner, instead of finding yet another pair of golden dresses in the wardrobe, I'm surprised to see there are several other outfits too, including the nightwear we arrived in which has been cleaned.

"Is that armor? For me?" Isla pronounces as she spots a small golden suit of armor.

Before I know it, she's pulling it on, her face all lit up. I can't help but smile.

"Do you think all the kids have this?" she asks.

"Maybe. I think I know who sent yours though," I say gently.

"Who?"

"Tharin, the First Defender."

"Really?" she asks, staring at the armor with surprise in her eyes. "We learnt about him today. He's a proper hero." She pauses, a slight crease in her pretty brow. "Is Tharin your Prime, Mommy?"

I swallow. So it looks like we're having this conversation then. "Yes, he is."

"That means he thinks he's my dad?"

"Yep. But there's no proof of that," I quickly add.

"Have you *met* Tharin?"

I nod. "Yesterday and today."

"What's he like? Is he kind?"

"I suppose he is kind, yes," I admit.

She thinks about it for a while and then sighs. "I don't believe he's my dad. But as long as he's kind and doesn't hurt you, I guess I'll let him live."

I laugh. "Lucky him."

She looks me up and down. "Shouldn't you get changed, Mommy?"

"I guess I should." I look for an outfit for myself. Still no bras or knickers. Don't they wear underwear here? I finally settle on a soft gold jumpsuit that looks reasonably sensible. When I put it on, I have to roll my eyes at how tight the high-necked top is around my large breasts. It'll have to do.

When Adin greets us outside, I can see something is playing on his mind. I'm about to ask him what's wrong when he notices what Isla is wearing and amusement replaces the worry in his eyes. "First Commander of the Skarsdonian fleet," he says, crossing his arms over his vast chest and bowing. "Come, Commander. Let me walk you to your battle feast."

Isla smiles up at him and walks alongside him, her armor clinking like his. I suppose they *are* uncle and niece. That's nice. Richard and I don't have siblings, so she's never had aunts or uncles.

"So what entertainment is on the menu tonight? Any more executions?"

Adin sighs. "They are very rare, Kate."

"'Hmm." We walk into the busy corridor ahead. The women look me up and down, obviously noticing I'm wearing something different.

"Nice," Charlotte says. "Where can I get one of those? These dresses are beginning to do my nut in." She pulls uncomfortably at her bronze dress.

"I would say ask your Prime, but you don't have one."

"They supposedly have one lined up for me when we land." She leans in close, lowering her voice. "I'm going to tell them I'm a witch. Apparently, they're superstitious like that, and no Obrothean will touch me."

I smile at her ingenuity. "Worth a try."

Anaya comes up to us then. "Hey, have you heard the news?"

"What news?" Charlotte and I ask at the same time.

"The Grand Sovran collapsed. I heard our defender talking about it."

That explains Adin's stony expression. I think instantly of Tharin. He'll be worried about his father. "Exactly how unwell is he?" I ask.

Anaya shrugs. "No idea."

"Maybe it's a good thing," Charlotte whispers. "Maybe with him out of the way, they'll change their minds about all this."

"Or maybe it'll make things unstable," Helena butts in, "and any semblance of politeness and restraint they have with us will be thrown out of the window." She looks me up and down. "How come *you* get a new outfit?"

"She's the First Defender's human," Adin replies proudly.

Shit.

"No way," Anaya says as Helena narrows her eyes at me.

"Wow, your dad is the First Defender, Isla!" Henry says in his posh British accent.

"We don't know that for sure," I quickly reply, squeezing Isla's shoulder.

"What's he like?" Louisa asks me.

"Is he as beautiful up close?" Anaya asks.

I feel my face flush. "I've not really spoken to him much."

"She shouted at him, and he kicked her out the first day," Charlotte says.

"But he is a prince," Henry says.

"So are you, but I still shout at you," Isla says.

He sighs. "Very true. But do you realize what this means, Isla? You're royalty like I was on Earth." We step into the hall, and as Isla runs off with the other children to look out of the windows, I find myself searching the stage for Tharin. His brothers are there now, but I can't see any sign of him. Maybe he's with his father? I go to the table, keeping an eye on Isla. More exotic looking dishes have been laid out for us.

"I can't believe you didn't tell us Tharin's your Prime," Charlotte says as we all eat. "Why didn't you? Helena was telling anyone who'd listen when she started dating Prince Alex."

"We're not *dating*," I say. "As for why I didn't say anything, I don't know. I guess it was overwhelming enough being in this situation. Add that to the fact my Prime is the future Grand Sovran… It was just too much to admit."

"So you don't mind using the word Prime now?" Anaya asks me with a cheeky grin.

"Looks like it's stuck in my head now. Like disgusting chewing gum in my hair," I add. They two women laugh.

"So what's he like?" Charlotte asks me. "Seriously?"

I think about it. "At first, I didn't like him. But he's growing on me. He does all these little things to show he listens, like getting me more books and outfits. He's actually quite intelligent too."

"Intelligent and hot," Charlotte says with a raised eyebrow.

"Do you like him though?" Anaya asks.

I frown. "I can't deny there's chemistry between us."

"You know, Teach, you really do keep your cards close to your chest," she says as she sips her drink. "You should have told us about him. Us girls need to stick together."

"I know that, but Isla and I are so isolated in our corridor."

"Your *special* corridor," Helena snaps, "with your *special* clothes."

"You can't always be the one with the privileges, Helena," Charlotte snaps back. "Kate didn't have a choice, you know."

"Exactly," I say, narrowing my eyes at Helena. "I might have my own corridor and more clothes, but I'd swap it all for a shared area like you guys have. It's not fair that Isla and I don't have the chance to socialize with you all."

It is lonely being on my own in that corridor. I brood over it all as I eat, quiet as the other girls chatter and Isla and Henry play some strange card game. They really seem to get on. How funny that my daughter's becoming friends with the future heir to the British throne. Of course, Henry has no status now, and *Isla* is a future heir. I shake my head, unable to quite wrap my mind around it all.

"Hello, Kate." I look up, surprised to see Isla's scribe, Castian, smiling down at me. He's wearing the usual pale-blue scribe outfit, and his dark hair is in a bun at the top of his head. He seems almost asexual. If I passed him on the street on Earth, I wouldn't be sure if he was a male or female.

"May I join you?" he asks, gesturing to the unoccupied seat next to me.

I shrug. "Sure."

"You look sad," he says as he sits with me. "Is it because Tharin isn't here?"

I laugh. "I'm sad because I miss my home." I peer towards the high table. "I presume Tharin is with his father. Is the Grand Sovran very ill?"

Castian sighs. "Yes, it has been happening more and more lately. He has a heart condition."

"Your healers can't deal with that?"

"They are good, but they are not miracle workers. However, a healer specializing in matters of the heart has been called in from Gatika. He will see the Grand Sovran as soon as we land. Still, Tharin is very worried," Castian says. "His father is hard on him, but they are close nonetheless."

"At least he gets to see his father," I say. "I bet there are women here who have ill parents they can't see."

Castian nods sadly. "You are right, of course. I admire your emotional intelligence, as I did when we talked ten years ago too. You know, we spent quite a few hours talking on this very vessel." He leans close, lowering his voice to a whisper. "Strictly, Pledged weren't allowed to speak to anyone other than their Primes, but Tharin allowed it."

I raise an eyebrow. "How did I find the time to make

friends in-between being abducted and forced to conceive a child?"

He laughs. "Oh, Kate. You make me laugh. You know there was no forcing involved."

"No, I don't know that, because my memories were *sucked* from me."

"I know this is difficult for you."

"How can you possibly know how I feel?"

He gestures to the other scribes around him. "We were taken against our will too, you know. Whenever the Grand Sovran wins a battle, he brings back the brightest men and women from whichever region he has pillaged to teach Skarsdonian children, to be his scribes, as he calls us."

"Jesus, this family just gets more and more cruel. Where are you from then?"

"The forest region of Fostinia. I was just a child when we were brought to Skarsdon. My mother was chosen to teach Tharin and his brothers. I grew up with them. They are not as bad as you seem to think."

"Really? They allowed the abductions to happen."

Castian sighs. "You must not be so dismissive. They have been through a lot."

"Like losing their mother and sister?"

"Yes, exactly that." He regards the high table with a soft gaze. "I know they may seem...brutal and clueless at times, but there is a light within some of the men up there."

"I can't see it myself." Except I can, can't I? I saw it today in Tharin. I pour myself some juice and offer some to Castian. He shakes his head with a soft smile.

"It's so delicious," I say, taking a sip.

"It's made from the nectar of the pemelonian flowers. You will see them when we land. They are really quite something to behold."

When we land. That's just two days away. A mixture of

sadness and excitement rushes through me at the realization. The truth is, I will be stepping foot on a brand-new planet, something I never dreamed I would be able to do. But will the thrilling novelty be enough to help me ignore the fact that I will be brought there against my will?

"I wish I could be more excited about the prospect of landing," I say.

"Being with Tharin will make it less daunting."

"But I don't know him."

"Deep down, you do. It is a great tragedy you do not remember the time you spent together."

I bite my lip. "Castian, can I ask you something?"

He nods.

I get the impression something bad happened between Tharin and I ten years ago. I mean, Ethos hinted at something and Tharin told me earlier he was dreading seeing me again. If we were really into each other like you say, why would that be the case?"

Castian's large green eyes flicker before he readjusts his expression. "I think that is something you must ask Tharin." He peers towards the waterfall. I follow his gaze and am surprised to see Tharin standing there watching us with curious eyes. My breath catches in my throat at the sight of him. His hair is away from his face in a plait, and he's wearing a white tunic and brown leather breeches. He stands out against the crowds with his vast form and imposing muscles. His beauty too.

"You should talk to him. Check he is okay." Castian says as he stands and walks off.

I continue watching Tharin. Maybe Castian is right?

Tharin

A mixture of emotions run through me as I watch Kate and Castian talk. I remember doing the same that third night when I snuck Kate out to meet him. I'd been telling her of Obrothea's version of teachers, and she had asked if she could meet one of our scribes. It was against the rules to let her leave my suite of rooms, but I have never been one to follow all the rules... *especially* when it comes to Kate.

So I took her to Castian's room. He was surprised to see her, but once they started talking, I saw how happy he was to properly meet the human subjects he'd read so much about. As we drank pemelonian juice and talked, Castian had taken the opportunity to tell Kate what a brilliant warrior and loved prince I was. Though she rolled her eyes, it seemed to penetrate. When we went back to my rooms, she had seemed lighter, giddier. The pemelonian had relaxed her. She'd even allowed me to sit close to her as she read one of my books. I had breathed in her beautiful scent, my hands aching to touch her.

Before she lay back on my bed ready to be beamed back, she pulled me towards her, pressing her soft, wet lips against mine. "A little something to leave you with," she'd said before disappearing.

I spent the next day when I should have been sleeping and training running over the feel of her lips on mine. The frustration was unbearable.

I notice Ethos approach now, his spiteful face dragging me from my memories. "I have just seen Father," he says in his bored drawl. "He seems better."

I frown. "I would not say the same. I only just came back from seeing him twenty minutes ago, and to me, he seemed even weaker than ever."

"He asked me to speak to you," Ethos continues, ignoring my comment. He takes a small vial from his pocket and goes to slip it into the pocket of my breeches. "He asked me to give you this so Kate will be more…amenable the next time you see her."

I shake my head in disgust. "I don't know how many times I have to tell him that I never had to resort to using vevatia on Kate, and I will not now."

"There is nothing wrong with a little vevatia if it helps the weak little creatures along."

I shove his hand away. "I told you, I do not need it."

"Fine," he says, putting it back in his pocket. "If the problem is your cock, I have a potion that—"

"I have never had a problem with my cock, brother."

"Well, the sooner you get on with using it, the sooner Father will stop asking me to give you these ridiculous pep talks. Do you not see the importance of this, especially now as more people learn of his collapse? They can smell blood."

"Don't you mean you can smell blood? I know how much you want the crown."

"If you do not seed your woman, it might be easier than I first thought for me to attain the crown when our father dies."

"The Goddess Tsuki help us all if you ever become the Grand Sovran."

He gives me a stern look and then storms off. I curl my hands into fists. That was a threat. As much as it pains me, he is right about our father though. People will be smelling blood, none more so than Ethos's supporters. Yes, my supporters outnumber his…for now. But if I do not prove my worth, there is every chance he could snatch power away the moment my father dies. It pains me to think of my father's demise, but think of it I must.

I might let Ethos take the power if he were a worthy option as Grand Sovran. This is not something I asked for. I have always been content to fight for the people , but the truth is, Skarsdon would flounder under his rule. My father knows it, most of my brothers do too. My sister used to know it as well. Two years before she died, Thesera told me if she were to die without heirs, she would want me to be Grand Sovran. "You are the war hero, Tharin," she'd said. "And you are loved by so many."

I had laughed, telling her Ethos would be better suited to the role seeing as he loved power so much.

"Never," she'd said. "I love Ethos. He is my brother, after all, but he would make a disastrous ruler. Skarsdon would crumble beneath him."

"And it wouldn't crumble beneath me?" I'd asked. "I know nothing of politics."

"Being a good leader isn't about politics," my sister had replied. "It is about empathy. Those who might support you as a leader won't do so because you are a war hero. It is because you also possess empathy and compassion. You love our people, and you listen to them. This is a skill Ethos will never have."

She had that opinion right until the very end. Adin told me as she lay dying in his arms after the explosion that ripped through the library, our mother already dead beside her, she'd begged him to ensure I took over when our father died, not Ethos.

I must keep that promise to her. If I do not secure my position by producing more strong, powerful heirs like Isla–the type of heirs I can only produce with Kate–then Thesera's worst fears might come true. As I think that, I notice Kate walk towards me, as though my sister is guiding her to me. She looks beautiful. The way the thin material of the jumpsuit I arranged to have delivered to her room clings to her breasts only serves to make my cock throb even harder. I take a deep breath and press my fingers hard into my wound.

Calm yourself.

"I'm sorry about your father, Tharin," she says when she gets to me. "Is he okay?"

"He is resting. He will be well tomorrow, as he always is after spells like this."

"Good." She looks down at her outfit. "Thank you for the extra clothes, by the way."

"I take it Isla likes her battle armor?"

"Yes, she was delighted."

We both watch as Isla approaches a younger child on the stage, helping her with an instrument. I feel a rush of pride as I watch my daughter. "She is already a leader," I say. "Look how she is with the other child."

Kate smiles. It's good to see her smile. "She's always been like that."

"Like her mother," I say.

"And her father. Richard has always held managerial positions."

A burst of frustration flares inside me. Will she ever stop with such nonsense? I take a sharp breath to calm myself and quickly release it. I need to take her away from this place so I can focus. It's too loud, too hot. "I want to show you something. Come." I put my hand out for her. She hesitates, eyes going to Isla. I love how protective she is of our daughter. "Castian is with her. He will not leave her, nor will Adin. Now come." She sighs and takes my hand, and I lead her towards the waterfall.

THIRTEEN

Kate

I hesitate as Tharin steps into the lake in front of the waterfall. "I'll get wet."

"You have been wet before, no?" he asks. Do I imagine him raise an eyebrow, his gaze traveling down to the area between my thighs? I clear my throat. I see what he's doing. I'm not going to play the game.

"Sure, no big deal." I clamber over the small wall and step into the water with him. It isn't like the water I'm used to, despite *looking* like it. It feels thick, almost furry, warm too. As we walk towards the waterfall, the lake grows deeper. While the water splashes around his knees, it is waist high on me. I splash clumsily, and Tharin strengthens his grip on my hand, smiling.

"Do not fall. You will get even more wet."

I roll my eyes and follow him towards the waterfall. It's truly beautiful, a plethora of colors splashing into the lake. I hold back as Tharin disappears into the waterfall, still holding my hand. His head peeks back out of the stream, his long blond hair now drenched, his long eyelashes watery spikes.

"Aren't you coming in? Do not tell me you are scared?" he asks, a glint in his green eyes. He really does seem lighter this evening, more mischievous and charming.

Resolve wells up inside me. "I'm not scared."

I follow him through, the strange water seeming to part as I do. When I step out the other side, I let out a gasp. We're standing in a brand-new globe-shaped room, except all the windows are clear and look right out into space here. The floor is dominated by misty water too, apart from a golden platform in the middle. I look around me in awe as stars spark in the darkness and a comet shoots past.

"Is this for real?" I whisper.

Tharin nods. "Very real. Come, you can see more from here." He leads me to a small floating circular platform in the middle of the lake, and I can't help but notice his pants are now see-through, revealing the taut muscles of his butt as he walks. I don't even want to *think* about what I'll see when he turns around. And what about how *I* must look? I peer down and see my breasts are visible through the soaked material of my top, as is the triangle of hair between my legs.

Great.

I step onto the platform, relieved to see Tharin still has his back to me as he messes about with something in the middle of the platform. He turns, and I have to avert my eyes. Yep, I *can* see pretty much everything. The outline of his huge cock strains against his drenched breeches, and his shirt clings to his gorgeous muscled chest. I have never seen anything quite so stunning. He's taking me in too, gaze hungrily traveling all over me.

He quickly turns his back to me, and I can see he is rubbing as his palm again, flinching. Does he do that to control himself? I think I need to as well.

"So," I say, trying to focus. "What's that you've got

there?" *And I don't just mean your impressive cock.* I berate myself. Clearly, that pemelonian juice is making me frisky.

"It's a telescope," he says. "Not quite what you're used to on Earth. Come see." I go to stand next to him. In front of us is a sphere about the size of a large watermelon that sits on a golden stand. "Look through," Tharin says, moving out of the way so I can take his place. His cock brushes against my side as he does, and I take in a sharp breath.

Come on, Kate. Control yourself.

"So I just look through the globe?" I ask. Tharin nods, and I stand on tiptoes and look through the globe. Suddenly, it's like I'm right there in space, up close with the stars. The telescope is so strong, I can see the fiery orange of the stars up close.

"Is this safe?" I ask, quickly moving my eyes away. "For my eyes I mean?"

"Very safe, it has a protective layer." Tharin leans close to me, his breath on my cheek. "Turn the globe and you will see more." He places his hand over mine and helps me turn it. The feel of his skin sends electric currents through me, and I gasp as a planet comes into view. Its land is a patchwork of vibrant colors, and instead of blue oceans, they are inky black. Criss-crossed around it all are bright neon-green scars that add to the strange, alien vibe.

"Obrothea," I whisper.

"Yes. And this is my mother's telescope."

I peer over my shoulder at him. "Really?"

He nods. "She was much like you, Kate. She adored watching the stars. Many a time, I would find her looking through this very telescope. She would have liked you very much."

He moves even closer to me, his hand still over mine, his skin pulsating red and purple. I feel my breath quicken. *No, Kate. No!* I quickly snatch my hand out from under his. He lets out a pained groan and clutches his hand to his mammoth chest.

"Oh God, sorry," I quickly say. "Did I hurt your injured hand doing that?"

"It is nothing," he says, jaw clenching as he puts his hand behind his back, hiding it from view.

"Let me look."

He shakes his head, still clearly in pain. "I said it is nothing."

"And *I* said let me look." We hold each other's gaze, as stubborn as each other. Then he sighs and brings his hand out from behind his back. I hold his with both of mine and watch as he unfurls his long fingers. It makes me think of a lion opening its injured paw to be inspected. There's a jagged, angry cut in the middle of the soft flesh still seeping blood.

"How long has it been like this?" I ask, grazing my thumb over the raised red flesh around it.

"Two days."

"You've not had it treated?"

"It'll be fine," he says, snatching it away. "I have had many wounds."

"But I presume you usually get them treated by a healer? We should go to them..."

"No!" His shout rebounds off the glass panes around us. "No," he says, calmer. "You don't understand. It...helps me."

"*Helps* you?"

"Yes. The pain controls my...urges."

I can't help my gaze from dropping to the outline of his cock that is straining hard and huge against the wet fabric of his pants. I quickly avert my eyes. So he has purposefully hurt himself to avoid... What? Losing control and pouncing on me? I don't know how to feel about that. "I guess it's worth it so you can avoid dying like Loxley."

He frowns. "I don't need *pain* to remind me not to

commit such a heinous act. No, it's—" He suddenly stops himself.

"It's what?" I ask.

"I promised myself I wouldn't fall for you again. I do this," he says, gesturing to his wound, "to remind myself to push any emotions away."

"Oh. So-so did something happen between us to make you so averse to feeling anything for me?" I feel weak asking. Even weaker at the disappointment I feel *when* asking. But I'm curious.

He turns away. "It doesn't matter."

I grab his wrist. "Tharin, please tell me."

"Your actions led to the death of my mother and sister," he suddenly says.

My mouth drops open. "I-I don't understand." He doesn't say anything, face pained. "Tharin, please tell me!"

"Fine. You made a video on the penultimate night we were on the vessel ten years ago," he says, face anguished. "You knew your memories would be taken, and I presume you wanted a way to remember everything. The video you made for yourself in the communications room was intercepted by Fostinians monitoring our ships. They learnt our best warriors were light years away. It was their chance to invade Skarsdon."

I blink, tears flooding my eyes as I put my hand to my mouth. It explains so much. Why he is so resistant to me. Why he didn't want to see me again. "Oh God, I'm so sorry."

His vast shoulders slump. "You weren't to know."

"But my actions led to their deaths. Everyone must hate me." I walk away, a sob escaping my mouth. I logically know it's not my fault. Who can blame me for trying to salvage memories I knew would soon be taken? But still, the guilt is overwhelming.

I feel Tharin's presence behind me as he treads through

the water to follow me. "Kate," he says, catching up with me and gently taking my hand. "Look at me." I turn around. "The only person who must shoulder the blame is Ryker," he says, "and he is dead now."

"But every time you look at me, you must think of what I did."

"I thought that would be the case," he says, his hand still around mine. "And, yes, I can't deny it crosses my mind. But mainly, I remember the good over the bad. How we began to develop true feelings for one other in such a short amount of time. How we—" He swallows, face flushing purple. "How we touched each other."

We both look down at our connected hands and then up into each other eyes. The air around us fizzes with electricity and strange but somehow familiar feelings.

"I wish I could remember," I whisper.

"I think you do, deep inside. The feelings anyway. I see it in your expression sometimes." His eyes drop to my lips. "I want to kiss you so much right now."

"Then you should."

He softly pulls my body snug against his. He tilts my chin up with his finger and leans down to gently press his lips against mine. All those feelings he talked about—yes, they are there, sleeper memories of emotion ignited in his presence —come rushing to the surface. I stand on tiptoes, reaching up to tangle my fingers through his long, wet hair. I skim the palm of my other hand over his stubbled jaw as his tongue finds mine and our lips move against each other.

He hitches his hands under my butt and lifts me as I wrap my sodden legs around his waist. We stare into each other eyes, his hardness pressing between my thighs, the wet material of his breeches and my trousers a frustrating barrier. All of him is softly vibrating with what must be the acrenium beneath his skin. Even his cock is pulsing against me in a way that is much too delicious, and I think I can fill his arcism too.

I lean back as he trails his lips down my neck, the soft growl he makes throbbing with my pulse. Around us, the water oscillates from red to black to purple to blue, reflecting his emotions. His fingers reach up, grazing my hardened nipples and his other hand hitches his shirt up to reveal his amazing abs…and what looks like a second belly button. I think back to what Anaya had told me about their arcism, and how having it pressed against your clit is indescribable.

He moves me up his body slightly and his arcism latches on to the outline of my clit through the thin material of my jumpsuit. I let out a gasp as I feel a sucking and pulsing sensation—throbs of delicate pressure—that swirl around my clit. All the time, Tharin watches me, his fingers stroking my nipple as his other hand supports my weight against him.

"Oh my God!" I moan. I realize Tharin is moaning too, his eyes glazed with desire. Does it do something to him as well?

He leans down, nibbling at my ear. "I can feel your small, swollen clitoris within me, even clothed," he whispers. "It's making my cock even harder." That does it. The combination of that amazing suction, the feel of his broad, muscled chest against me, and the sound of his voice saying those things sends me to the edge.

"Are you coming?" he asks.

"*Yes.*"

He quickly carries my trembling body towards the platform and lays me down. "Good. Let me quickly seed you now, as you come. It will help with the rousing."

I freeze against him, my orgasm still rocking through me. "What did you just say?" I stammer.

"I'm just saying this will be the perfect opportunity." I try to push him away, and he frowns. "What's wrong?"

"Let me go," I shout. He stands up, and so do I, body still trembling from my orgasm. What the hell was I thinking, allowing myself to get tangled up with this alien kidnapper? "So that's why you brought me here," I say. "To seed me. It's all I am for you now, isn't it? A vessel for your future heirs. I mean, I did cause your mother's and sister's deaths. How could I ever think I could be more than that to you?"

"Kate, it isn't like that."

"Then why talk about *seeding me*? Clearly, I'm a means to an end, Tharin. Well, forget it. I will not be used by you," I say and storm out.

Tharin

I watch Kate run out through the waterfall. "Stupid," I hiss. "Stupid, stupid."

Why did I used the word seeded? I know how she hates it. I sigh and go to my mother's telescope, looking through it and finding Obrothea again. It's an explosion of color. The black of the sea and the green, gold, and pink of the land are all struck through by the neon green of the acrenium scars. In just two days, I will be returning to my beloved Skarsdon with Kate and Isla. But what awaits us?

I remember thinking the same as I watched Earth from our vessel that fourth night we spent together ten years before, lying with Kate in my arms after I'd made her orgasm with my fingers and my arcism. She'd had no idea our objective was to impregnate the women onboard. She'd just thought it was some kind of social experiment. She did not know our plans for children who might be born either, that we would train them to become Skarsdon's most fearsome and talented army. She would never have agreed otherwise. I knew that even then.

So many times I dreamt of telling her everything all those years ago, but just like now, I had to put Skarsdon first. Back then, though we'd hoped Ethos's theories about the hybrid children we might produce with humans would be correct, there was no guarantee. If they ended up possessing normal human qualities, they would be left on Earth to be observed. Kate noticed my disquiet on the fifth night we were together, and when she pressed me for the reasons, I knew I needed to distract her, so I'd suggested she meet a scribe, my most trusted scribe, Castian.

Taking her outside our room was the first mistake I made. I explained the role of the communications area we passed as we made our way to Castian's room. If she hadn't seen that room, maybe she would not have gone there on our last night together to make that video? Maybe my mother and sister would still be alive? And here I am, making more mistakes and driving her away.

I hear noise behind me. Is Kate back? I go to turn but something strikes me from behind and everything goes black.

FOURTEEN

Kate

I sit gloomily in the darkness at the back of the auditorium. So I caused the death of Tharin's mother and sister, and his focus now is clearly on just "seeding" me as quickly as he can to avoid spending any more time than he needs to with me.

I shake my head, clenching my firsts. How is it my fault really though? They took my memories away. All I was trying to do was reclaim them by making a video. Not to mention the fact they were the ones who kidnapped me.

Tharin's need to seed just proves how completely medieval they all are when it comes to their views on women. We're just vessels for them. Mothers. Nurturers. Satisfiers. That's it. I guess it's not really his fault. This alien way of thinking is all he's ever known. *Ha, alien. Human* men struggle with this too, even after all this time. When I confronted my ex after discovering he'd cheated on me, the first thing he'd said was, "It's no big deal, Kate. It's just sex. You're the mother of my child, that's the most important thing in the world".

Most important thing in the world.

Is that the only value Richard saw in me and now Tharin too? As a mother? Not as a woman in my own right, with feelings and self-respect? After Richard, I told myself next time I met a guy, he'd have extracted himself from the Middle Ages. And yet I'd just been brought to orgasm by a being several lights years further in the past than Richard. And yet...Tharin is nothing like Richard. The connection I feel with this alien warrior is *insane*. It's like nothing I've ever known. I stifle a cry of frustration. It's all just so messed up.

I try to focus on Isla as she dances with the other children to some strange music. I can see a couple of Tharin's brothers are in there too, no doubt watching their Sacred children. When will these warriors get to meet the children they claim to have fathered? So far, I have seen no interaction between the children and the men. How will I feel when it comes to Isla meeting Tharin? I go to drink some more of that intoxicating drink I brought in with me and then pause when Adin rushes towards the brothers, an urgent look on his face. He says something to them, and they all suddenly stand, draw their weapons, and run out of the auditorium. Before the wall begins to solidify again, I see they're running towards the waterfall.

Tharin.

A ball of fear squirms in the pit of my stomach. Something isn't right. I can't help myself. I follow them, splashing through the strange thick water, the waterfall once again drenching me from above as I go under it. When I come through the waterfall, I see six of the huge brothers gathered around the raised platform in the middle. As I draw closer, I see Tharin collapsed over the shattered remains of the telescope, an ornate-looking dagger plunged into his back. I rush towards Tharin, but Ethos steps from the circle and shoves me out of the way. I stumble, landing with a splash in the water.

"She was with him here earlier," he shouts. "Surely this is too much of a coincidence when combined with what she did ten years ago? She must be taken to the fortalice to be questioned." The brothers all turn to regard me with suspicious eyes.

"I would never hurt Tharin," I shout. "I had nothing to do with this!"

One of the robed brothers—the girls call him the alien Jesus because of his shoulder-length hair and kind eyes—shakes his head. "Come now, brother. Kate would never hurt Tharin. She loves him."

"Does she really, Remus?" Ethos retorts. "Do you not remember what she did? Until we know for sure, we *must* imprison her." He comes towards me, and I push myself back, legs scooting in the water, my gaze not leaving Tharin.

He's not moving. Oh God, he's not moving. Is he…?

A glass door bursts open, and the slender beings who tended to the injured woman and defender on our first day stride towards Tharin. The brothers part, faces pained as one of the beings hovers their palm down over Tharin's wound with his eyes closed. The air around the wound vibrates, and the healer opens his eyes with a sigh. "He is barely breathing. He must be brought to the healing room immediately."

I let out a gasp, putting my hand to my mouth.

The brothers all gather around Tharin and gently lift him. Tears slide down my cheeks. Never has he looked more vulnerable as he's carried away, his muscular arms dangling down beside him, his soaked hair trailing over his unconscious face.

"What of Kate?" Remus asks, worry in his eyes.

One of the twins, the robed one, turns to look at me. "Ethos is right. She must be taken to the fortalice until we know for sure." Defenders march towards me, and I scream as they grab at me.

I sit in the darkness with my head in my hands. I don't even know where I am. I can feel a bump by my temple, and when I touch it, blood comes away on my hand. I must have been knocked unconscious, because I woke here in coal-like blackness. I can't even see my hands in front of my face. I don't know how long I've been sitting here since I woke. An hour maybe? God knows how long I was unconscious. All I can think of is Tharin.

I squeeze my eyes shut as though it will stop the images of that dagger in Tharin's back coming back to me. Who would do that to him? Ethos clearly thinks it's me. Some of the other brothers do too. I'm not surprised really. They surely blame me for the deaths of their mother and sister. I shiver as I consider what this all means for me. More importantly, what it means for *Isla*. If rape is punished with death, then surely the attempted murder of a Highborn and heir to the throne holds the same sentence? Isla will be left here alone.

I lean my head against the wall. I thought it was bad being kidnapped, but this is even worse. The idea of losing Tharin isn't sitting well with me either. Okay, that's an understatement. The thought of him dying makes *me* feel like dying too. And yet I barely know him. Except I don't *barely* know him, do I? He told me himself that we spent seven intense nights together ten years ago. And from what others have said, I developed feelings for him. What was is his brother Remus said? That I *loved* him? The more I get to know Tharin, the more I see how very possible that is.

Despite my memories being wiped away, the feelings clearly remain. I feel them in my soul. The thought that he might die *tortures* me. I have to finally admit it. I loved this being. Maybe I still do. The feelings I once had still beat strong within me, even if I don't remember or understand them. I wrap my arms around myself. "Tharin," I whisper. "Please live."

A noise awakens me. I must have fallen asleep again. Or fallen unconscious. I touch my fingertips to my temple and feel dried blood there. What if I'm badly hurt? Is it right to be falling in and out of consciousness? Do I have a concussion?

As long as Isla is okay, I'm fine, a small voice says. *As long as Tharin is okay, I'm fine.*

There's another noise, and a slice of light rips through the darkness. I huddle in the corner of the room, arms around my legs, as a huge form fills the doorway. I realize then it's Remus, and he's carrying a small tray. He peers behind him and nods. The door closes, throwing us into darkness again, but then a small light switches on above. He comes to me, kneels down beside me, and places the tray on the floor. There's some bread on there, some soup-like substance, and one of the strange fruits they sometimes serve us.

"Is Isla okay?" I croak through dried lips.

"She is safe. We allowed her to stay overnight with the Charlotte and Helena. She is now at school with Castian."

"Where does she think I am?"

"She has been told you are staying away overnight as part of the Pledged rituals. I'm not sure she believed Castian when he told her," Remus adds with a small chuckle. "He told me she gave him a rather dubious look. My niece is no fool."

My niece...

"At least she's safe. And—" I swallow, almost too scared to ask. "Tharin?"

"He is alive."

My shoulders collapse in relief. "Thank God. I didn't do it, Remus. I never would. You know that, right?"

"Of course I know that," Remus says. "When Tharin finds out you have been brought here..." He shudders. "His anger will empty the universe of its stars."

"How long have I been here?" I ask, taking a bite of the bread, welcoming its delicious warmth.

"Twelve hours."

"That long?" I put my hand to my sore head again.

Remus frowns, examining my head in the semi-darkness. "Oh, Goddess Tsuki, forget what I uttered of the stars. The universe will be ripped of its planets and its suns too. Who did this to you?"

"I have no idea. One of the other defenders, I imagine. I don't remember."

Fury sparks in his green eyes. He rips some cloth from his robes and presses it against my wound. "Do not fear, Kate. There are many of us working to ensure your freedom. Defenders. Scribes. Healers. My brothers too, of course. Well, some of them," he adds with a sigh.

"Not Ethos, I presume. Why does he think I did this?"

"Ethos has his own reasons."

"What kind of reasons?"

"You are aware, of course, that Tharin is the eldest of us. Therefore, it is he who will become Grand Sovran when our father passes on to the Zenoth. And that, I fear, may be sooner than we all thought."

"He's that bad?"

He sighs. "He has slipped into unconsciousness. The shock of learning that Tharin was…" He shakes his head, eyes filling with tears. "I know he is not scared of the Zenoth, but I am scared of losing him."

"I'm so sorry. He seems strong from what I know of him. Hopefully, he can get through this." I look down at my hands. The question is, can I get through this? "What is the Zenoth by the way?"

He looks at me with surprise. "Has Tharin not told you of our beliefs?"

"I get the impression he's not the religious type."

Remus smiles. "You would be right about that. The Zenoth is, I suppose, like your heaven. It's the realm where our consciousness passes to once our bodies cease to function. It's a truly beautiful place."

"You talk like you've seen it."

"I have," he says matter-of-factly.

"What do you mean?"

"There are substances found both here, and on your planet too—for example, in some tree bark—that allows us to enter the Zenoth, the middle realm of consciousness."

"You mean DMT? I read an article about people reporting shared images when taking the stuff."

Remus nods. "Yes, that is right. Tsuki, our All Creator, is the most common sight, a truly beautiful being made of colors and shapes we cannot even define."

"Is that who's in your hologram images?"

"Yes." He smiles. "Nobody really dies, Kate. This is not a mere belief. It is a truth. There have been too many shared experiences to deny it. There isn't one person on Obrothea who does not believe this. We find it strange how you humans are so cynical."

I think about it for a moment. To have such a strong belief that there is life after death is rather comforting in a way. When my mom died, one of the things I struggled with was not knowing for sure I'd see her again. It was the same when my dad died a couple of years ago. I've never been overly religious, so I don't have the same faith in the afterlife that others might. Maybe if I'd grown up on Obrothea, I wouldn't have had to endure that part of my grief.

"So with the Grand Sovran being ill," I say, "and Tharin injured, things must be in a fragile state."

"Yes. It is why I believe Tharin was targeted."

"The future heir to the throne." I raise an eyebrow. "Ethos could benefit from him being out of the way."

Remus sighs. "The thought did occur to me."

"But would he really *stab* his own brother?"

"He more likely got someone else to."

"And then blamed me for it, like he does for your mother's and sister's deaths."

Remus's face looks pained. "That was not your fault, Kate. You did not know what that video would lead to."

"Ethos seems to imply I did know."

"He has this ridiculous theory that you conspired with Ryker and sent the video to him on purpose."

"How could I have even known Ryker if he was back on Obrothea?"

"Ethos is convinced you were communicating somehow on the ship. Anyway, revenge would not be his main motive. He knows if you and Tharin produce more heirs like Isla, it will eclipse any power he might gain."

"Tharin will be okay though, won't he?"

Remus frowns. "The dagger penetrated his lung and made it collapse, and there was excessive bleeding. This might have killed a normal Skarsdonian, but Tharin is strong, and our healers managed to get to him just in time. We just need to see if their healing will work. All we can do is wait."

"And what of me? I can't stay in here. Isla is alone."

"Truthfully, I do not know what will happen. But know this," he says firmly, "Isla will be well cared for. I will ensure that even if you can't." I let out a sob, and Remus softly grabs my arm and looks me in the eye. "You must remain strong for the battle ahead, Kate."

"What battle?"

"The Grand Sovran's life hangs in the balance. Pawns are being moved around the board, positions being decided." He stands with a sigh. "Not to mention the battle that is sure to come when Tharin is well again and learns what has been done to you." He peers behind him. "I must take my leave. There is much to be discussed outside these walls. I will try to return with more food though. The provisions here are... limited. Remember, be strong for Tharin and for Isla."

I nod. "I will." But as I say that, I have to wonder what hope I have of getting out of this cell while my protector is debilitated?

Tharin

I am sitting at a grand table, my mother on one side, my sister, Thesera, on the other. My grandfather, the Grand Sovran Balon, is at the head of the table sitting across from my great great grandmother, Bedicia. Before us stands the All Creator, Tsuki, who watches us eat a great feast with joy on her face. She hovers cross-legged in the air, her skin a dance of geometric shapes and otherworldly colors. She is as beautiful as they say. My mother takes my hand and smiles as my sister leans her head on my shoulder. It is all that I dreamed of, to see them both again. And yet something is missing.

Kate.

As I think of her, the food before me begins to wilt and rot. A shadow falls over the sun, and my mother frowns. I quickly stand.

"Do not go," Thesera says, grabbing my hand.

"He must, Thesera," my mother whispers.

The scene around me disintegrates, and I'm back in the healing room. I sit up with a gasp. Pain shudders through the muscles and bones of my back, and I howl. A healer rushes to me, another nearby runs from the room shouting, "He is awake. Tharin is awake!"

"Kate?" I say, looking around me.

"Be careful, sire," the healer says. "You are injured."

I pull a tube from my arm. I look down and see my chest and stomach are swaddled in gold strips of healing lace. "What happened?" I ask.

"Sire, your brothers will explain—"

"What happened?" I roar.

The healer swallows nervously. "You were struck with a dagger, sire. In your back."

I twist around to look over my shoulder and see my back is wrapped with more golden lattice. Who would do this? My last memory is of me talking to my mother near her telescope and then searing pain. The door bursts open, and my brother Kiah runs in. "Brother! You are alive!"

"Who did this?" I ask him, trying to get up from the bed as the healer pushes me back down. "Where is Kate?" My brother opens his mouth and then shuts it. "Where. Is. Kate?" I roar.

Kiah and the healer exchange glances. I go to swing my legs off the bed, but the healer pushes me back again. I growl and grab him by the scruff of his tunic, lifting him high above me as he thrashes about. "Where is Kate?" I shout for what feels like the millionth time. "Tell me, or you shall be thrown off the ship. By the Goddess Tsuki, I will do it!"

"The fortalice," the healer gasps.

"The fortalice? Why is Kate being imprisoned at the fortalice?"

Kiah puts his head in his hands. "Oh shit, as the humans would say."

FIFTEEN

Kate

At first, I think the roaring sound is my stomach rumbling. God knows, I'm hungry after being here all afternoon and evening without food. But then it gets louder and closer, and I realize it sounds more like the roar of a giant bear.

"Which one is she in?"

Tharin!

I stand up, heart thumping.

"I said which one?" he roars. There's the sound of objects being thrown about, followed by a cry of pain. The wall before me shimmers and disappears to reveal Tharin, trails of golden, bloody bandages dangling from his massive chest that swirls with colors of rage. His green eyes fire with anger. He marches towards me, picks me up with one huge arm. I latch onto him and wrap my arms around his neck, my legs around his hips, and he carries me from the inky cell into what looks like a circular dungeon.

A large defender runs at him. "Sire, I am sorry. I have to do this. We have been ordered by Ethos to prevent anyone, even you, from taking the human woman."

"What does Ethos's word matter? Where's my father?"

"Your father's unconscious, Tharin," I quickly say.

I can see the deep pain in his eyes, and I wrap my arms even tighter around him. He turns to the defender standing in his way, lifting his free arm to reveal he's carrying a dagger. "One last chance, Weldius," he warns.

The defender flinches. "I have sworn my loyalty to Ethos." He rushes at Tharin, who sighs and swipes the dagger across the defender's neck, slicing the skin.

The defender staggers back, gurgling and clutching at his throat. Another defender runs at us from the other side. I kick my leg out, connecting with his chest, and he stumbles back. Tharin gives me a look of pride and then drives his dagger down the top of the defender's breast plate. Blood spurts all over my face. I press my cheek into Tharin's warm chest as he strides down the corridor.

More defenders come our way, but before they can even get close, Tharin lashes and stabs at them with the dagger, leaving a trail of blood and cries of pain and horror in his wake. I can hear him wince in pain himself, and I wonder whether he has even healed properly. All the time, I keep my bloody face buried in his chest, listening to the furious beat of his heart. Soon, the attacks dwindle, and I hear whispers of Tharin's name. I look up to see a line of defenders either side of us as Tharin strides down the corridors with me in his arms. They are all watching him with their strange green eyes, saying his name over and over in a low chant, in rhythm with his heartbeat. As he passes them, they turn and walk away as though they were stationed there to ease his path towards his room.

When we get inside his room, the wall solidifies behind us, and I realize we're not alone. Remus is there with two more of Tharin's brothers—the youngest of the warrior brothers who reminds me of an Abercrombie & Finch model with golden wavy hair to his shoulders and a wide, handsome grin. Next to him is the warrior twin with the long scar down his cheek.

"Brother, are you well?" Remus asks, walking over to examine Tharin's wound. Tharin flinches, and Remus shakes his head. "You need more healing time."

"He'll need even more healing if Ethos gets his hands on him," the scarred brother says. I notice he regards me with cold eyes and remember again what Tharin told me of that video I made.

The youngest brother nods. "Yes, Heldran is right, you killed some of Ethos's most loyal defenders," he says with a sparkle in his eyes. "Which is *very* impressive, might I add."

Tharin's nostrils flare as he looks down at me. He's still holding me, his one strong arm around my waist keeping me against him with ease. I press my cheek against his warm chest, never wanting him to let me go. I can hear his heart-beat, slow and steady, see the colors of anger quiver under his skin. "It was worth it," he says, eyes still locked on mine.

"Am I safe here?" I ask. "And Isla? Will she be safe after what just happened?"

"Adin is with her," Remus explains. "Castian too. They will bring her to you after her schooling."

"This room is impenetrable," Tharin reassures me. "We can remain here until we've gathered our thoughts." He turns to Remus. "Is it true? Is Father unconscious?" Remus nods, and his two other brothers hang their heads. A mixture of sadness and anger flickers over Tharin's face. "So Ethos is taking his chance?"

"So it seems," Remus says.

I can see Tharin is struggling with the idea his brother would stab him.

"I will kill him for you if I must, Tharin," the youngest brother says.

"Hopefully, it will not come to that, Kiah," Tharin says. "We must think of our next steps."

"We can discuss that if you put your human down," Heldran snaps. "You standing there holding her as though she is a monkey is rather distracting."

"No," Tharin says, handsome face serious.

"It's not good for your wound, Brother," Remus says.

"He's right, Tharin," I say reluctantly. "You should let me down. Please?"

He sighs and does as I ask. I stand on wobbly legs, looking down at the remains of my blood-drenched clothes. Tharin follows my gaze and then grabs a golden shirt. He wraps it around my shoulders and makes me sit down on one of the large armchairs in the room. I should be the one looking after him, but I'm too tired and confused to argue.

"You're injured." He crouches down in front of me to look at the wound on my head. "Who did this?"

I shrug. "I-I don't know."

"Ethos's defenders were pretty rough when they took her," Kiah admits.

Tharin jumps up and marches to the door, his face is sparking with anger. "How about I kill Ethos now and be done with it?"

His three brothers stride after him and grab him.

"That is not the answer, brother," Remus says. "We need time to think about our next step."

"Remus is right," Heldran says, running his large, calloused hand over his shaven head. "You may have beaten some of Ethos's loyal defenders with pure adrenaline, but it may not be so easy to fight the others, especially with your wound."

"You're the First Defender," I say to Tharin. "Surely they should be loyal to you first? Well, after your father anyway."

"Not all my men are led by loyalty and courage," Tharin

says with a sigh. "Some, especially those in the city, see coin as more of a draw."

"Or blackmail. Ethos has his little spies camped all over the city," Kiah explains. "He makes it his business to know all there is to know so he can hold secrets over their heads."

Remus places his hand on Tharin's shoulder. "I fear that the time has come for one side to overcome the other. As reluctant as you are, Tharin, you are going to have to prepare yourself for battle against Ethos. I cannot see Father emerging from his illness any time soon."

Tharin shrugs his brother's hand off and begins pacing up and down. With his golden hair lifting with each step and his clothes filthy with blood, he's quite the sight. "Damn Ethos."

I eye his wound, which is seeping with blood. "They'll be no chance of you winning battle if you don't give yourself some time to recover from your wound," I say to Tharin. "We're landing some time tomorrow, right?"

He nods.

"Then we use this time for you to recover," I suggest, "and figure out what to do when we land." I turn to Tharin's brothers. "Maybe you guys can gather some intelligence to see where we stand? It would also make me feel better knowing you're both out there making sure Isla is okay. She can be brought back here, right?"

The three brothers look at Tharin for permission. He nods.

Kiah examines my face. "Hmm, turns out these human women are rather wise."

"You should never have doubted us," I say, giving him a strong stare.

He shrugs. "That is what Tharin has been telling us from the start." He pats his brother on the back. "Take care, brother. Let your wise human woman tend to you. We will be back later."

Remus nods at Tharin. "I will try my best to gather more intelligence."

After they all leave, Tharin begins pacing the room again, deep in thought. I go to him and place my hand on his arm. "You really do need to rest, Tharin. We both do. And maybe have a shower," I add, looking down at my bloody clothes and hair.

He turns his attention to me. "Yes, you are rather filthy. Let me clean you."

I laugh, embarrassed. "No, *you're* the injured one, remember. You need to get yourself clean before the wound becomes infected. Do you have a shower you can use?" I ask, looking around the room.

"No, just that." I follow his gaze to a jug of water and a cloth nearby.

"Wow, that really is quite medieval," I say. "Fine, looks like I'll have to help you." I lead him over to it, pour water onto the cloth, and gently clean his face. I probably don't really need to do this, but I feel this urgent need to look after him.

God, he really is so beautiful with those green long-lashed eyes of his blinking down at me, his full lips slightly parted. I can't help remembering the kisses we shared…and the incredible orgasm he gave me. He is silent as I help him, his eyes never leaving mine. I try not to let my body react. This is purely medical. I go to check his back, but he grabs my wrist, flinching.

"Leave it be," he says.

"I'm worried it got dirty from all the other men's blood."

"I will be fine. It's a mere scratch."

I laugh. "You're being ridiculous. You were stabbed. Let me see to it." He sighs and loosens his grip on me. I walk around him to look at his huge bare back. It swirls with color, purples and reds. The golden dressings on it are saturated in blood. Some must be from the defenders he was forced to kill, but I have a feeling much of Tharin's is mixed in there too. Tears spring to my eyes as I remember seeing him stabbed. It all comes rushing back then, the sight of this strong man looking so vulnerable.

"It was so horrible to see you like that," I admit as I gently clean his wound. "I knew something was wrong, I ran through the waterfall and was terrified when I saw you—"

He peers over his shoulder at me. "It sounds like you were worried?"

"Of course I was."

"Even after what I said about seeding you."

"It's not your fault you act like a primeval ape."

He raises a golden eyebrow. "So you forgive me for being such an ape, seeing as I'm the father of your child."

"Yeah, well, we don't know if that bit's true."

He turns around, looking down at me with an intensity in his green eyes that almost takes my breath away. "Can you not admit what is so clear to everyone else? I'm Isla's father." He moves closer to me, so close I have to lean my head even farther back to look at him. "What if I had died without ever hearing you say it out loud? Look me in the eye and finally admit that I *am* Isla's father."

I purse my lips, blinking back tears. Of course, I know he is. Not just because of the green eyes they share or the shape of their perfect noses. But because of the courage they share. Their zest for life. The way they both hold themselves. "Yes, Tharin, there may well be a possibility you are my daughter's father," I admit.

His face lights up. "Finally."

"Don't look so happy with yourself. It's not like I ever agreed to it."

"But you did. Deep down, you know you did."

I can't answer that, because he's right. I don't remember

anything from ten years ago, but everything inside me tells me that yes, I must have agreed to sleep with him...*and* therefore get pregnant with him.

"Is that all I am though?" I ask. "The mother of your Sacred child?"

"You know that's not true. I began to develop true feelings for you." He swallows, Adam's apple boxing up and down. "I even tried to convince my father to allow you to come to Obrothea with us. I couldn't bear the thought of parting from you, and you felt the same by the last night we spent together."

I look at him in surprise. "Really? I said I'd go to another planet? Willingly?"

He nods, face softening. "Yes. You were excited."

I think of the promises I once made myself to have a normal life, not to wish for a life of adventure like my parents had. "I find that hard to believe."

He sighs and gently places his palm on my cheek. "I know all your dreams of adventure were ruined by your mother's death, Kate."

"Ah-huh," I say.

"Was she like you, your mother?"

I smile. "I think so. She loved singing and dancing. Campfires and hikes. That was why the commune was so magical for her to begin with. Me too." I frown. "But then the dream turned into a nightmare."

"Yes, I remember you telling me she began to feel unsafe there."

I nod. "A lot of the people there were pretty unstable, to be honest. I found out later, from another commune member, that Mom actually asked Dad if they could leave a few days before she died. He said no, of course." I look up at Tharin. "If I asked, do you think you'd take me back to Earth?"

He frowns. "Is that what you want?"

154

"I just want to know whether you would let me?"

He sighs. "If you asked, I would find a way."

I look at him in surprise. "Really?"

"Yes. I do not want you thinking you are my prisoner. I never have. I want you to be here by choice. Taking you human women to our ship against your will never sat well with me. Especially as I began to fall in love with you."

"Fall in love? But it was just seven nights. How can such feelings develop over seven nights?"

"They do for many people."

I know he's right. Some of my friends have had short holiday romances that turned into marriages. I once thought I was in love with the teenage boy I met at the commune after knowing him five days.

"I wish I could remember those nights," I say with a sigh.

"I wish you could too."

"I'm not sure I'd want to remember the actions that led to the death of your mother and sister though," I add. His hand slips from my face, and he turns his gaze away from me. "I would never have understood the consequences of that video, Tharin."

"I know," he admits.

"Did-did we even talk about it?"

I notice his eyes flicker with pain. "We did, yes. When we learnt about the invasion on the last night."

"So I sent the video the night before, and they invaded the next day?"

Tharin nods.

"You must have hated me," I add, feeling terrible.

"I hated Ryker. He is the one who caused their deaths."

"Remus told me Ethos thinks I actually conspired with Ryker. You don't think that? Do you?" He avoids my gaze, and I reach up to make him look at me. "Do you?"

"I did, for a while. My grief and anger made me weak.

But as the intensity of my emotions faded, I knew you would not do that to me. How can I blame you for wanting to retain your memories? It's Ethos's stupid experiments that are to blame."

"Experiments that led to Isla being born," I remind him.

His face softens. "Yes. Even with all the consequences, how can I regret that?"

"And us? Do you regret the feelings you had for me?"

He looks deep into my eyes. "No," he says. "I thought I did, but standing here in front of you... No. I would do it a hundred times over."

"Even if you knew your mother and sister would die as a consequence?"

His face flickers with pain. "Maybe. Yes. No." He roars, looks up at the ceiling, and shakes his head.

"Sorry, I shouldn't have asked. I'm also so sorry you had to go through all that," I say, stroking his arm.

He takes deep breaths, calming himself. When he looks back down at me, his eyes are soft. "What's done is done. I can change nothing now. All I know is the feelings I had ten years ago are still here." He curls his vast hand into a fist and punches it against his chest. "Stronger than ever."

"I feel the same. I don't know how. I remember hardly anything, and yet I *know* there are strong feelings there." I swallow. "I also know I want to kiss you again."

"Then your wish is my command." He sweeps everything off the table behind me, encircles his large hands around my waist, and lifts me onto the table's surface. His lips are hard and warm against mine. I part my lips, and his tongue slides inside my mouth as I let out a moan. I reach one hand up, tangling my fingers in his bloody hair, then place my other hand flat against his huge, muscular chest, feeling the skin vibrate against me.

Why the hell can't I resist this being? Why am I so weak?

As I think that, there's a buzzing sound from the door area. Tharin lets out a frustrated cry against my lips.

I gently push him away. "You should answer."

Tharin watches me for a few moments, taking deep breaths as his skin fluctuates purple. Then he closes his eyes until he grows calmer. "Yes?" he calls out in irritation.

"Isla will be here in ten minutes," Adin's voice calls through. "We have arranged for her to be released early from her schooling."

I feel my heart leap with joy. I haven't seen my girl for nearly two days. Then I realize what a mess I am. "She can't see me like this. All the blood…"

"Of course," Tharin quickly says, lifting me back off the table. "Come."

I follow him to the other side of the room and watch as he presses his bloody palm against the wall. It shimmers and disappears, and I shake my head in disbelief. We're standing in what looks like a huge bathing area with views out to space.

"We could have done this before," I say to Tharin. "Why the act with the jug of water and cloth?"

He shrugs. "I liked the idea of you cleaning me like that."

I shake her head. "You're a bad boy."

"You have no idea." His gaze travels over me, and he takes a sharp breath in, looking away. "I will leave you to bathe. There are towels on the side."

"What about you?" I ask.

"I have a jug of water, remember?" he says with a raised eyebrow. His face grows serious. "If I join you in here, I can't guarantee what will happen." He backs away, and the wall solidifies behind him.

I only have time for a quick dip in the amazing baths and a rinse of my hair before I hear movement in the next room. I get out and wrap a towel around me before rushing in to find

Isla bursting into the room with Castian. Tharin has done a decent job of cleaning himself and has changed into soft brown leather breeches and a black tunic. His hair is wet and tied back. He watches Isla with a small smile on his face.

I open my arms to her. She throws herself into them, and I swing her around as she giggles. "You're all wet, Mommy, have you been swimming?"

"I just had a bath," I explain. "I didn't shower for nearly two days. I was stinky."

"Ew," she says, wrinkling her nose. "Gross." Then Isla catches sight of Tharin. She goes shy, squeezing her face into my shoulder. It must be strange meeting the alien who proclaims to be your father.

"So here is the famous warrior I hear talk of," Tharin says to her.

"*You're* more famous than me," Isla retorts. "We learnt about you in class."

"Well, from what I have heard from Castian, I suspect stories will also be written about *you*."

"Yep, Castian says I will make an *awesome* Skarsdonian warrior," Isla says proudly.

"That you will," Tharin says, laughing.

"That you *won't*," I say, shooting Tharin a look.

"Is this your room?" Isla asks Tharin.

"Rooms, don't you mean?" Tharin says. "Let me show you to yours."

"There are *more* rooms?" I ask.

He nods and leads us to a wall. "Place your palm against the wall," he instructs Isla. She smiles and does as he asks. A door appears, and the three of us step through into a large room with a window looking out into space. Isla's eyes light up, and I can't blame her. This is the room of her dreams. It's like Tharin knows her inside out. A huge window draped with black starred curtains and a massive green cabin bed dominate the middle of the room. Sparkling black shelves are dominated by books and magazines. There's a huge desk with realms of paper, notepads, pens, and more on it, and around it all is a host of unusual looking games and toys.

"I filled it with all the things I'm told a human child of her age loves—games and dolls and papers and pens," Tharin whispers to me as Isla rushes to a strange-looking doll house made from glass. "They're different from what she is used to on Earth, but I hope she'll like it."

"It's amazing, Tharin," I whisper.

Isla wanders around, amazed. "What's this?" she asks, gesturing to a large board game with figurines and a dark wall down its middle.

"This is the game Drango," Tharin explains, going to her. "It depicts the Great War that took place five hundred Earth years ago, where your ancestors fought off Yarabion warriors who tried to penetrate the great wall of Drango."

"My ancestors," Isla whispers, eyes sparkling with excitement. I notice a hint of pain. The conflict between loving the idea of this war hero and future king possibly being her real father while also missing Richard must be so difficult for her. For all his faults, Richard is still the man she knew as her father.

"Is this you?" she asks Tharin, holding up a small, muscular figure that looks just like him.

He nods. "This game was updated to feature the best defenders in Obrothean history. Naturally, I am among them.'

I smile. He certainly isn't modest.

"Who's this?" Isla asks, holding up a figure of a man with long dark hair. "I think I recognize him from a book I read. It's Ryker, your half-brother, right? He was like you, a great warrior on the battlefield."

Tharin's eyes flash with anger. He takes the figurine from

her and curls his fists around it. "He is not meant to be in it anymore. He is dead."

"Why?" Isla asks.

"He betrayed us. He is *not* a good man. Now, who do you wish to be? Monsters or warriors?'

She picks up the figurine of Tharin and smiles. "Warriors, like you."

I sink down into a nearby chair and watch as they play. Richard never played with Isla like this. He preferred to do the social-media-friendly kind of bonding—cinema trips and visits to pretty places so he could take photos to post and show what an amazing dad he was. Except as soon as the photos were taken, he would stare at his phone, hardly paying attention to our daughter. It's not like I wasn't guilty of some-times turning to my phone too, but at least I made an effort.

It occurs to me then that I have lived three days without my smart phone and Isla without her iPad, and here she is playing a game with her hero father. Tharin throws himself into the game like a child, putting on funny voices, which makes Isla giggle endlessly. When her figurine kills his, he pretends to be mortally wounded, collapsing his giant body against the ground. I can't help but feel emotions pull at my heart.

I think again of what Tharin told me earlier. Would I really have agreed to go to Obrothea with him, knowing all I did about its battle-torn past? I must have. But then I made that stupid video. Tharin catches my eye and mouths a *thank you*. Is he thanking me for letting him spend time with his daughter? My heart catches again. If this weren't such an awful situation, with us kidnapped and being delivered to a war-torn planet, I might love this little scene. I have to remind myself it's wrong. I must be careful. I cannot let the mesmer-izing effect Tharin has on me make me weak.

Tharin

Kate is quiet as we eat dinner with Adin and Castian that evening while everyone else feasts in the great hall. We are sitting at a table by the main baths, looking out to space. Does she regret the kiss we shared, our second since she arrived? I have no regrets. The feel of her soft, wet lips against mine and her arms around me brought back memories, good memories of when we kissed before. Kisses that, on the fifth night, led to her finally agreeing to me sinking my cock into her. I shiver at the memory now. We were not able to control ourselves. As soon as she woke on my bed, we fell into each other arms and undressed. That night, we made love, as she made me call it, three times. My cock could not get enough of her. I knew with a certainty she would fall pregnant. My seed combined with the way she orgasmed as I came inside her made the possibility too strong to ignore. She thought her strange human contraceptive pill would stop her falling pregnant, but I knew it did nothing to stop it.

As she lay in my arms after, I thought of the fact that at that very moment, my seed was racing to meet her eggs. It made my desire to keep her with me even stronger. That was when I broached the subject of her coming to Obrothea. I thought she would refuse, but her eyes had lit up.

"Is that a possibility?" she'd asked.

The next day, I asked my father during one of our communication calls, but he had instantly said no. "No one will accept a Highborn being officially Pledged with a human. It can only happen when we are sure the children produced are as Ethos predicts."

"But that is ten years away," I had said to him. "Why

can't the women just come with us now, and we can raise our children with them?"

"It is too unstable. We know Ryker is readying an army in the forests, and the Gatikan Mad Prince is salivating for revenge after you killed his father. We cannot have these vulnerable humans and their children on Obrothea yet, not until we are sure the children will develop their strength as puberty approaches."

I knew he was right. I was asking my father to allow me to bring my precious human, and potentially our unborn child, into an unstable world.

Am I not asking the same now? I thought Skarsdon was more stable with Ryker dead. Though the Mad Prince still remains alive, seething in his blackened castle with his concoctions and potions protecting him, I hear he is too addled by those same concoctions to truly focus on building an army. But now I have a new enemy, it seems. My brother. And tomorrow, we land in a region bound to be on edge with news that their Grand Sovran is gravely ill. I know what needs to be done…for Skarsdon.

Yet for once, Skarsdon does not feel like a priority. Kate and Isla do.

I look at Kate now, desperate to kiss her again. She's wearing a golden dress Adin brought from her rooms, so short I can see her exquisite thighs. I try to catch her eye, but she continues to look pensively out to space. I must try to alleviate her worries.

After we eat dinner, Kate takes Isla to her room. My daughter is such an amazing young girl. She has all the grit and the charm I dreamt a child of mine would have. After a while, I can't help but join them, taking a moment to watch Isla read to her mother.

Kate looks up and notices me. "Why don't you read to a real life Skarsdonian hero?" she asks Isla. Isla nods and Kate stands, giving our daughter a kiss on her forehead. As she passes me to walk out, I grasp her arm softly and smile at her, thankful she is giving me this chance. I sit on the bed with Isla as she begins reading to me, voice sleepy. She pauses and peers up at me. "Do you really think you're my dad?"

I sigh. "I know it's a lot to take in, but yes, Isla, I am your father, and I am very proud of that fact." Her brow creases. "Of course, I need to earn that right," I quickly add. "The father you knew, Richard, has been there over the years. A father isn't just biological."

Isla nods. "That's what Mommy says. You're doing a pretty good job of convincing me though." I can't help but smile. She lets out a yawn. "I'm super tired."

"Then sleep." I watch as she sinks into the mists and her eyes close.

I watch her for a while, imagining reading with her each night. Is it really possible for us Skarsdonian warriors to have a true family, like the humans have? I once thought my life would be spent on the battlefields, returning home rarely to see to my Pledged Skarsdonian woman and our brood of children. It is not the way for Skarsdonian men to tend to women and children, other then to keep their women satisfied and pregnant, and their children healthy and well fed.

I see now the problems that can cause. When I was tormented with grief and sorrow after my mother and sister's deaths, a human touch would have made the difference, but we were made to put on a brave face.

What if things could be different?

———

Kate

When I get back to the poolside table, Remus, Kiah, and Heldran have joined Castian and Adin, all of them apart from Adin drinking pemelonian juice and talking in low voices. Castian and Remus are sitting very close to one another, and for a moment, I wonder if there's something going on between them. They all stop talking as I approach.

"Don't stop on my account," I say.

"Castian and I were just remarking how human Tharin seems lately," Remus says.

I frown, taking the seat across from Castian and pouring myself a small cup of pemelonian. "Human?"

"Obrothean fathers are not like human men on Earth," Castian explains. "They divide their time between battling, saging, scribing, or whatever other job they have. They return home to sleep and eat."

"And fuck," Kiah says with a laugh. I give him a look, and he grimaces into his drink.

"My brother is right," Remus says with a smile, "even if he does express it in a rather brutal way. It is important for Skarsdonians in particular to produce as many children as possible. The more children you have, the more power."

"Doesn't sound very nice for the women," I remark.

"Our women are happy," Heldran says in his gruff voice. "Happier than human women, from what I have seen. Nightly orgasms, all the possessions they wish, servants, many healthy children to care for."

I laugh. "Orgasms. Well, as long as there are orgasms." I sigh. "Don't your women get bored? Some of us aren't content to just be mothers."

"Once the children are of age," Kiah says, "the mothers are free to do as they wish. They can return to their jobs or take new ones. They can even take on as many lovers as they wish if their Primes are away."

I shake my head, smiling. "It's just a whole other world... literally. Why do you think Tharin seems so different?"

"What is he doing now?" Heldran says with a bitter laugh as he peers in the direction of Isla's room. "He is reading with his daughter. We warriors do not do such things."

"Well, that's just sad if you don't," I say.

"Oh, come now, Heldran," Kiah says. "Tharin is a big softie beneath it all. We all know that. He was always our mother's favorite, our sister's too. They taught him all their soft ways."

The table goes quiet at the mention of the two women. Heldran in particular seems to be struggling to control his emotions, and his large fingers tighten around his glass. "It is not them who made him soft," he hisses. He raises his eyes to meet mine. "It is you."

"Heldran, calm down," Remus says.

"You've all seen the way he's been the past ten years without her," Heldran spits back.

"What do you mean?" I ask.

"Oh, he's been a mess," Kiah says. "He blamed it on the grief, but we could all see he was also mourning not being with you."

My face flushes.

"He's right," Remus says. "Among all the Highborn and their Pledged, there is not one couple who could match the feelings you two have for one another."

Tharin strolls in then, and we all go quiet. I watch him, feeling yet more anger and frustration at the memories that were stolen from me...and slightly unnerved by how hostile Heldran is with me.

"She is asleep," he says, a contented look on his face. Kiah and Remus exchange a smile as Heldran continues to fester.

"I thought that would be the case," I say.

"So," Tharin says, pouring himself some pemelonian, "what news, brothers?"

"We're at an impasse," Remus says. "I can tell from the discreet conversations at dinner earlier that the other brothers feel much the same. They are very aware of the anger you feel at Kate being detained. The amount of blood spilt to save her makes that very clear. Waiting until we land tomorrow is definitely the best course of action."

Tomorrow. Hearing them say that reminds me of just how soon it will be before I set foot on another planet. It fills me with a mixture of excitement and concern. Tharin must see the look on my face, because he goes to stand behind me and squeezes my shoulder.

"Tomorrow is a big day," he says. "Kate and I need to be alone."

When the other men leave the room, Tharin takes the seat next to me and looks out of the vast window towards space. "How are you feeling about tomorrow?" he asks as he sips his juice.

"Nervous. Excited," I admit.

"I'm pleased you feel some excitement. I understand what a...difficult experience this is for you."

"That's an understatement. I'm almost sick thinking about it."

He sighs. "Then we will not talk of it. I'd rather know all I missed out on. Tell me all about your pregnancy, the birth. Isla's first steps, her first day at school. I wish to know it all." Over the next hour, we talk of our daughter. Lost first teeth and grazes. First day at school and her special achievements. I tell Tharin about my life as a teacher too. I only qualified after I had Isla.

"It doesn't surprise me you became a teacher," he says, pouring me more pemelonian. "But I'm sad you didn't pursue your dreams of getting a—what was it you called it—a masters in space studies. I remember you talking so passionately about it."

I sigh. "Reality gets in the way of adventure. We had a mortgage to pay after Isla came along, healthcare to cover."

"We," Tharin repeats, a flicker of jealousy in his green eyes.

"I presume you know I got married, right? I heard from the other girls we were all monitored from afar?"

"Yes, I received regular reports. What is this Richard like then?"

"An idiot. He cheated on me."

He looks at me in surprise. "I didn't know this."

"Well, now you do. I caught him with my hairdresser. The aftermath anyway. They were dressing after a quickie in our house. I came back because I forgot something, and there they were."

Anger flits across his face. "He would be executed on Obrothea, infidelity is forbidden for men."

"But not for women? Kiah told me women are allowed to take lovers on Obrothea."

"A women can't just be left without pleasure when her man is at battle."

"Really? How would you feel about me taking on a lover?" The anger flares in his eyes again, and I laugh. "Truth is, Richard was never right for me anyway, nor I for him." I swallow, looking down at my hands. "And now I know why. Something was always missing. I just felt it in the core of me. I mean, with Isla, it was perfect. She's everything. But the other side of my life." I peer back up at him. "I now know what the problem was. I didn't have *you* in my life."

I can't believe I'm saying it. But it's true. It really is.

Joy floods his face, and he takes my hand in his huge, warm one. "I have felt the same," he says. "I've thrown myself into battle over the years, into…other things too, but my life has been empty without you."

I look up at him, taking all of him in. This beautiful giant of a man with his fierce green eyes and long golden hair.

"Look at us both," I whisper, "two lost souls until now."

He strokes my face and pulls my chair towards his, his vast hands sliding up my thighs. I shift even closer, desperate to get as close to him as I can as our lips connect, my tongue circling his. He moves his hands farther up and under my skirt, his massive thumbs gliding right towards the heat of me. I shift even closer to him so his thumbs graze the bare lips of my sex. He stops, holding my gaze as his thumbs sink into my wetness. I let out a groan, and he kisses my neck as I circle my hips in rhythm to his thumbs moving in and out of me.

Tharin stands, carries me to one of the large daybeds, and lowers me onto it. The mist rises and welcomes me, covering me in a delicious purple warmth. He kneels down in front of the daybed and softly grasps my ankles, pulling me towards him so his head is between my legs. I cross my legs. I'm not wearing any underwear thanks to their stupid no-underwear policy.

"You're so shy," he whispers. "Can I not taste you?"

The way he says it like that… I bite my lip. "What if Isla wakes?"

"I will hear an alarm announcing movement in her room."

"Paranoid much?"

"I told you, both of you will always be safe with me. So *can* I taste you?" he asks again.

"I love the way you ask like that."

"Let me continue then. May I stroke your clitoris softly with my tongue?" he whispers, his breath on my bare thighs as he trails his lips up them. "I would like to plunge my fingers into you too, feel your wetness around my knuckles." He pauses, peering up at me. "If you wish me to, that is?"

"Yes, yes, I do wish." I raise my hips towards him, desperate for him to do what he's taking about, but he continues to tease me, his lips stopping just before the most intimate part of me. The walls and water oscillate purple with our desire, and I can feel his skin buzzing as I place my fingers in his silky hair and try to push his head towards me. He laughs softly, and then I feel the wet flat surface of his tongue against my clit. I let out a moan as he begins lapping up and down my pussy.

"Harder, faster," I whisper. He does as I ask, sucking and lapping at my clit as he reaches up and drags the neckline of my dress down with one hand to expose my breasts. He circles my nipples with his fingers, and I draw my legs up to my stomach to press myself even more into his face, rocking as the first waves of orgasm already begin swelling through me. "Oh," I murmur. "Oh-oh-ohhhhhhh."

He moves up the bed, fingers still inside me as he watches me come, his cock pressing hard and long against the inside of my thigh. It's so tempting to just reposition myself, take his cock out of his breeches, and draw him into me, but I don't want to get pregnant, so I close my legs. A look of disappointment flashes across his face but then it's quickly replaced by lust.

Tharin

I watch Kate as she comes. Her body shudders, and her pussy contracts around my fingers. I press my cock, still shrouded in the cloth of my breeches, against the wetness of her thighs. I want to release it and plunge it into her. I think she wants

169

the same, but she closes her legs, turning away. I'm disappointed but I know we can not rush this. I gently remove my fingers from her and draw her into my arms, looking down at her exposed breasts and stomach. I am amazed by her beauty. Her full breasts, her curved legs, and the rise and fall of her luscious hips. Obrothean women tend to be muscular. In contrast, Kate is soft and round and perfect. She bites her lip, almost looking embarrassed, which just makes me want her even more. I graze my fingers over the scar that lines her lower stomach. "This is where Isla came out?"

"Yes," she says. "She was stubborn and refused to turn."

"Stubborn like her mother."

"And her father," she says, raising an eyebrow.

"It's a beautiful scar." I smile.

"You really think that?"

"Of course, why would I not? It's a symbol of our daughter's life, etched onto your skin."

"Richard never liked it."

I feel anger build at the mention of that human's name. "Then he's even more of a fool than I thought."

"I don't want to talk about him." She gives me a mischievous look and gently pushes me back against the daybed. "Now it's your turn." She leans over me, kissing my neck, trailing her lips down and tonguing each of my nipples. The sensation connects with my cock, making it pulse. She slowly lowers herself, gliding her lips down my stomach as I tangle my fingers in her dark hair. She pauses at my arcism and stares at it a moment, then softly licks it. I groan. "You like that?" She asks.

"Yes."

She licks me again and the sensation bubbles inside me, my cock straining against the fabric of my breeches. She moves down slightly so she's level with my cock, and I see from the way her pretty eyes widen that she is happy with its outline. She licks her lips, unlaces my breeches, and pulls the full length of me out. Her eyes widen even more. Some pre-seed slips out from the slit in my cock, and she darts her tiny tongue out and licks it. I put my head back, moaning. This is unbearable. Her lips encircle my shaft, embracing the top half of it, sucking softly. I am overwhelmed with how it feels to be with her again.

My beautiful Kate.

She looks up at me with her fathomless brown eyes, and it takes everything to stop myself spurting into her mouth right then and there. She moves her lips down my shaft, her hands now hard on my buttocks. The pain of my wound is strong, but my need to come in her mouth is stronger. She uses her hands to make me thrust forward, my cock plunging deeper into the soft, warm wetness of her mouth. She gags slightly, and I go to move away, but she circles the base of my cock with both her hands, making me stay hard and long in her mouth, her dark gaze still locked on mine.

The sight of my cock thrusting in and out of her pretty mouth is enough to set me off quicker than I would usually, spasms making me arch my neck back as my colorful seed explodes inside the soft cushions of her mouth. There is so much it spills from her pretty mouth, a rainbow on her skin. We hold each other's gazes as I continue to come, my hips rocking lazily back and forth as my fingers gently caress her hair.

When I'm done, I slowly pull my length from her mouth and reach down to wipe away some come that has dribbled down her chin. I pull her up to lie with me, my arms tightly around her as I catch my breath.

"Was it always like this?" she asks. "Those nights we spent together?"

"You resisted at first. But in the end, you could no longer resist me."

I lift a strand of her hair. "Your hair is just as I remember. So dark."

"Like the Fostinians. Your slaves."

He shakes his head. "I told you, they are no longer slaves."

"No longer?"

"Yes, they now have the choice. It's something I fought for, in memory of my mother. It's why I have so much support in the northern regions of Skarsdon, on the border with Fostinia."

"That's good for what's to come, right?"

I smile wickedly. "Definitely. Ethos will certainly regret campaigning against their emancipation." I notice something out of the window. "Kate, look."

She follows my gaze and her mouth drops open. "Obrothea."

Pride rushes through me at the sight of my home planet in the distance. Its colors—greens and purples from where we are—are vivid against the darkness of space. Its electric-green scars are more prominent too, zigzagging across its surface.

"It will be your home soon," I whisper. "I know that's hard for you to take in, Kate, but I'm confident you will grow to love Obrothea as I do."

I draw Kate into my arms before I have the chance to see the doubt in her eyes. She leans her cheek softly against my chest and raises her hand to my face, tracing it with her tiny fingers as though checking I am still here. She sighs, contented, so tired she begins to fall asleep.

As she sleeps, I carry her back into our bedroom and lay down with her on the bed. I stroke her silky hair and breathe in her smell. This is what I dreamed of for ten years, the chance to watch Kate sleep again, her long dark eyelashes shadows over her cheeks, her hair a dark wave around her head. Despite what passed between us, I could not help but dream of how things could have gone differently. But what lies ahead of us now? Ethos may be biding his time, yes, but I know how impatient my brother is. He will strike soon.

Will my home be too dangerous for a child? Will it be too dangerous for Kate?

I pull Kate even closer to me. No, Kate and Isla will always be safe with me. Always.

Kate

My eyes flutter open, and I realize we're back in Tharin's room now. The man himself is strutting around the room right now very naked. I let my gaze lazily follow him as he walks back from his wardrobe, the muscles in his beautiful butt gliding beneath his skin. He's like a Greek god. Huge and muscular with long golden hair. He looks down at me as he passes by, brushing his fingers against my cheek with a look of want in his eyes.

God, he's beautiful.

I grab his hand and pull him towards me, taking his giant, already-hard cock in my hands.

"Tharin? I have news," a voice calls. It's Adin. Tharin ignores him, leaning his head back and moaning as he moves his cock close to my mouth.

"Tharin! It's important!"

Tharin sighs and moves away. "Later," he mouths down to me with his succulent lips. "Give us a moment, Adin," he shouts through the wall. He throws me a golden tunic, and I pull it on as he changes into some trousers. "Come," he shouts out again.

The wall dissolves, and Adin walks in with Remus and Kiah. They both look very serious.

"We have heard word defenders loyal to Ethos are gathering at the landing station in Skarsdon City," Kiah says.

"What does this mean?" I ask.

Remus meets my gaze. "We cannot guess their plans, but it's not good."

"It will be impossible to fight them," Adin adds, "even with some of your loyal defenders onboard, Tharin."

Tharin nods. "We'll be overwhelmed."

Something occurs to me. "You said defenders in the northern part of Skarsdon are more loyal to you?"

Tharin nods.

"Well, can we land there instead of the city?"

They all grow quiet, exchanging looks.

"That could work," Kiah says.

"Yes, it could work," Tharin says, squeezing my hand.

Remus shakes his head firmly. "But how do you hope to divert this vessel towards a completely different landing area?"

"I happened to save the captain's entire family when Gatika's Mad Prince went on his rampage," Tharin says. "He owes me." He turns to Kiah. "Can you get word to him?"

Kiah nods. "I will go now." He marches out of the room.

Tharin comes to me and wraps his muscled arms round me. "You are a genius, Kate. We men may have our physical strength, but you women have your wits."

I smile. "So it's been said." But despite the good vibes in the room, I feel a trickle of apprehension. Soon, we will be landing in a brand-new planet, and we have no idea what awaits us.

SIXTEEN

Kate

I walk down the corridor with Tharin wearing a long-sleeved golden dress that pools around my feet. Tharin told me it's important to give the right impression when we land. I am his Pledged after all. Isla walks between us wearing a tunic dress the same color as mine. As for Tharin, he looks very regal in the cloak that's draped around his huge shoulders. It's beautiful, threaded with gold and undulating with color. He told me it belonged to his mother and represents both his Fostinian and Skarsdonian blood. His father, who still lies unconscious ready to be carried out of the vessel, apparently doesn't like these cloaks. He prefers the golden cloaks, but Tharin said this cloak shows his ties to the northern region and Fostinia. I am proud of him for taking a stand like this. It rams home even more what he is—royalty, but royalty that knows his own mind.

Adin strides in front of us, his hand on the hilt of his sword. He looks troubled. I can tell he's not sure about my plan. He certainly seemed dubious when we told him. But Tharin thinks it's the right plan, and I have to believe he knows what he's doing. He's the only anchor I can rely on here. I realized that as he strode away from the prison with me in his arms. The way he dispatched those giant men without a second glance. The way he held me and made me feel so secure and protected despite the battle unfolding around us. I have to trust him to keep me and Isla safe, because if he can't, what hope is there for us?

Nerves flutter in my stomach as we approach the corridor along from the one Tharin and I share. I let out a breath of relief when I see none of the other woman are here. I'm not sure what they will think about all this. When we get to the wall separating us from the hall, Adin pauses. I look up at Tharin, and he nods, green eyes very serious. Adin presses his hand against the wall, and it dissolves.

We walk into the sound of hubbub. It looks like all the women and children are here, but instead of sitting at the tables, they're crowding at the windows, trying to get a look at the new planet we're to call home. From where I'm standing, I catch sight of golden-tipped mountains and purple frosted trees. My heart soars with excitement as my tummy turns with nerves. At the high table, Tharin's brothers peer out of the vast windows, confused expressions on the faces of the two sage brothers who have sided with Ethos as they realize we're not landing according to plan. Ethos looks particularly angry, his nostrils flaring.

Good.

"We're on the border between Skarsdon—" Tharin gestures to the golden mountains, "—and Fostinia." He points to the purple treetops.

"Can I go look with the other children?" Isla asks.

Tharin puts his huge hand gently on her shoulder. "Not now, Isla. But fear not, you will see it all close up soon enough."

I know how she feels, I want to run to the window and get

a good look, but I know I must stay here by Tharin's side. Tharin takes my hand and leads us into the room. The crowd goes quiet, turning to regard us. I wonder what they've been told. I catch Charlotte's eye, and she opens her hands to me as though to say, "What the hell happened?"

Ethos notices Tharin then. He begins clapping his large hands. "Very clever, brother," he says, walking down the stairs from the raised area and heading towards us. I move closer to Tharin, and he places a protective arm around my shoulders.

"Very clever indeed to arrange for us to land in a place you know you are adored," Ethos continues.

"I wouldn't have had to," Tharin replies in his strong, deep voice, "if you had not arranged to have defenders waiting for us in the city, no doubt ready to imprison us."

Ethos raises an eyebrow. "What *are* you talking about?"

"Don't pretend you don't know," I say, unable to help myself. Tharin squeezes my hand and shakes his head slightly. Maybe he thinks it's not my place to say such things. But his brother imprisoned me and took me away from my daughter.

"This is not your battle to fight, human," Ethos snaps. "Skarsdon ways are very different from earthly ways. You cannot begin to fathom them."

"So betrayal and treachery towards one's own family is acceptable here?" I snap back.

"You go, girl," I hear Charlotte shout out.

"You are making many assumptions," Ethos says, cold eyes drilling into me. "There are many Obrotheans who would gain much from Tharin's demise." He turns his gaze towards me. "The demise of some humans too. My brother would do well to remember that before accusing his own family."

Tharin shakes his head in disgust. "Your lying knows no

bounds, Ethos. Be careful, or it will get you killed one day," he adds, caressing the hilt of his sword.

Ethos gives him a hard look and turns to the crowds. "We must get ready to disembark. There is much to organize now our plans have changed," he adds bitterly and then strides out of the room with two of his sage brothers. While Remus and Kiah remain behind, I notice Heldran seems conflicted, watching as his twin walks away. Then he looks over at Tharin and sighs, leaving the stage with Remus and Kiah to join Tharin. It must be difficult for Heldran to take a different path from his twin brother—a path that includes me, a woman he clearly isn't sure about. I realize then how brave Remus is to choose to side with the warriors instead of his sage brothers.

Tharin nods at his three brothers, clearly grateful, then he fixes a smile on his face and looks down at Isla. "Would you like to go on my shoulders to get a better view?" he asks her.

"Yes, *please!*" she exclaims. He scoops her up onto his huge shoulders, and she giggles as we head towards the windows. The women and children part for us, regarding Tharin with fascination and whispering as they look at me. When we get to the front, I take in the land below and let out a gasp. It is rich with color. To the right are golden mountains that hardly look real, and to the left, a vast, sprawling purple forest. Intersecting across them both are jagged green scars that are just like the kinds of ruptures you might see after an earthquake, some large enough to create valleys in amongst the mountains and harsh green trails in the forest floor. I stand on my tiptoes as a large purple sphere glistening atop a tall mountain closest to the forest comes into view.

"Is that your mother's palace?" I ask Tharin.

He nods. "We'll stay there."

"It's so pretty," Isla whispers.

I take her hand. "It is, isn't it?" We're silent as the vessel glides over the golden mountains, casting a huge oval shadow over the land. Eventually, a clearing comes into view between two mountains, not far from the palace. I'm shocked to see crowds below, staring up at the vessel with joy on their faces.

Tharin squeezes my hand. "Let's go."

I let him lead us to the back of the hall and into a larger hall. Ethos and the two other sage brothers are already standing at one end before a vast golden wall. Tharin and the rest of us take our place at the other end. The vessel touches down with a shudder, and the golden wall before us disintegrates to reveal the huge crowd waiting before us. Among them are many defenders who stand in their bronze armor, beating long spears against the ground in unison to make a loud throbbing beat. There are scribes too, and religious sages holding their arms up in prayer. There are normal people as well. Well, as normal as seven-foot beings with oscillating skin can be. They're all wearing plain bronze clothes and are a mixture of golden and dark haired. We've landed in what looks like a massive sandpit surrounded on all sides by those vivid gold mountains. They really are gold and sparkle in the sunlight.

"Mommy, look!" Isla shouts, tugging at my hand. "Look at the sun!" I peer up to see a sun the same size as ours but more red in color and fringed with neon green.

"You should see our three moons," Tharin whispers to her.

"I can't wait," she says, clapping her hands in excitement.

I shake my head. Am I really here on a new planet, in a completely different solar system from the one I know? I breathe in the air. It smells like it does on Earth before a storm. There's also a sweet musky smell too, like Tharin. A set of golden stairs are rolled to the front of the vessel. Ethos steps forward, and the crowd goes silent. The dislike they feel for him is clear. But as Tharin takes steps forward, a massive, almost deafening cheer rings out around the pit.

My God, they love him.

Will they love me though? Just how many of these beings know about the role I played in the death of what must have been two beloved women? I try to find the hatred in their eyes as they regard me, but all I see is intense curiosity.

"Why are they cheering?" Isla shouts above the noise.

"Tharin's a hero, remember?" I say, feeling intense pride as I say that.

She smiles and looks up at him. I do too. He looks like a god up here, a giant among men. There is emotion in his green eyes, sadness too. It must be difficult coming here with all his memories of his mother and the circumstances in which we find ourselves now. I squeeze his hand, and he looks down at me, face softening.

"Now do you feel protected?" he asks, gesturing to the huge defenders standing in the crowd before us.

"Yes," I say. "Mainly because of you though."

He smiles, pride in his own green eyes. "Good, because you should." He narrows his eyes at Ethos, who is now talking into some kind of circular instrument—maybe their version of mobile phones?

"Where will Ethos and your two other brothers go?" I ask Tharin.

"To the city," Tharin says. "Where he has the most support."

"And your father?" I ask gently.

"He will stay with us in the Globe Palace of course. I can't trust Ethos with him. I have arranged for the specialist heart healer to be there waiting for him." As he says that, Remus comes to join us, Kiah and Heldran too, their three Pledged women and Sacred children with them. I'm shocked to realize that Louisa, the Irish redhead, is with Remus, who stands with his hand on the shoulder of their red-headed son. She never mentioned anything about being pledged to a prince, but then I didn't at first. Heldran's Pledged is a tall black woman who looks tired and bored. Their son is in awe of the crowds. The woman standing with Kiah is a very beautiful Chinese woman with thick black hair in a bob and red lips. Their child is equally as gorgeous, a small girl who smiles shyly at Isla. I realize the girl is much younger than the other children, maybe only four or five. A thought occurs to me then. Did they do a special trip back to Earth for the youngest highborn son? Kiah would have been barely a teenager ten years ago.

As they join us, more Primes and their families go to stand behind Tharin, at least two thirds of the vessel's occupants. I'm pleased to see Helena and Charlotte among them beside a warrior with a long plait of white hair down his back.

"I hope you have lots of room in the palace?" Kiah says when he gets to us. "It seems your support is even greater than we thought."

I can see Tharin's trying not to show too much emotion, but his green eyes give him away as they beam with pride and happiness. "There are over a hundred suites. That will be plenty."

"Wait a minute," Isla says. "A hundred suites? How *big* is this place?"

"You'll see," Tharin says with a chuckle.

"How are we getting there?" I look around for any sign of transport.

He gestures to our right, and I let out a gasp. Several huge elephant-like creatures are being led towards the vessel by defenders. I say elephants because they have trunks like an elephant. Yes, *trunks,* two of them curling majestically into the air. They are double the size of the elephants on Earth, and they have Obrothean skin that fluctuates between pink, blue, and yellow. They are magnificent and "wows" echo around us from the human children.

"They're called tuskians," Kiah explains to his daughter. "Disobedient beasts most of the time, but magnificently violent in war. We have vessels to transport us too but the use of tuskians is a Highborn tradition."

The platform beneath our feet begins to move towards the tuskians. Isla giggles, holding Tharin's arm as we are raised high enough to be able to get onto the first of the beasts. Its top is shrouded with a golden saddle. Tharin lifts Isla onto it first, then me before he smoothly jumps onto its back. I wrap my arms around Isla, and Tharin wraps his arm around me. Then he lifts some golden reins and whispers something into the tuskian's ear. The tuskian responds, moving through the crowds. The people around us cheer, and some reach up to touch Tharin's feet. As we leave the landing area, we enter a path that winds up through the mountains. Small, sphere-like buildings jut out of them, and as we pass, people come out and wave in delight at Tharin, their hero. There are children among them, and it's good to see them looking happy and healthy. I feel Tharin's arms tighten around me, protecting me as I lean my head back against his chest.

I still can't quite believe this is happening. Exactly this time four days ago, I was dropping Isla off at her dance class before going food shopping. And now here I am dressed in gold and being transported by alien elephants through the mesmerizing landscape of another planet.

Not just that. I'm really falling for Tharin. From being dead set against him, I now can't imagine being without him, especially not here on this strange planet. As I think that, the Globe Palace, a vast sphere that fluctuates with color comes into view. It's set on the top of a mountain like a snow globe.

"The Globe Palace," Tharin says, emotion in his voice. "It was once part of Fostinia. When my father invaded over thirty years ago, he insisted on claiming it as part of Skarsdon."

"That must be a sore point for the Fostinians," I say. *No wonder they invaded Skarsdon ten years ago,* I want to add but don't. It's what took his mother and sister from him, after all.

Tharin nods. "I think he claimed the palace for my mother. While he never allowed Mother to step foot back into Fostinia, she was allowed in the Globe Palace after it was officially made part of Skarsdon. From there, she had views of Fostinia."

"Why wouldn't he allow her to return to her homeland?"

"He is a possessive man, Kate. He did not want her pining for the life she once had without him."

I think of my own pining for Earth. Isn't Tharin keeping me from my home, as his father did? I have to hope he is different from his father. Maybe there's hope one day he will allow me to return? He indicated he might but do I really believe that?

"Not that she listened to him, of course," Tharin adds with a small chuckle. "She would secretly take us into Fostinia when he was away and we stayed at the Globe Palace."

The tuskian carries us up the steep mountain in front of the long line of Tharin's supporters from the vessel, and more crowds come out to see their great First Defender. As we get higher, I catch more glimpses of the huge tangled forest on the other side with trees such a vivid purple, they don't seem real. When we come to a stop at the front of the palace, I'm unable to believe my eyes. The way the palace hovers right on top of the jagged golden mountain makes it almost feel like it might roll and topple over us. It looks like a giant marble swirling with color.

Tharin kisses the top of my head and jumps off the

tuskian. A section of the globe in front of us dissolves, and several men and women file out of it. They're all dark-haired. Fostinians, I presume. But they're wearing the bronze of Skarsdon. I also notice three healers among them, led by a female healer who is wearing a more ornate outfit than the others. A small vessel suddenly appears and lands nearby. The healers approach as the vessel's doors open, and the Grand Sovran is carried out by four defenders on a golden stretcher. It's strange to see him lying there, covered by a golden shroud. Pale and still. I glance at Tharin who frowns, his eyes filling with tears. This must be hard for him. I squeeze his hand as his father is taken into the palace. When he disappears from sight, Tharin helps me and Isla down, and the tuskian is instantly led away by one of the Fostinians. Behind us, Tharin's supporters come to a stop too. It must have taken courage to openly defy a man such as Ethos. I catch Charlotte's eye and smile. I'm pleased she's among them.

Tharin walks towards a beautiful Fostinian woman with plaited brown hair down her back. She looks to be about fifty. "Welcome, sire," she says, inclining her head. I notice her gaze catch on me. She won't have seen a human in the flesh before. Then she turns to Isla, her curiosity even more noticeable.

"Jerelda," Tharin says to her, "each Highborn and his Pledged are to be placed in a suite with their Sacred child. You can decide where. But my brothers Remus and Kiah will have their usual suites. Naturally, Kate and Isla will be with me."

"Of course, sire," the woman says. She looks at me again then turns to the other Fostinians, barking some orders. They scurry towards the others.

"Can you make sure Helena and Charlotte are near us?" I whisper to Tharin. "They're my friends."

He follows my gaze towards the two sisters and frowns. "The human princess and…the witch?"

I can't help but smile. So Charlotte's plan of getting them all to think she is a witch has worked. "She's harmless," I say. "Isla really gets on with Henry too."

"*Please?*" Isla begs, putting her palms together in a begging gesture as she peers up at Tharin with her big green eyes.

He smiles. "How can I say no to you two?" He beckons one of the Fostinians over and instructs them to move Helena, Charlotte, and Henry into the suite below us with Helena's Pledged. Then he turns to his supporters. "You will each receive your own suite, and meals will be taken in the grand hall or in your suite, if you prefer. Just let your attendants know. Men, we will convene in the battle rooms as soon as you have settled. We have much to discuss."

"Men?" I ask. "Don't you think this affects us women too?"

"Yes, it does, Kate. But for now, I need to talk to those among us who are used to our ways and know our politics." He takes my hand. "Come, see inside. You'll love it."

We follow him up some golden stairs and gasp. It's truly like we're standing in a globe. We have views of the outside from every direction of the spherical hallway we're standing in, the mountains to the right and the vast forest to the left.

"The palace is created out of several globes within each other, like a circular Russian doll," Tharin explains. "This hallway is at the center with ten more layers around it."

"How come we can see everything outside if there are other layers around us?" Isla asks.

"What you're seeing is a projection of the view outside," Tharin explains to her. "But we occupy the outer level, so our views are real."

He leads us to the back of the hallway and presses his

palm against it. The wall dissolves, and we walk into a circular golden lift. He presses one of the weird symbols on a pad on the wall, and the lift shoots upwards. Isla giggles as it comes to an abrupt stop. Tharin places his palm against the wall again, and it dissolves, revealing a large living area. "Here we are," he says.

We follow Tharin into a vast curved space with seating areas, tables, and shelves. There's a softness here that speaks of a woman's touch. Golden fur throws are draped across the purple ornate chairs and thick black rugs adorn the misty floors. A mixture of Skarsdon and Fostinia. Isla clearly thinks it's beautiful, and she hurries around, touching and sniffing everything. There are several telescopes dotted around too, positioned to look at the skies beyond. There are also book-shelves filled with scientific tomes featuring pictures of planets and stars I don't recognize. Has Tharin arranged for them to all be placed here for me?

I take Tharin's hand, and he smiles down at me. "Do you like it?"

"It's beautiful." I can see in his eyes he's distracted though. I know his brothers and the other men will be keen for his attention. He gives me a soft, drawn-out kiss. "I'll be back later. But anything you want, anything at all, ask Jerelda." As he says that, the Fostinian woman he spoke to earlier appears. She inclines her head at me.

"Hello, Jerelda," I say, feeling strange greeting someone who is essentially my maid.

Tharin smiles at Isla. "Her first task can be to show you your room, Isla. Of course, I was not aware we would be coming here, but it is the room I had as a child, so I think you'll like it. Jerelda, Kate and I will have my mother's old room."

My body fizzes at the thought of spending another night with him, this time on this beautiful planet. Tharin gives me another quick kiss before walking through the space Jerelda just came through.

Isla looks up at me, raising an eyebrow. "He *kissed* you."

My face flushes. It feels so natural that I didn't even consider Isla might wonder what the hell's going on. "Yes, darling. About that—"

She smiles. "It's cool. I like him."

I smile. Kids can be so smart, sometimes.

She turns to Jerelda. "Can I see my room now, please?"

"Of course," Jerelda says, smiling.

"Is there a kitchen where I can make us some food?" I ask.

"Nonsense," Jerelda scolds. "You are the First Defender's Pledged. You will never have to cook again."

"Oh." I rather enjoy cooking when I have the time, but from the look on this woman's face, the idea I might want to cook myself is a form of blasphemy.

"First to your room, little warrior," Jerelda says to Isla, "and then food. I will arrange for a cold platter to be placed in the dining area for you."

Warrior. Why do these people seem to think my daughter is a warrior?

I look around the vast area. "Is there any way of contacting the other human women?" I ask.

"Of course. I can pass any messages on."

"No, I mean can I call them or anything? I saw one of the brothers use some kind of communication device."

Jerelda gives me a pinched look. "I've not been told that's allowed."

I frown. Is it because of the video I sent ten years ago? Does she know about it? I do sense a coldness in her attitude to me.

"As I said, I can pass on a message," Jerelda repeats. "Who would you like the message to be passed to?"

"There are two British sisters," I say. "Helena and Charlotte. And an Irish redheaded woman called Louisa. Oh, and an Australian called Anaya. Maybe they'd like to join us for something to eat while the men are occupied. It'll be good for Isla to see the other kids."

Jerelda inclines her head. "Of course."

"You really are enjoying all the benefits of being the First Defender's Pledged, aren't you?" Helena says.

We're standing in what is to be mine and Tharin's large bedroom with Helena, Charlotte, Louisa, and Anaya. The kids chase each other around the vast hallway outside. The bedroom *is* huge, with a large window offering views of the forest. *Real* views seeing as it's the outer layer of the sphere. On a raised platform in the middle of the curved oblong room is a misty bed, the four posters around it made from ornately curved purple wood. The floor is covered with thick white and golden furs, the mist rising through them. There is a huge bookshelf to one side of the room with two large chairs and a massive telescope.

"Um, Helena, your room is huge too," Charlotte says. "I've been confined to a bloody kids room tucked into the corner. Even Henry's is bigger than mine."

"Well, he is a Sacred child," Helena huffs.

"It's very nice, Kate," Louisa says. "The wood they've used for the bed posters is pretty."

"Perfect for hanging on to while the First Defender bangs you," Anaya adds.

I can't help but laugh as Louisa blushes.

"The wood must be from the forest," Charlotte says, going to the window and looking out. "I mean, have you seen *anything* like it? What I'd give to go explore with my bow and arrow."

"Not that you'd shoot anything other than the trees," Helena says with an eye roll. "Charlotte hates having to shoot any deer when we go hunting with the royal family," Helena explains to me.

Charlotte ignores her, turning to Louisa. "What about you, Louisa? You kept your prince Pledged a secret. Have you got a huge room too?"

"It's not as big as this," she says.

"Can we eat?" Anaya asks. "I'm starving. The kids might have demolished our food by now."

I smile, and we walk out of the room towards the large dining area. It's double the length of the bedroom, with a large floating purple wooden table and benches in the middle, and white globe lights hanging above it. A delicious looking cold buffet has been laid out with breads and what looks like cheeses and meats, plus the usual strange vegetables and fruit. We each sit down, the children having too much fun exploring to join us, which is just as well, as it isn't long before the subject becomes *way* too inappropriate for them.

"So you were locked away in Tharin's rooms overnight," Anaya says, slathering some buttery substance on her bread. "How was that?" she asks, wiggling her eyebrows.

I avert my eyes, pretending to focus on buttering my own bread. "It was fine. We were safe, and that's what counts."

"Did you get much *sleep*?" Helena asks, her blue eyes drilling into mine.

"Helena, leave her alone,' Charlotte says. Then she turns to me, her eyes sparkling. "But *did* you get much sleep?"

I flick one of the strange see-through napkins at her. "None of your business."

"So you *have* done the deed," Anaya says.

"Actually, no. Not yet."

189

"I bet he's a demon in bed," Anaya says. "A proper alpha."

"It's not all about sex, Anaya," Louisa reprimands. "Remus and I have not even kissed yet. We're trying to make a connection first."

Anaya laughs. "You keep telling yourself that. I mean, it's *clear* the guy is gay."

Louisa scowls at her. "As long as he's kind, I don't care."

"What about you?" Anaya asks Helena. "Please tell me you've had a little fun with the white-haired Persean," she says, referring to Helena's Prime. "I mean, how *old* is he? He looks about fifty."

"Old enough to own a huge chunk of land on this strange planet," Helena says, gesturing out of the window. "That will do me. And, yes, maybe we have dabbled a little bit, not that that's *any* of your business."

"I bet you're jealous of Louisa and Kate," Anaya says, clearly enjoying goading Helena. "Both of them are with princes, when you've left yours behind on Earth."

Helena's eyes flash with anger. "I'd rather a rich lord than a brutal First Defender."

I give her a look. "You've changed your tune. Anyway, Tharin gives the impression of being a cold-hearted warrior prince, but he's really a softie. And the way he is with Isla is just the cutest. I never thought I'd say this, but I actually feel safe with him. Safer than I ever have with anyone."

Helena laughs. "Safe? Are you joking? These beings have plucked us from the true safety of our planet and brought us to this savage world." She gestures to the forest outside. "You realize the Grand Sovran stole his second wife from Fostinia? *Killed* her first husband and her parents. He was about to execute her before he decided to keep her alive at the last minute and make her his wife."

I frown. Tharin never told me that bit. "Really?"

Louisa nods. "Helena is right, I read it one of the books. When the Fostinians tried to rise up against him thirty-one years ago, the Grand Sovran went into their settlements and kidnapped the warriors' children and wives, turning them into the slaves we see today."

"Slaves that Tharin fought to emancipate," I say. "Look, I get what you're saying. I feel the same at times. But we need to remember they are a different species from us. They have a whole different way of living and of thinking. I truly think Tharin is trying to change things. He changed the pronouncement about Highborns being exempt from crimes like rape, didn't he? I think he'll make a great Grand Sovran when the time comes."

"Wow," Charlotte says, smiling. "You really do like him, don't you?"

"Yes, I do," I admit.

She places her hand over mine. "I'm pleased for you," she says. "Really. Just remember what Helena said though. You can never really say for sure that you're safe with him, Kate. Not here on a planet like this."

"*Especially* with Tharin the First Defender," Helena says with a raised eyebrow, "the man who is, according to the history books, the most vicious warrior this planet has ever seen. The man who even killed his own brother, Ryker."

"Oh, leave it, Helena," Charlotte says. "You were only telling me the other day how hot you think Tharin is. Anyway, can you really blame Tharin for killing Ryker? He did start the invasion that killed his mother and sister."

I look down at my splayed hands on the table. *And I made the video that propelled him to.* "Look, guys," I say. "I'm not going to deny I've fallen for Tharin big time, but Isla always comes first. Even when my heart is telling me to go a hundred and ten percent in, rest assured I listen to my head too. I'm aways cautious, for Isla's sake. I wouldn't just throw myself into this without thinking."

"Good," Charlotte says. But her sister doesn't seem convinced, giving me a skeptical look.

"Wow, ladies, look," Louisa says, pointing out of the window. I see the kids have stopped running around too, their mouths open as they stare out of the windows. Three moons are beginning to appear in the darkening skies. One very large one, and two small ones overlapping each other. Though they omit a silvery light like our moon, the largest of them is circled with the very same neon green that scars this planet and circles the sun too.

It is all so beautiful but also so very, very different. I realize in that moment just how little we know of this planet, and quite honestly, how out of depth we are. I've stupidly allowed the excitement of setting foot on a new planet and the time I have spent with Tharin to cloud my judgment. I *must* remain vigilant.

SEVENTEEN

Tharin

I look at the men crowded into our battle room. From here, we can just about see the training camp where most of us once trained together. I may have seen many wars in my thirty years, but the battle that is on the horizon will be my most important, for this time, Kate and Isla are here in Obrothea too.

"First, let me express my how grateful and proud I am to see so many of you here," I begin as I look at each of the men. "To risk the wrath of Ethos and his supporters... Your loyalty means everything to me."

The men bang their fists on the table.

"Though lines have been drawn," I continue, "lines that divide us here at the Globe Palace from Ethos in Skarsdon City, they are not yet battle lines."

"You are right," one of the men says. He is a tall, broad-shouldered man called Persean, who is pledged to Kate's friend, Helena. He is a good man. As a child, my brothers and I spent time on his family's sprawling estate not far from here. "But when word gets out about what happened to you, Tharin," Persean continues, "the people will rise up."

"We do not know yet who was responsible for attacking Tharin," Heldran cautions.

"Surely it was Ethos," Kiah says. "It may not have been his hand that plunged in the dagger, but he was the puppeteer."

"There is no proof," Heldran says.

I examine my brother's wary face. I know it has been hard on him to turn his back on his twin, Tygrve. They are close, despite the different routes they have chosen. I also know it's hard for him to trust Kate. For a while, he truly believed she had betrayed us on purpose. But I had hoped I convinced him it was just an error on her part. His history with women makes it difficult for him to trust any of them. It is not Kate's fault. Though he is scarred and gruff, he is as ruled by his emotions when it comes to women as I find myself being ruled when it comes to Kate. His heart was once broken. It was hard for him to come back from that.

I nod at him now. "Heldran is right. I have learnt lately how important it is to gather evidence first before jumping to conclusions."

"Is this something you have learnt from your Pledged?" Persean teases. "Helena told me Kate was angry after you killed the rapist without a trial."

"Yes, Kate has certainly been showing me some of the benefits of the earthly judicial system," I admit.

"I bet they are not the only benefits she has been showing you," Kiah remarks, and the others laugh. "These human women cannot get enough of our cocks, and I bet she is even more insatiable with you."

"You will not talk of my Pledged like that, Kiah." I slam my fist onto the table. Kiah clamps his mouth shut, and the other men grow quiet.

"Sorry, Tharin," Kiah says, lowering his head. "I did not mean to disrespect your Pledged."

"I told you, he is like a puppy dog around her," Persean says, rolling his eyes.

"Be careful, Tharin," Heldran says. "Remember what happened ten years ago. Are you sure you can trust her?"

Some of the men around us look confused. Not many know of that video Kate made.

I resist the urge to slam my fist into the table again, giving Heldran a warning look. "Of course I trust her."

"But what if the rumors of her conspiring with Ryker are true?" Heldran says.

The confused expressions on the men's faces turn to shock. Damn Heldran for saying all this in front of them. I give him a look which I hope shows my displeasure.

"You will not question the sincerity of my Pledged," I say in a loud, firm voice to Heldran, "or this puppy dog will turn into a wolf, you hear me?" They all quickly nod as Heldran bows his head. "Anyway, that is not what we are here to discuss." I pace around the room as I think. "If it is indeed Ethos who arranged the attack on me, we need proof. The idea of a Highborn trying to kill another, let alone his brother and future heir to the throne while Skarsdon's leader lays unconscious, will be enough to drain any support he has." I turn to Remus. "Remus and Persean, you will lead a team focused on gathering intelligence regarding what happened on the vessel." Remus nods. "And Kiah and Heldran, your jobs are to prepare for any form of battle. I will help you. We can visit the training camp and the local settlements. See who we can rally to our cause if it is needed. Regardless of whether Ethos is behind all this or not, someone is, and we need to be ready to face whoever is responsible when the time comes." I swallow, thinking of my father being treated by his healers. "And my father, when he wakes, can rest knowing all is in hand."

The men begin thumping their fists on the table again. As they do, I peer towards the forest where I tracked Ryker down ten years ago and thrust my sword into him. A small thought occurs to me. What if I'm wrong about Kate? What if she really was conspiring with Ryker as revenge for taking human women from their beds in the night? Maybe she learnt of our plans to get the women pregnant with hybrid children we would one day seek to turn into an army? I trample that thought away. I must trust her.

Kate

Tharin doesn't return until the early hours. When he does, he sinks into bed and reaches for me. I turn to him and see how exhausted he looks.

"Are you okay?" I whisper.

"I'm fine now I'm with you."

"How's your father?"

"Still unconscious. But let us not talk of sad things." He presses himself against me, and I realize he's naked. A thrill of desire threads through me, and I reach for his huge, hard cock. His hand glides up my thighs and cups my sex, his fingers pushing into me. He kisses me with urgency, and I kiss him back, tangling my fingers in his long hair.

I want him inside me. The thought scorches its way into my sleepy mind, and I go to whisper it into Tharin's ear but then pause. I don't have any contraception, and I *don't* want to get pregnant, not right now. Surely they have some kind of contraception here? But how can I bring it up with Tharin without ruining the moment? I just have to resist him…for now.

So I turn my back on him, but all that does is make his cock nudge hard against my back. He moves his hand around to cup my breasts and plays with my nipples as I lean against him, moaning. The skirt of my nightgown rides up, and it would take just a small movement for him to slip into me.

"I want you," he whispers.

"I want you too," I reply. "But I don't want to get pregnant. It just doesn't feel right."

He moves away from me. "It doesn't feel right, having another child with me?"

I turn to face him. He looks wounded, so I kiss his stiff jaw. "You make it sound horrible. I don't mean it as an insult, but I don't want to get pregnant when I'm still trying to wrap my head around what's happened to me. Can you understand that?"

He sighs, twisting a lock of my hair around his finger. "I understand. I can arrange for Jerelda to bring you a special tea each morning to stop you falling pregnant." He sighs. "But it can take three days to work."

"Well, there is other stuff we can do in the meantime." I kiss him on the lips and begin moving my hand up and down his shaft as he caresses my nipples.

"God, I've missed you, Kate," he says in a husky voice.

"I've missed you too," I whisper, my hand moving faster, the sound of his moans in my ear making me wet. He kisses my neck, my collarbone, his breath growing shallow as I use the pre-come squeezing from his tip to help my hand glide even faster over his cock. He reaches down and finds the nub of my clitoris as his lips circle my nipple, sucking and pulling until it's as hard as a pebble.

I feel an orgasm building and can tell he's feeling the same. Eventually, he lets out a gasp, and his warm rainbow-colored seed spills over my hands as I feel my own contractions begin.

Over the next couple of nights, the routine is similar. Tharin disappears all day and returns in the night for us to steal sweet touches and kisses, no more until the herb takes effect. Though Charlotte and the others sometimes come over, and Castian often stays to chat after he brings Isla back from her day of learning, there are periods when I'm alone. I can't help but wonder: if this is how my life will be from now on, waiting for my "husband" to return at night from his heroic duties?

Isla's lucky. She's being taught all sorts of fascinating things by Castian as part of her tutoring in the classroom set up for the kids. But I'm not even allowed to go out and explore. This is a different planet in a different solar system. The frustration at not even being able to see it properly is intense. Tharin says things are too unstable at the moment, that I must stay safe inside. Part of me wonders if it's more about trust. I did send a video that led to the region's invasion, after all. Does he really trust me?

I consider just going out for a walk anyway. I'm not some pretty little kept creature like the birds in the strange aviary on the first level. Then I remind myself that I have no idea what I'm dealing with out there.

One day, Remus pops by to speak to Tharin. "He's still out," I say. "He's *always* out."

He frowns. "Are you okay, Kate?"

I sigh. "Just, you know, *bored.* I was like Castian once, teaching all day, every day. It could be a pain in the butt sometimes, but I *miss* it. I wish I could help teach the kids here."

"You do not know enough of our history and our ways, Kate." He tilts his head and smiles. "Maybe it's time *you* did some learning. Look around you," he says, gesturing to the bookshelves nearby. "Our mother was a vivacious reader and acquired many wonderful books, especially on the subject of space and astronomy. You should read, learn."

"I have been reading." I gesture to the golden reading glasses on my head that are keeping my hair out of the way. "But I need more than that."

"Then set yourself a task," he says, going to a nearby desk. "Use her writing sets to map stars you didn't know about. Tharin tells me you once did that as a child. We could arrange to get them published. Imagine, the Pledged of the great First Defender Tharin providing beautiful maps of our stars for the people of Obrothea."

I walk over and look at the paper he's gesturing to and the stunning set of unusual pens oscillating with color. "Maybe you're right."

"I am *always* right."

So that's what I end up doing. I focus on the telescopes, turning to them in the evenings to map the skies, creating star maps using Tharin's mother's beautiful calligraphy sets. On the third evening, I'm surprised to see Adin heading into the forest through my telescope. He peers over his shoulder to check nobody is looking and then walks in among the trees. What is he up to? I wonder about telling Tharin, but maybe Adin is like his mother and just misses his people. When Adin comes by to do his guarding duties the next morning, I show him the maps I've created. I haven't had a chance to show Tharin. We barely see one another.

Adin's green eyes spark with joy when he sees the maps. "You have a true talent, Kate."

"I have some *amazing* subject matter. I never dreamed I'd get to see a whole new solar system."

He strolls over and picks up a book I discovered earlier about the moons of this solar system. "Mother liked this one. Our father gave it to her."

"What was she like?"

"Sometimes strong, sometimes soft, sometimes happy, sometimes angry…like Tharin."

"That about sums him up," I say with a smile. "Did the Grand Sovran really kidnap her?"

Adin nods sadly. "Yes, over thirty years ago," he says. "Our grandfather, the Great King of Fostinia, made moves to claim more of the land they always argued over. So the Grand Sovran invaded Fostinia. He killed our grandparents, our father too, a great Fostinian warrior."

"I'm so sorry, Adin. How can you bear to be here, especially after what happened with Ryker as well?"

Adin shrugs. "It is in the past. At least the Grand Sovran saved our mother and spared us. He was planning to kill her, but when he saw her, he decided to take her for his wife."

"And you and your bother as his sons?"

Adin shakes his head. "We remained in Fostinia for many years."

"My God, that must have been horrific for her and for you," I say. "To be parted from one another."

Adin nods, dropping his gaze from me. "She would never have allowed it, but she knew the Grand Sovran would slaughter us and more of her people if she fought too hard. She also knew our uncle would care for us. Anyway," he says, lowering his voice as his eyes sparkle, "she'd sometimes find ways to sneak back to see us."

Sneak back…like Adin did into the forest the night before? I go to the recent history books and flick through them until I find a photo of Ryker. He's often depicted as a tall, dark-haired beast of a being striding through battlefields wielding a huge war hammer, his long brown hair and muscled chest bare and filthy with blood. "How did you and Ryker end up here then?" I ask.

"The Grand Sovran arranged for us to be trained at the Skarsdon training camp when I was thirteen and Ryker was fourteen. He saw our potential."

"How did you mother feel about that?"

"She was pleased. It meant seeing us more."

"But it meant thrusting you into battle."

"You do not understand, Kate. We were grateful to have the opportunity to train at our planet's most revered training camp."

"And what about Ryker? Was he proud?"

Adin goes stiff. "It never sat well on his shoulders. As the eldest of us, if the Grand Sovran had not invaded Fostinia all those years ago, Ryker would have been king of the region. He blamed the Grand Sovran for stripping it all away from him. But he also saw the chance to train at Obrothea's most lauded grounds with its most celebrated warriors as a chance he could not turn down."

"I heard he had an argument with the Grand Sovran and was banished?"

Adin nods sadly. "After Ryker helped Tharin kill the Gatikan king, he asked the Grand Sovran to grant us with some Fostinian land as reward, and also let our mother officially return to visit too. But the Grand Sovran refused. They argued, Ryker was his usual self, speaking rashly before thinking. The Grand Sovran banished him."

"But you stayed?" I ask. "Why?"

"Because I am not like my brother. I know invasions and counter invasions are the way of this world. Thrones are taken and taken again. It is like a game of Drango. It is all just a game. At least I could train in Skarsdon. I could live in relative luxury instead of in the creature-infested forest. I could be with my brothers...and my mother and Thesera."

"What was Thesera like?"

He smiles. "Mischievous. Clever. Though we were not related by blood, she treated Ryker and I like brothers."

"And yet his invasion led to her death."

"He would not have wanted that."

"How did it happen?"

Adin sighs. "I only came in during the aftermath. I was hunting in the next region. It took me hours to return after I learned of the invasion. When I did, I found the library they'd been in bombed. My mother was dead, and Thesera lay dying nearby."

"Oh God, it's all so awful."

The wall dissolves then, and Tharin walks through. He looks as beautiful as ever. His long blond hair is swept away from his face in a ponytail, and most of his chest is bare, apart from the shoulder armor he wears. I feel ridiculously excited as I look at him. He is back early. It seems such a long time since I've seen him in daylight.

He puts his hand out to me. "Come, let's get out of this palace."

EIGHTEEN

Tharin

I see from the way Kate's brown eyes light up that she is supremely happy for a chance to leave the palace. I have been feeling guilty for leaving her alone in my mother's Globe Palace, but it has been essential for her and Isla's safety. By securing the support of the defenders in this area, we have more chance of winning any battle that might come. I know Ethos and my other brothers will be doing all they can to do the same. So I must work harder, faster. Just a few days of this for a lifetime of happiness and security… Well, maybe not a lifetime, but as much as I can secure anyway. Skarsdon is never without some kind of trouble.

It's not just that though. I could tell from the questions posed by the men the past few days that some do not trust Kate after what Heldran said. He is contrite. He tells me he forgot not everyone knew. Maybe he is the one I cannot trust? But he has always been on my side, not to mention the time he saved my life when I stormed the Gatikan palace a few years back. I have to believe he would not purposely risk my Pledged's life. He is known for speaking before he thinks.

Either way, I can't risk a move being made to harm Kate as some form of misinformed revenge. I trust my men, but I do not trust all the people they speak to...nor the eyes that watch as Kate moves around the palace. Only a select few knew about that video. Heldran bringing it up means that "select few" has become many.

I try to drive all those thoughts away as I help Kate onto the tuskian that awaits us, enjoying the feel of her shapely behind in my hand as I do so. It has been difficult for me not to see her as much as I'd like. Our love is only beginning to blossom again, and yet I am away from her during the daylight hours. We have our nights though. Her tender moans and the wet, soft feel of her sating me is just enough. But I want to see her in the light too, to talk to her... and to feel my cock inside her, finally.

So now is our chance. I climb on top of the tuskian and wrap my arms around her from behind. She leans back against me, and I breathe in the smell of her shampoo. It is strange to smell this Skarsdonian scent on her, but it feels right somehow too. This is her home now. She is a Skars-donian in my eyes.

The tuskian begins walking lazily down the hill, treading a trail between the golden mountains. The sun shines above us, a blot of fierce red in sky. I point out the sights as we descend, like the path of purple herlecian trees.

"Wow, what are they?" she asks as we pass them. "Their blossoms are beautiful."

"Do not be deceived by their beauty," I say. "The blossoms on herlecian trees can be very dangerous. They may look beautiful, but one touch can have devastating consequences." I feel her shiver against me. "Surely you have such dangers in your world?" I ask.

"You're right," she replies. "I guess it's just strange to see it all so out in the open."

As we begin to ascend one of the golden mountains, pretty enty birds soar through the skies above us, their soft pink feathers merging with the purple clouds.

"They're so pretty," she whispers. "Like mini flamingos."

I spot a huge kravray in the distance and point to it, delighted to be graced with such a creature. "Watch this!" I say to Kate, slowing our tuskian down. The kravray swoops towards one of the smaller enty and snatches it into its mouth. "We call them the sharks of the sky. It is magnificent, is it not?"

"Oh," Kate says, frowning. "I'm not sure I'd say magnificent."

I smile at her fragility. Surely she knows of the food chain. It is the only way the ecosystem survives. Even the luminous stident fungus that grows in the forest and by the lakes plays their part.

As we near the top half of the mountain, the tuskian begins to struggle. The trail here is steep and risky. The tuskian's grand claws knock golden rocks down to the rocky terrain below. Kate watches with wide eyes, clutching my arms which remain around her waist tightly. I know she is brave, but there are times like this when I see her fear and it makes me proud that I can protect her. As we turn a corner, the ancient cave at the top comes into view. It sits like a golden hood, shrouding the darkness within. We draw closer, and the darkness within lights up, the acrenium rocks that line its inner walls igniting at my presence. My own skin throbs a colorful response, and Kate takes it all in, wide-eyed.

"It's beautiful," she whispers.

I smile down at her. "Like you."

The tuskian comes to a stop, and I jump off with ease and reach up to help Kate off. As I lower her to the ground, she kisses my mouth, and my cock stirs in response. She pats my tuskian and smiles.

"They're such amazing creatures. They're a lot like our elephants. I remember taking Isla to the zoo last year, and an elephant snorted water at her through his trunk. She loved it."

I laugh. "No fear of tuskians doing such things. They're scared of water. It was a problem when we fought in Gatika, where there is a great deal of water. But enough of those fickle beasts. Look at the view."

She turns, taking in the golden mountains of Skarsdon spread out before us, their crescents tinged red by the setting sun. "There's the city," I say, pointing into the distance towards a huge conglomerate of tall golden and white buildings. I see she is thinking the same thing I am. That our enemies are there right now, plotting our demise. But I do not wish to think of that today. "Come," I say, taking her hand and leading her to the cave. I must duck to get in, but Kate walks in easily, smiling in wonder as she looks around her at the pulsing colors, like jewels in the walls.

"Isla will love it here," she says.

"I will bring her."

I spread out the fur I brought with me and take out the snacks and pemelonian juice I had packed for us.

"We're having a picnic?" Kate asks as she sits down on the fur.

"Pick nick?" I ask, confused.

She laughs. "It's where you bring food out in the open like this and eat outside."

"Ah," I say, laying all the food out. "Strange phrase. I like it. Yes, we are having a picnic. And I have good news too: my father has woken."

Kate clutches my hand. "That's great news, Tharin."

I smile as I remember seeing my father earlier, sitting up in bed and eating. "His healer is the best in the land. It seems she has bought my father more time. He is still weak but the healer is sure he will regain his strength in a matter of weeks."

I sit down, and she leans against my arm as I kiss her forehead. "I've missed you," I whisper into her ear.

"God, I've missed you too."

"Have you been well on your own in the palace? I hear your friends come to visit you and you have been reading a great deal."

She nods, her eyes excited. "Actually, I've been mapping the skies. Your brother Remus gave me the idea. I've been using your mother's pen set and papers."

"That is wonderful news. I'll have to see what you've done when we return."

"Definitely." She nibbles on a small piece of fruit, and I can't help grow even harder at the sight of her lips doing that. I take a breath.

No, this is about talking, Tharin. Connecting.

"See there?" I say, pointing to a gap in the mountains and a jagged, broken structure.

Kate nods. "Yes, I noticed that. What is it?"

"It's the remains of the great wall of Drango, which the game is named after. It was ruined during the Great War with Yarabion. And there," I say, pointing to the mountain ahead, one side of it hollow, "a vessel belonging to the Malrisians crashed into the side, killing all the ice warriors on board."

Kate's brow puckers. "How sad."

I laugh. "It's not sad. They were our enemies."

"But they still left families behind."

"That's true," I say with a sigh. "But they were also responsible for the deaths of thousands of Skarsdonians during the Ice Wars."

I feel her sigh against me. "So many wars," she says, taking a sip of her pemelonian juice. "It's so...unstable here."

"It's just the Obrothean way," I say matter-of-factly.

She peers up at me with her big brown eyes. "You say it like it isn't an awful thing, Tharin. You thrive on battle, but I'm not used to it."

"Please don't worry," I say, pulling her towards me and stroking her dark hair. "You will always be safe and protected here. There hasn't been a war for many years now. And even if there is one, our women are kept safe."

"Safe like your mother was? Your sister?"

I stiffen. Why is she talking of this now? "Please, let us not talk of sad things. I don't know why you wish to steer the subject into such deep waters."

She moves away from me. "But you were the one who brought up wars."

"That's different. It's part of our glorious history."

"Glorious? People die in wars. That isn't glorious."

"Skarsdon has lowest number of casualties in all history," I say. "The warrior spirit runs in our blood. Of all the races in Obrothea, it is the Skarsdonians who are the strongest, and Isla will be the strongest of them all. When she is ready for battle, you'll see what I mean." Kate moves even farther away from me, fire in her eyes. Oh ye Goddess Tsuki, what have I said?

"I will never let Isla go into battle," she exclaims.

"It will be her choice. Already I see her desire to battle."

She laughs bitterly. "Her desire to battle? She is a child."

"A child that comes from my blood, from the unique combination of our DNA. She is a warrior," I say proudly, because I am proud of my warrior daughter.

Kate sits up and crosses her arms, her raven hair dark against the sinking red sun, her eyes regal. "You can't make judgements like this so early about our child. She has to find her own path."

"You are so beautiful when you are angry," I say, feeling

my cock throb against my breeches. I go to her, but she pushes me away. I frown. "Oh, come now, Kate."

"No, Tharin, I'm trying to be serious."

I smile. "My cock is very serious too." I go to her and kneel with her, wrapping my arms around her stiff body. She resists at first, but it is not long before she sinks into my arms, moaning as I kiss her neck.

Kate

Tharin traces his lips down my neck, and despite the anger bubbling inside, the impact of his touch overwhelms me like a tidal wave. I watch as his head dips over my breasts, yanking the material of my top down to reveal them, his soft lips enclosing each of my nipples. Electric darts of sensation throb through me as he nibbles and licks. I wish he wouldn't distract me so much. I wonder if he does it on purpose, aware I'm growing angry? It works though, right? *Oh God, yes, it works,* I think as his hands nudge my knees apart and his fingers reach under my skirt to find my clitoris.

"So wet," he whispers against my nipple, "always so wet for me."

I reach up and place my hands on his cheeks, making him look into my eyes as he moves one huge finger inside me, then two. We hold each other's gaze, and I see how turned on he is from the way his skin flushes purple and how his breath quickens. It turns me on too, how a giant warrior like him can be made to react like this thanks to me, a little earthling. I dip my hand into the waistband of his pants and pull his huge cock out. *I made this happen,* I think as I feel it pulse. *Me.*

I want to feel him inside me. It's been three days since I started taking the strange tea Jerelda's been serving me each morning with a disproving look. Three days for it to take effect. I lean over to whisper in his ear, "I'm ready. I want you inside me."

He pauses. "You really want this, Kate?"

"Yes," I breathe, realizing I have never wanted anything more.

His green eyes flare with desire and mischief. "Are you sure?"

I moan in frustration. "Yes. Tharin, *please*."

"Say it again. Say *please* again," he asks, voice husky.

"*Please*, Tharin. Fuck me. *Seed* me."

A look of triumph crosses his beautiful face. His cheeks are flushed, and his green eyes are heavy with desire...and something else. Anger? Sadness? I don't get the chance to think too deeply about it, because he lifts me onto his lap and slowly slides me down his full length. First, the engorged head, then the rest, his eyes never leaving mine as he does so. I gasp, arching my back as he fills me up, the sensation at once familiar and unfamiliar.

Tharin presses his lips hard against mine, stifling a moan that's about to escape. He lifts me up off his cock again, his hands strong on my waist, and then thrusts me down onto him even harder this time, his arcism brushing against my clit. I straddle his waist even firmer with my thighs, trying to get as much of him inside me as I can as he circles his hips and grinds into me from below. The joint sensation of his cock and that airflow from his arcism drives me to the edge. It's not just that. It's the desire and emotion in his eyes too. It's as much of a turn on as the way his cock feels inside me.

But then his mind seems to go somewhere else and an angered expression crosses his face while he plunges into me, deeper this time, almost painfully. The walls of the cave respond, threading with red and navy blue among the purple. His movements grow even harder as he pummels into me and

I moan, that part of my brain worried about why he seems so damn angry muffled by the way his cock and his arcism are making me feel. He tangles his arms around me, his face close to mine, lips hard on mine as he circles his hips, crushing into me, forcing sensations to vibrate through me as I cry out in agony and ecstasy.

His movements grow even more urgent, and he suddenly swivels me around so I'm on all fours, looking out of the cave as he slides in and out of me from behind. I catch sight of the ravished wall in the distance. The unbelievable way he's making me feel battles with the sight of war, of death, of disaster before me.

"Kate!" he shouts. I feel his cock grow even huger inside me and then his hot liquid fills me as he cries out.

Tharin

Kate curls against me. She seems somber as she looks out at the view before us.

"What's wrong?" I ask, kissing her shoulder. "Did I hurt you?"

She smiles up at me. "No. Well, it was a bit ouchy at times. You are huge." I frown, and she laughs. "It was a good kind of ouchy, and trust me, there was a lot more ecstasy than ouchy."

I relax. "Good. My aim is to provide you with ecstasy daily."

She raises a dark eyebrow. "Daily?"

"Okay, twice, maybe thrice daily."

She laughs. "I look forward to it." She rests her cheek on my chest, her fingers tracing across it and stopping at a jagged scar. "What's this from?" she asks.

"Five years ago, when we stormed Gatika again. The Mad Prince did it." I frown at the memory. "I was foolish that day. I rushed into the Gatikan Palace without heeding the advice of Heldran, who only a few moments before reminded me of the prince's expertise in creating hazes to stupefy and slow."

"This prince sounds nasty."

"He is, and he's intent on getting revenge for me killing his father. That was why we were there. We heard rumors he was building an army, but this was no normal army. They were addled with a special concoction he'd created to make them stronger than ever." I shake my head at the memory. "We saw it ourselves as we fought those men on the black beaches of Gatika, their movements lightning quick, their usually green eyes blotted white." I do not add how it made my father hope even more that Ethos's experiments worked, for it would mean we might be able to match any army the Mad Prince formed with one of our own, created with our hybrid Sacred children.

"Is this army something I need to worry about?" Kate asks me.

"Not for now. I saw how unstable the haze made his soldiers too, meaning they were much easier to overcome than the Mad Prince hoped. Not a surprise considering the rumors of his own addiction to the concoctions he made."

"Was it the Mad Prince who did this?" Kate asks, fingering my scar.

I nod. "When I walked into the palace, I was over-whelmed by a strange haze, so overwhelmed the Mad Prince was able to attack me, driving his sword into my chest. But then Heldran came and fought him off."

"Heldran saved your life."

"Yes."

"I get the impression he doesn't like me."

I sigh. "Heldran is a complicated man, but he would never

hurt you. The fact is, I ran into that palace without heeding his warnings because I was still addled by grief and thoughts of you. I wasn't thinking straight. I was desperate to drive memories away with battle."

"That's so sad," Kate whispers, stroking my face. She then turns to regard the remains of the Skarsdon wall.

"Are you still troubled by our war-torn history?" I ask her.

She nods. "It's difficult not to be." She bites her lip and rests her chin on my chest as she peers up at me. It makes me want to take her all over again. Already I can feel my cock hardening.

"I just know how messed up tragedies can make people, you know?" she continues. "I mean, this Mad Prince, the death of his father probably made him that way."

"I don't know. He has always been a strange one, from what I've heard."

"Still, with so much death and destruction, there must be more than the fair share of deranged lunatics like him. And wounded warriors who rush into battle when they shouldn't."

I sigh. "You are right. I was wrong to do that. But since then, I have learnt to live with my pain."

"Have you though?"

"What do you mean?"

"Just now, when we were…making love. You seemed angry at times, sad."

I clench my jaw. "You were imagining it. I felt nothing but ecstasy." I make myself smile, but she does not seem convinced. Can I blame her? As much as I try to stave off the past and her role in it, it sits in the pit of me like coal. The anger and pain boils with the lust and turns into a poisonous, sickening broth. I realized that as I looked at Kate's face. It was why I had to turn her around. As beautiful and as mesmerizing as that face is to me, it is also the one that appears in the video that led to my mother's and sister's deaths. I stretch and sigh, keen to change the subject. "We must sadly return," I say. "But there is always tonight, when I return...if you won't be too ouchy?"

She smiles. "I look forward to it."

Kate is quiet as we head back. I know it is connected to the talk of war and death. I can see it worries her. I need to prove to her how powerful I am. How I can protect her and Isla. Obviously, I have not made that clear enough. It keeps me awake that night and Kate notices.

"Can't you sleep?" she asks in a sleepy voice.

"I'm too busy watching you. I am too busy," I add, gently kissing her lips, "thinking about how much I want to make love to you."

"Again? You're insatiable."

"Are you too sore?"

"Yes, but I don't mind." She wraps her small leg around mine, shifting herself even closer to me. I look into her eyes, trailing my fingers down her beautiful cheek as she reaches down, finding my cock and encircling it with her hand. She kisses my neck, my cheeks, my lips as she moves her hand up and down my shaft. What she's doing to me, the way she's touching me and looking at me... Nothing feels better.

I slide my cock into her. She moves slowly against me, the wet walls of her pussy traveling down the length of me. I feel my arcism latch on to her clitoris, and she moans, gyrating her hips in that special way I remember, circling as my cock grows huge and all encompassing.

This is what I have wanted for so long. To fill her up with my cock and my love. Not once do our eyes leave each other, and I know this is the way I should have fucked her earlier.

We move against each other, more intense, more urgent, until I can no longer stop myself. My seed bursts inside her, coming so hard I shake.

The look in her eyes is all I need to go to sleep. I just need to make sure that passion is mixed with a feeling of security too. The next morning, I do something I've never done before. I allow a Pledged into our training grounds. It will be a surprise for Kate. Isla knows though. Her eyes lit up in excitement when I whispered it to her. My brave warrior daughter.

As our tuskian takes us down the mountain, people come out to watch. Word spreads that the First Defender, his Pledged, and his Sacred child are out of the palace together. I can see it makes Kate uncomfortable. She is a strange being, but that's why I love her. Isla smiles though and waves. She is very much suited to the life of a future Grand Sovran. Pride swells inside me. I am sure once Kate sees our magnificent defenders, she will feel the same.

The training grounds come into view. They're made up of a vast circle squatting right on the edge of a dramatic cliff. Encircling it are viewing platforms and walkways accessing the quarters for the warriors who train here. At the top is a whole floor dedicated to our healers. We approach the vast gates of Skarsdon. They stretch high into the sky and are surrounded on each side by golden walls that protect the training camp. Only those with royal blood can pass. The technology weaved into the gates sense us and open automatically in our presence. "There will be a time," I whisper in Kate's ear, "when I have planted enough seed in you that the gates will recognize you too."

She looks at me in surprise. "What on earth are you talking about?"

"Because of the unique combination of our DNA, Ethos believes Fortifying will occur."

"Oh, yes. Actually I did hear something about that."

"It's rare, but Ethos is convinced it will happen for us due to our genetics. It occurs when enough of my seed sinks into you and your DNA begins to replicate my DNA."

"It doesn't sound medically safe," Kate says. "And it's a tad unethical for my DNA to be changed."

I laugh. What strange views she has. "Mine will change too from your secretions, and is Isla not the embodiment of this fortification?"

She shrugs. "I guess."

Our tuskian walks through the gates and comes to a stop in front of the camp. I jump off, lifting both Kate and Isla off too. We stride in, and I see my defenders are in the middle of the grounds already, going through their moves. What an impressive sight, the very best Skarsdon has to offer, the fiercest and most deadly male and female warriors on the planet. Isla watches with bright eyes.

"Are they training?" she asks in awe, gesturing to three children who are among the warriors.

I nod. "One day, you will be among them." Kate gives me a sharp look. "Only if your mother agrees," I quickly add.

"How old are they?" Isla whispers.

"They can begin to train from twelve, depending on their skills."

When our presence is noticed, all the defenders stop and form into a semi-circle, raising their swords in greeting and calling out my name. The battle scribes emerge from inside too.

"There are teachers here like Castian," Isla declares.

"Yes, they are here to teach the more strategic side of war, not to mention our great battle history. We train healers here too for battlefield healing."

"It's all so cool," Isla says.

I notice Kate is quiet, surveying the grounds with unreadable eyes. "It is impressive, isn't it?" I whisper to her.

She blinks slightly. "Yes, very."

"Is that blood?" Isla asks, noticing a patch of it on the ground below.

"Yes," I reply. "Blood is shed during training, but our healers are always at hand."

Kate stares at the blood, wide-eyed. Maybe it was a mistake bringing her here? No, when she sees them train, she will feel better. I lead her and Isla to a nearby viewing platform where food has been laid out for us. Isla tucks in, but Kate shakes her head, saying she is not hungry.

"Watch," I say. "See how strong these defenders are. They will fight to the death to protect you and Isla and any other children we may produce."

While Isla is fascinated, Kate flinches, turning away as one defender thrusts his sword into another. "I'm not sure Isla should be watching this," she says.

"Why not?" I say. "Each wound makes these defenders stronger. Defenders need to experience pain so they're not surprised when it comes in battle." Isla is a much more enthusiastic observer. "I cannot tell you the number of times I have been wounded. Look." I gesture to a scar on my arm. "My own brother Kiah did this when we were training, the little imp." I lift my armor to show her the scar left by the Mad Prince. "And this is from a sword being thrust right through me."

"Wow," Isla says, tracing her fingers over it.

"It's not wow," Kate says. "It's horrible."

I look at her in surprise. "You didn't think my scar was horrible yesterday."

She takes in a deep breath. "Not the scar itself, but the action that caused it. Jesus, Tharin, why did you bring us here?"

"To show you how strong the warriors who defend you are. I could see you were worried yesterday. I thought this would put your mind at ease. Clearly, I was wrong."

"Yes, you were wrong." She watches a healer run to tend to a young man who is writhing on the floor in pain. "I mean, how old is that kid? Fourteen? Fifteen? And you hope that will be Isla in less than three years?"

Isla frowns as she watches the boy.

"I did say only if you agree," I reply. "The earlier she begins her training, the more skilled she will be at avoiding being wounded. Can't you understand that? It is to protect her."

"You don't get it," Kate says. "My duty as a parent is to protect my child!"

"And so is mine, Kate," I say. "This is all for her, for you. All this training is to protect you both."

"But this isn't my idea of protecting my child," she shouts, and defenders turn to look.

I see Isla is also looking at us in alarm. I do not wish her to be upset. "Kate, lower your voice," I murmur.

She suddenly stands. "No, I will not lower my voice, and I will not put my daughter in danger like this. I will not do what my father did to me and my mother by dragging us to that commune." She grabs Isla's arm and pulls her away.

NINETEEN

Tharin

"The problem with human women," Kiah slurs, "is that they think they are clever. Best to stamp that confidence down." The other defenders at our table laugh, but Remus, who is quietly playing a board game with Castian nearby, rolls his eyes.

"Comments like that do not help me, brother," I say, downing more pemelonian. We are sitting in the great hall at the center of the globe while Kate sulks in our bedroom.

"Itsh true," Kiah says, hiccuping. "They have an answer for every argument." He turns to Adin, who is standing at the door, always on guard. "What do you think, Adin?"

"How would I know?" Adin says. "I will never know a human woman like you will."

I see he is desperate to go back upstairs and guard my quarters, but Kate refused to allow him, insisting she didn't want any warriors near her for the night. I think that includes me too. My shoulders sink. I had been looking forward to sinking my cock into her again and hearing her small moans of pleasure.

"I'm sure we can arrange it, Adin. It is time you lost your virginity," Heldran says. "I know of many Pledged human women who would be happy to taste your impressive cock."

"Our Pledged are not objects to be handed around," I say in disgust.

"Some like to be," Kiah retorts as Castian shakes his head in disapproval. "I'm jushhhtt stating a fact," he slurs. "My Pledged invited a friend to join us in bed. Her friend's Pledged told me he is exhausted with her insatiable needs, and I can tell you, brother, by the end of our session, so was I." The other men roar with laughter.

"I cannot figure Kate out," I say. "One moment she talks about feeling scared, then she grows angry when I dare to show her why she shouldn't be scared."

Remus smiles to himself.

"What?" I ask him. "What are you thinking?"

"I am thinking what an oaf you are," he says, "to think you can show a human woman we are a cuddly, protective, secure species by taking her to a blood-ridden training ground for warriors."

Of course, now he says it like that, I realize he's right. "But this is Skarsdon," I say. "We are a planet of warriors."

"And she is a mother wanting to protect her child," Castian adds.

"Remus and Castian are right," Persean says. "A western-ized human woman like Kate isn't used to the horrors of war. I have seen that with Helena and her sister. You have thrown Kate into this, Tharin. Of course it worries her deeply."

"But she always wanted adventure," I say. "She even wanted to live in Obrothea at one point."

"But isn't adventure what caused her mother's death?" Castian asks. "That's what she told me ten years ago, anyway. The stray bullet on the commune she lived on as a child?"

I put my head in my hands. "You are right, I am an oaf."

Kate

I think I can hear the men laughing in the distant layers of the palace. They're probably laughing at me, a silly pathetic human who's scared of war and blood. Let them laugh. Nothing will stop me putting my daughter's safety first. All my fears come rushing back. I've been so stupid, allowing Tharin's cock, lips, and fingers to smooth away my initial fears. The fact is, I am a kidnap victim who has been forced into a brutal, bloody new world with my daughter. I allowed myself to be taken in by a beautiful warrior, typical Stockholm Syndrome.

I hear the door open, and I turn away and pretend to be asleep. I don't want to see Tharin. I don't want him *near* me, but I can see the glow of his skin through my eyelids and smell his musky scent. It sends an unwitting dart of desire though me. I feel his heavy weight on the bed, the mists no doubt swirling around him in excitement.

"I know you're not sleeping, Kate." He's slurring. Great, so now I have a drunk alien warrior in my bed. I don't say anything, squeezing my eyes shut even more.

"I am an oaf," he says. I bite back the need to agree wholeheartedly. "I was a fool to show you more blood when it is bloodshed you despise and fear."

Well, he's right there. The bed shifts again, and I feel his breath on my cheek. *Focus, Kate, focus.*

"Worst of all," he whispers, "I did not think of your mother." My stomach drops at the mention of her. "I know you think her own adventures led to her death, but have you ever considered you may be wrong?"

Anger swells inside, and I turn to him. He is staring down at me with sad green eyes, his beautiful golden hair in his

221

face. "How can you say that? My mother died because we were living a life of adventure in that damn commune."

"She died because of an accident," he says gently. "You told me your father owned guns even before you moved to the commune. Imagine if your mother had stayed in her safe suburban life, as you once called it. She would not have tasted adventure. Is it not better to live a happy life full of adventure rather than being bored and sad?"

"Bored and sad is fine if it meant she would stay alive," I retort. "Bored and sad is fine if it means keeping my child safe."

"Can we not have both? I can offer you security *while* you adventure."

I shove him away, ignoring his wounded look as I do. He doesn't get it. "I'm tired. I don't want to talk about it."

Over the next few minutes, I feel him breathing next to me, but after a while, he gets up and leaves the room. I can't lie, his absence makes my gut ache. It's the first night since we arrived on this planet without him beside me. But how else can I get him to understand?

Tharin

The next morning, I do what I always do when my mind is in turmoil. I fight. Luckily, Warliur, the defender who has travelled to meet us today, is a worthy opponent. When I suggested we conduct our meeting over some training and lunch, he was delighted. Warliur is a giant, standing eight foot tall above me, but of course I can defeat him. There is not a Obrothean I can't defeat.

"Brother, are you sure this is a good idea?" Kiah asks, gesturing at the huge defender warming up across from me.

"You drank a great deal of pemelonian last night, and your mind is distracted with thoughts of Kate's disapproval."

"He will not defeat me. It is impossible."

"I do not mean he will defeat you," Kiah says. "I mean you may defeat him. Even kill him."

I laugh. "Are you a fool? Of course I won't."

"You are distracted, brother. As you have been ever since you met Kate. You have said it yourself over the past ten years, you struggle to control yourself when she's on your mind. You have killed many in a rage on the battlefield to take your mind off her. What if you return to your old habits? If you fatally injure this defender, all is lost. He has much influence on defenders beyond this part of Skarsdon."

I shove him away. "I will not kill him. What are you thinking? You are the one who is still addled from last night's pemelonian."

I stride away from him, shaking my head as I approach the giant. He is standing with his entourage, several warriors of the same stature as him. My defenders look excited. They love a challenge. As do I, clearly, since I have chosen to love the most challenging of females. Her coldness last night and the way she turned her back to me makes fury roar inside.

Maybe it was too much to ask that we start anew? Maybe I misread the look of love her eyes. I should have stuck to my original plan of no feelings, just seeding. The irony of it all, as humans would say, is that I have not seeded her thanks to Jerelda's concoction of herbs I agreed she could have. I am weak. Pathetic. I clench my sword tightly.

I fight the giant with a ferocity and strength I usually save for the battlefield. I see it both impresses him and scares him. That makes me feel good, electric. When I draw blood, it fuels my hunger for more. I hear Kiah shout my name, but I ignore him. I thrash my sword at the giant's neck. He blocks it with impressive strength. It makes me think of the way

Kate blocked my advances the night before, and that boils my blood. I swivel and dart behind him, lifting my sword above my head. I will stab him in the back as I was stabbed on the vessel. I roar and begin to bring my knife down.

"Tharin!" I hear Kiah shout.

I pause, blinking. What was I thinking? Kiah was right, I never should have fought after a night like the one I just had. I drop my sword to the ground before it becomes my people's poison. But the giant is angry now and has found his advantage, thrusting his dagger into my side.

TWENTY

Kate

I sit by the window reading a book about this solar system's black holes, looking out every now and again for Tharin. I have no idea when he will be back or whether I will even talk to him when he does. The one thing I do know is that I need to see him. I feel a little bad about last night. He did seem genuinely contrite, and it must have been difficult for him to see me turn my back to him.

Adin's brow is heavy as he guards us. I don't know how he just stands there. Does he ever sleep or drink? His devotion to the family who took his mother and his brother away from him amazes me.

A huge defender bursts into the room, and Adin draws his sword and then relaxes. "Secilin, it is just you. What is it?"

"The sire," the defender says, out of breath. "He is wounded."

I jump up, heart hammering in fear. "Where is he?"

"At the training ground. It was an accident. He will be fine, but he is asking for you, his Pledged."

"That damn training ground," I shout. "We have to go."

"Of course," Adin says, and we run outside. Adin whistles for his tuskian, and it gallops over from the stables. Adin jumps onto it and leans down to help me up in front of him. He kicks at the beast with his legs, and it goes faster than I knew it was capable of, galloping like a stallion the whole way to the training ground as Adin stiffly holds the reins, trying his best not to touch me.

During the journey, I can't help but panic. What if Tharin *isn't* going be fine? Oh God, why did I ignore him last night? He doesn't understand my fears. How can he when he has never experienced the comforts of a peaceful life like I have? He *tries* to understand, that's what counts, and I threw it back in his face. The gates slide open, clearly sensing Adin's blood. When we arrive, I don't need Adin to lift me off the tuskian. Somehow, I manage to jump down and run towards the entrance to the training camp.

"Where is he?" I shout to the defenders guarding it. They point up a flight of stairs. I take them two at a time, noticing a giant being standing in the center of the training ground, head hung low, blood before him on the ground. Is this who hurt Tharin? I hope not. He's *huge*. As I get to the landing, I hear Tharin's roar of pain before I see him. I run towards the sound, Adin following me. Tharin is lying on his side on a quartz slab in a curved golden room, two healers attending to a deep, bloody gash in his side. His gorgeous face is screwed up in pain as they sweep their strange hands over his wound.

"Tharin!"

His eyes snap open, and he puts his hand out. I run to him and take his bloody hand in mine, kissing his pained face. "What happened?" I ask him.

"Didn't. Focus," he hisses through his teeth.

I wonder if it's because of what happened between us the night before? "Will he be okay?" I ask the healers. They both nod, and I feel a sense of relief.

Over the next twenty minutes, I watch in fascination as the healers do their work, moving their palms over Tharin's wound as he winces and moans. It must have been deep, maybe fatal if he were on Earth. Thank God, we're here on this planet. I realize in that moment that these healers' miraculous abilities mean the injuries of war really aren't like they are on Earth. So many can be healed quickly. Maybe I've been wrong to worry so much?

Soon, Tharin's wound begins to close right before my eyes, and he starts to relax. I place my hand against his sweaty face, and he kisses my fingers.

"I'm sorry," he says, peering up at me.

"No, *I'm* sorry," I say back. "I didn't listen to you, not properly. Things are different here. More violent, yes, but maybe safer too," I say, gesturing towards the healers.

"It looks like we really are both sorry," he says, "and we have much to make up for."

That night, we make love slowly and tenderly. Though Tharin is still in pain, he thrusts even deeper into me than he dared to before, taking his time to allow me to expand around him and give over completely to him. As his movements quicken, so do the incredible sensations as the pressure of his arcism hums on my most sensitive part, building and building until the crescendo of sensation erupts inside me.

As it does, I get a sudden image of doing the same, but in a different place. Specifically, a small pod-like room with golden walls. Not the room I first had on the transporter vessel. Another room. A deeply familiar room. There is a book lying on the side, its spine exposed: *The Great Forests of Obrothea*. Discarded plates of food lie on the misty floors, and Tharin is above me, moving in and out of me as I come. But he looks different, younger. The scar on his chest is gone, and his hair shorter and to his shoulders.

I snap my eyes open just as Tharin comes now, his warm seed spilling into me.

"I remember something."

He looks down at me, breathing heavily, his cock still pulsing inside me. "What do you remember?"

"It was from ten years ago, I think. Were we in your room? There was a book, *The Great Forests of Obrothea.*" I reach up, fingering his scar. "Your scar was gone. Can I really be remembering?"

He frowns and pulls out of me, going to his table to get a cloth to wipe himself. He doesn't usually do that after we make love. He clearly doesn't want me to see his face. I go up on my elbows to look at him. "Is it possible? Could my memories be coming back?"

"Maybe."

"Why won't you look at me, Tharin?"

He turns to me. "I am looking at you."

I clench my jaw. I can see he's angry that I'm remembering. But why? What is he so afraid I will recall?

Tharin is quiet over breakfast. Even Isla notices it, frowning down into her bowl. He leaves earlier than usual, kissing Isla's head and my lips, still avoiding my gaze. As Isla changes for her lessons, I go to Castian while he waits for her. "Castian, can we have a quick chat?"

He bows. "Of course."

I gesture to the chairs by the bookshelves. He sits in one, smoothing his robes over his long legs. "Is everything well, Kate?" he asks, concern in his green eyes.

"Yes. It's just… I think my memories from before are coming back."

He leans forward. "When did this start happening?"

"Last night."

"Very interesting. The dose of liptus you were all given on your last night ten years ago should have been enough to offer very potent, long-term memory loss. May I ask, is there anything in particular that triggered this memory?"

I bite my lip, my face flushing. "It was after Tharin and I had sex."

"At what point exactly?" he asks, unfazed.

"It was after we…orgasmed. Or during."

Castian stands and starts pacing the room. "Can it really be possible?" he murmurs to himself.

"What's possible?"

"His seed is having such a potent effect on you that it is somehow bringing your memories back."

"You think it's from when he comes inside me?"

Castian nods. "I believe you visited the training camp to see him when he was wounded yesterday?" I nod. "Tell me, did the gates open for you?"

"They opened for Adin."

"No," Castian says with a head shake. "They would not open for him. Adin does not have the Grand Sovran's blood. They only open for those with the Grand Sovran's DNA. It means you must have opened them. It is the Fortification, and it is happening *much* sooner than we thought it might."

"Fortifying. Tharin told me about that. Something about it changing my DNA?"

"Yes, Tharin's seed is already causing your blood to match his. The more he seeds you, the more your enzymes will mix." He turns away from me, silent for a moment. "It would make sense that the fortification is causing the liptus to wear off. It does strengthen your immune response and defenses, after all."

My heart pounds in excitement. "Does it mean my memories will come back eventually?"

"Yes," Castian says, still deep in thought. "Yes, they will, Kate."

Part of me is happy. The other part worries about Tharin's reaction. He really doesn't seem to like the idea of my memories coming back.

"What's all the excitement about?' We turn to see Charlotte at the door. I invited her over for bunch. I run up to her and take her hands. "Tharin and I are already Fortifying. Remember Anaya mentioned it?"

"Yeah, I've read about it too." She frowns. "But I thought that won't be for ages."

"Yep, me too."

"Looks like we need to celebrate this strange genetic miracle," Charlotte says, squeezing my hand. "Pemelonian brunch sound good?"

I laugh. "What the hell?"

The rest of the day passes in a fun blur as we both get intoxicated on that delicious pemelonian. By the time dinner arrives, I can barely control my excitement about telling Tharin. But when he walks in, I can tell he knows already. He comes up to me and pulls me into his arms.

"We are invincible," he whispers in my ear.

I smile. "How did you know?"

"Word is spreading." I wonder if he knows it's related to my memories returning? I think he would be less happy then. "Now," he says, "where is my little warrior? I have something for her."

"Isla!" I call out.

She runs from her room with Henry as Tharin pulls out a small sword. It glitters and swirls with color, and Isla's eyes light up.

"That's cool," Henry says.

I frown, and Tharin laughs. "It is blunt, Mother Bear," he says to me.

"Oh," Isla says, disappointed.

He walks to her and ruffles her dark hair. "Fear not. I will sharpen it when you turn ten." I roll my eyes. "Now, let's celebrate," Tharin declares. "We have so much to be happy for. Your early Fortifying *plus* the grand banquet I have planned to bring all our allies together in one place. I have prepared an exquisite dress for you."

"You're having a banquet?"

"Yes, I decided today. We can announce our fortification there. It will make our position even stronger."

Over the next couple of hours, we enjoy a feast with our closest allies in the palace. It almost feels like I'm back at home having a dinner party, except for the fact there are three moons outside instead of one. Tharin sits with me, pulling my chair close to his. He's respectful in Isla's presence, keeping a distance and only occasionally stroking my arm or squeezing my knee beneath the table. But when she is not looking, he's much more free with his affection, placing his arm protectively around my shoulders and kissing my neck. I lean into him, feeling his newly washed hair on my cheek.

When our pudding is brought out, gasps go up around the table. It's presented in stunning, ornate goblets with smoke pouring out of them.

"A Skarsdonian delicacy," Tharin declares. "Zooba plants mixed with the cocoa we brought over from Earth. I think we will serve this as the banquet in two days."

I lift my spoon and breathe in its exotic smells. There's a scent mingling with the others that feels so familiar. What *is* it? I lean close, sniffing the dessert. An image suddenly comes to me. I'm sitting in that same pod that I remembered the night before. A hand reaches out, pressing some soft, purple petals into my palm. The memory dissipates, and I stand up. The movement makes the table rock, and things spill and crash to the floor.

Tharin jumps up with me. "What's wrong, Kate?"

"I just remembered something. I… I remember someone giving me purple petals on the vessel ten years ago. I remember the smell. It was so distinctive." I look at the goblet of mousse before me. "It smells like this mousse."

Everyone exchanges shocked looks. Tharin grabs my spoon, lifts it to his nose, and sniffs. His face erupts in rage. "Herlecian petals. Someone is trying to poison Kate!"

TWENTY-ONE

Tharin

Castian dips the sample he took from Kate's mousse into his identifier.

"Will this definitely tell us if there are traces of herlecian blossom in there?" I ask.

"Yes, Tharin. It will take a few moments."

I pace the room, clenching and unclenching my fists. "Who would do this?" The thought drives me to distraction. Isla was about to eat some too, what if there was some in her mousse?

Kate comes to me and takes my hand. "Calm down, Tharin. Their plan didn't work, did it?"

Remus and Kiah walk in then. "The kitchen workers are all waiting in the library, brother," Remus says.

"All of them?" I ask, going to him and placing my hand on his shoulders. "I must be sure, brother. Not one of them escaped?"

"The kitchen lead showed me a list of workers tonight," Remus confirms. "They are all there being guarded by Adin, Persean, and Heldran."

"Good, good," I say.

"What if we got it wrong though?" Kate says. "There are probably lots of flowers with purple petals, I imagine?"

"But that smell is distinctive," Tharin says. "It is definitely herlecian."

"It'll be what triggered the memory from ten years ago too," Kate says. "You know how smells can trigger memories."

Castian looks at me with surprise. "Smell triggers memories for humans?" Kate shakes her head. "How interesting. When I think I know everything about humans, I learn something new." He looks back down at the screen and sighs. "The results are in. It looks like Kate's mousse did contain herlecian, but not the other mousses."

It takes all of my control not to pull the room apart in a rage. Instead, I pull Kate's trembling body into my arms and kiss her forehead. "They will not get away with it."

"But why would someone target me?" Kate whispers. "Is it because of my video?"

"It's more likely Ethos trying to stop you having more Sacred children like Isla," Kiah suggests. "It puts Tharin in too powerful a position to have the most powerful heirs."

"Or it's to stop me remembering what happened ten years ago," Kate suggests. "I did recall someone pressing those very same petals into my hands. Clearly, someone tried to poison me then too, and now that they know I'm remembering more, they want to make sure I don't remember that specific moment." She frowns. "But then why didn't I die or become seriously ill if they're poison?"

"The petals need to be consumed to be fatal," Castian explains. "Something must have stopped you eating them."

I pull Kate even closer, rage making my heart thump against her temple. Who would do this to her? Then something occurs to me. "How would they know you're remembering more?"

"The Fortification is eroding the long-term effects of the liptus," Castian explains. "We think it is helping her remember."

I try to control my emotions. Kate will remember...everything? Including those harsh words I threw at her that last night? I fear that memory will break us, no matter how strong we are now.

Just before Kate arrived for her final night on the ship, word came through that Skarsdon had been invaded...and that my mother and sister were dead. Not only that. A video was found on a Fostinian communication device. A video Kate had made, talking to camera about her experiences on our vessel and all she had learnt. It gave the Fostinians the momentum they needed, a chance to invade while "all Skarsdon's best warriors" as she called us in her video were occupied light-years away.

She must have gotten out of our room, found the communications area again, and recorded the video in the hope she could send it to herself on Earth. It must have somehow been intercepted by Ryker. Kate did not know how to cloak her messages as we did.

I was showed it just before Kate was due to return. Ethos was convinced it was proof that Kate had conspired with Ryker. That Ryker had somehow found a way to communicate with her the past few days. In my grief and anger, I ran to my room to confront her. She'd cowered in the corner of the room as I ranted and raved, telling her I wish I'd never laid eyes on her. She'd seemed confused about the video, claiming not to remember even sending it. The haze could have that effect sometimes. But we all knew it was her.

I stormed out, shouting that she must be returned to Earth

instantly, all her memories wiped. She was lucky we allowed her to leave. If Ethos had had his way, she would have been tortured to extract information. Maybe he wanted to see her dead now because of her memory of herlecian petals being pressed into her palm? Was *he* the one gave her the petals while she waited to see me that last night, or was it one of his minions? Had he tried to do it again tonight?

"Damn it," I say, sweeping my hand across the table and sending the identifier and samples toppling to the floor. Castian steps back, looking dismayed. I storm out of the room, and Kate and Remus chase me.

"Brother!" Remus says, "these Fostinian workers are of good, honest stock. Do not be too harsh."

"The person who did this is not good, nor are they honest," I hiss. "They deserve to die!"

Kate grabs my shoulder. "Please control your temper, Tharin," she says. "Remember how much trouble it's got you into lately," she adds, looking pointedly at the wound on my side, which still smarts. "You heard what Remus said, these are good people. Don't jump to conclusions." She turns to Castian. "Is there a way to quicken my memories returning? I mean, other than the obvious," she adds, blushing.

"I'm not sure it works like that, Kate," Castian replies.

"I have heard there may be herbs in the heart of the forest that help long-forgotten memories return," Kiah says.

"Maybe," Remus says, "but no fool would go into the middle of the forest unless they want to be eaten alive."

Good. I do not want Kate remembering.

"I will question the workers," I say. "Maybe I'll eat them alive too."

Kate puts her soft hand to my chest. "Take deep breaths."

I do as she asks, closing my eyes, and the anger dissipates a little. When I open them, I am calmer. Remus tilts his head, clearly intrigued by the effect Kate has on me.

"Fine," I say, "I promise to be calm and fair."

When we walk into the library, the workers are standing in a semi-circle. They are fearful, I can smell it in the room. They cannot meet my gaze, and one young girl trembles. Long ago, I would just torture them to get the information I need. But I have taken heed of Kate's words. I take a deep breath and walk up and down the line, looking into each of their eyes. There are ten dark-haired Fostinians here of all ages and sexes.

"We have just learnt that ground-up herlecian blossoms were found in my Pledged's food. As many of you will know, herlecian blossoms are poisonous." I stop before the large chef and place my hand on his shoulder. He shakes beneath me. I'm tempted to press my fingers together and tear his muscle away from his bone in the hope of forcing a confession. But again, I take heed of Kate's words. *One...two... three...* "Now," I say, letting him go and walking down the line again, "I am not suggesting any of you were the masterminds behind this plan, but maybe one among you agreed to do someone's bidding. Maybe that someone paid you handsomely in Skarsdonian coin to convince you to take such a risk. I imagine that you did it for your family. Goddess Tsuki knows I would do anything for my family, including killing. But I am a fair leader, so I shall give you a chance."

I stand in the middle of the room, observing the tears filling all the workers' eyes. "In fact," I say, "whoever did this will be paid double what they were offered if they confess now." I cross my arms and wait, but they all shake their heads in denial.

"I would never betray you, sire," the chef says dropping to his knees before me and raising his hands in prayer. "You are the great Quilesia's son," he adds, referring to my mother. "You have our Fostinian blood running through your veins. You are to be our savior, our hero."

The others follow suit, but it just makes me want to rip their heads off. "One of you did this," I roar. I grab one young man's throat and lift him. "I hear your Pledged is with child. What better incentive is there for making more coin?"

Kate runs to me and grabs my elbow. "Tharin, let him go." But I cannot, my rage is intoxicating.

"Daddy?" I turn to see Isla watching me with a heavy brow. I drop the young man, my shoulders sinking. This is not how I want my daughter to see me.

Kate

I look between Tharin and Isla. She called him Daddy, and yet she also did it just as he was about to choke a potentially innocent worker to death. I see Tharin realizes the same, and shame sweeps over his face. He storms from the room, shouting over his shoulder, "Question them, Adin!"

I think of following him, but what good will it do? He needs to calm down...alone. I usher Isla out of the room and take her to the living area.

"Is it true?" she asks. "Did someone try to poison you, Mommy?"

"No, darling." I don't want to scare her, but the fact is, someone *did* try to poison me, not just now, but also ten years ago if I'm right about that memory of someone pressing purple petals into my palm. How did I survive it? Did something make me stop taking it, as Castian suggested? Or was the Fortification occurring back then too? Was it so strong it saved me? I do recall being super sick back then but I put that down to being pregnant when I learnt I was carrying a child. But maybe it was the effects of the poison. If only I could remember who did it.

When Isla goes to sleep and there is still no sign of Tharin, I find Adin standing by the windows, looking out with a hooded brow. "Who do you think would do this to me, Adin?" I ask him.

His jaw tenses. "I don't know, Kate. It greatly displeases me."

"It would help if I could remember who gave me the petals ten years ago."

"It would. Hopefully, the Fortification will continue to strengthen you and you will remember soon."

"Not soon enough though." I follow his gaze to the forest. "You and your brother grew up in the forest, didn't you? I bet it's full of herbs and flowers and plants?"

"It is. What are you asking?"

"I heard there might be something in the forest that helps with memories?"

He nods. "It's called stident fungus."

"Can you get me some?"

He shakes his head. "It's better if you ask Tharin."

"But Tharin seems averse to me remembering. I'm not sure he'll agree. Please?"

"I don't think it's a sensible idea."

I cross my arms. Why do the men around here not let me do anything? "And I don't think you sneaking off into the forest at night is sensible either. I've seen you, Adin." His green eyes widen, and his face pales. I feel bad, but if it means I can get his help to remember, it's worth it. I sigh. "Look, I promise I won't say anything. You told me yourself your mother would sneak back to Fostinia to see her people, and I get it. I really do. If I could sneak back to Earth, I would." I put my hand on his arm, and his face flushes. "All I want is to remember. Can you help me?"

He takes in a deep breath. For a moment, I think he'll

refuse, but then he nods. "Fine," he says. "But you will have to come with me."

I think of what Remus said about being eaten alive out there. "Why can't you just go and retrieve it for me?"

"It has to be consumed as soon as it is plucked, otherwise it withers. Best to go tonight though, while the moons aren't full. That is when the creatures really get excited. I will be there to protect you though."

I shiver. *Creatures*. "Won't Tharin notice I'm gone?"

"I will ensure Tharin is occupied." I can see the idea of betraying his brother is killing Adin, but his desire to keep his visits into the forest secret obviously outweighs that. "I shall see you here at sunset. Wear a dark cloak," he instructs and strides off.

Skarsdon at night is even more astounding than it is during the day. Of course, I've seen it from the windows and the balconies. The way the sunset turns the sky purple and then indigo. But outside here, as I follow Adin towards the forest and breathe in the night air and hear the strange night creatures that squawk and hiss, it feels even more foreign to me. And now we're about to enter a whole different region, the Fostinia region I have heard so much about. Tharin would be fuming if he knew I was out here, but it has to be done.

"Keep close," Adin says, his glowing skin guiding me through the dark.

I do as he asks, walking close to him as we enter the vast purple forest. It feels like it is moving around us, a hive of hidden activity. The long trunks of the purple trees seem to take on a different form, like the ash-riddled columns of a burnt-out mansion. The ground below feels hazardous without daylight, even the light emitting from Adin's skin not enough to illuminate every little root I might trip over. Beyond the path, in amongst the trees, I see movement, flashes of eyes. I know in my rational mind it may simply be nocturnal animals, but it still makes me quicken my step, heart thumping loudly as I peer over my shoulder.

After a while, we reach a clearing surrounded by what looks like tree stumps glowing a luminous green. "I remember seeing these on the journey from the landing strip," I say.

"Yes, you will have seen it by the lakes."

"So we could have just gone to the lakes?"

"The lakes can be just as dangerous at night as the forest."

"So what is this stuff then?" I ask, eying the strange substance.

"It's known as stident fungus. It feeds off the rotting insides of dead trees and stagnant water."

"And I have to *eat* it?"

"It is harmless, like your Earth mushrooms. But it will help you remember."

He gets his dagger out and goes to one of the tree stumps. I wrap my arms around myself, eyes searching the darkness. Tharin really *would* be angry knowing I'm here at night guarded by just one defender. I watch as Adin scrapes at the strange fungus. When he's got enough, he walks back over, a small ball of the glowing green fungus between his thumb and forefinger.

"This should be enough," he says.

"And you're absolutely sure it's harmless?" I ask.

"Sure. My mother was a huntress and queen of this forest. She taught me everything she knew when she snuck out to visit us." He goes to hand some to me, but then there's a noise behind us. I turn to see a huge figure approaching in the darkness. Adin grabs me, pulling me close to him as a large man with long flowing brown hair steps out from the darkness.

"Now, now, brother, *what* do we have here?"

It's Ryker, the rebel pictured in all the war books. But how is that possible? Tharin killed him.

TWENTY-TWO

Tharin

I wake from a nightmare. It a bad one this time. I am watching the high table from behind a screen. I see my mother and my sister, along with my other dead ancestors. But there is a new addition. There's a beautiful woman with long brown flowing hair standing with her back to me. I bang on the glass, and the woman turns.

It is Kate…and she is standing with Ryker.

I wake up, strangling a scream. I reach for my love, desperate to see her with my own eyes to prove to myself she is alive.

"He's finally awake." I open my eyes to see Kiah laughing at me. He convinced me to join him to strategize and drink in the battle room last night. How could I have fallen asleep? Of course, the ointment the healers gave me do tire me, and I did spend much of the night before making love to Kate.

Kate. I need to feel her touch. I stand and stretch. "Your talk bores me, brother, that is why I am quick to fall asleep. I will retire to bed now."

Kiah stands with me, gripping my wrist. "Oh, come now. Surely there is more pemelonian to drink?"

I shove his hand off. "No, I'm tired and I want to see Kate."

He shrugs. "At least I tried."

"Tried what?"

"Nothing. Go seed your Pledged."

I go to the lift and let it take me to our suite, nodding at the defender who guards it as I walk inside. Strange it's not Adin, but then he is allowed time off. He's just usually so reluctant to take it. I go to check on Isla, who is sleeping soundly, then I head to mine and Kate's room, my cock already rising in anticipation of plunging it into Kate. But then I remember what Castian said. The more I seed her, the stronger she gets, and the more likely she is to remember. Will it be such a bad thing for her to remember though? It will lead us to whoever is trying to poison her, and there are more good memories than bad. But the idea of her remembering the argument we had makes me sick.

I go to the bed and pause. Kate is not there. What if something has happened to her as she sleeps? What if my dream was warning me? Fear darts through me. I check the toilet, the dressing room, the hallway, even Isla's room again, but Kate is nowhere to be seen. Then I catch sight of figures walking towards the forest in the darkness outside. One of them is Kate. I can tell from her tiny form. She is being taken from me. I've grown too complacent. I grab my sword, readying to gut the fool who has attempted to take my Pledged from me. Then something occurs to me. I recognize the gait of the warrior with her. It's Adin. Where is he taking her? I run outside, following their distant figures until they approach a clearing in the forest. As I'm about to call to them, I see another figure step out among the trees.

Ryker!

How is this possible? The last time I saw him, he was lying dead on the floor of this forest. I roar and run towards him. Adin goes to stand between us, but I sweep him out of the way and lunge at my brother, the betrayer, and grab him by the lapels of the fur draped around his shoulders.

"How are you alive?" I scream into his mocking face, holding my sword to his throat as he smiles at me, infuriating me even more. "How?"

"I saved him, Tharin," Adin says. "I told you he was dead, but he was not," he admits with a heavy sigh. "There was just a faint heartbeat. When you left, I took him into the forest and paid a healer to say they had burnt his body."

"Nice touch there, brother," Ryker says. "Stab me in the heart and then asking a healer to burn me."

"I am not your brother," I shout, spittle landing on Ryker's stubbled cheeks. I glare at Adin. "You betrayed me."

"Never," Adin replies vehemently. "I just saved my brother. I have always been loyal to you first."

"And yet you are here meeting with him," I say, a whirlwind of emotions threatening to overwhelm me. "And Kate?" I say, turning to her. The sight of her standing across from Ryker is a dagger to my heart. "Is it true what they say? Did you betray me on purpose with that video? Have you been in alliance with him all along?"

"No," Kate shouts. "How could I when I was only on the vessel seven nights, and he was here on Obrothea?"

"How would you know? You don't remember much from that time," I retort.

"I do," Ryker says, his lips curling into a smile as he looks Kate up and down. "We were communicating all that time on the ship. You know how women are around me once I get chatting."

I go very still as Kate shakes her head. "He's lying. I wouldn't do that."

"Am I?" Ryker says. "We had the same cause after all, overthrow the men who had forced us away from our homes."

Kate tries to come towards me with her hand out, but I step away from her, dragging Ryker with me.

"Step back," I command, my voice so loud and angry it sends night creatures flocking away in the darkness. "There is nothing you can say to explain this. You betrayed me, just as others warned me you did."

Kate

The expression of disgust on Tharin's face almost kills me. I look at the tall, dark man he is clutching. He's not even struggling, just glaring at Tharin with a malicious glint in his green eyes. Could Ryker be telling the truth? Did I conspire with him? Surely not. If the feelings I had ten years ago match how I feel now, I would never betray Tharin. And yet...

I *was* kidnapped then, as I am now. Maybe I *would* have resorted to something like that? How can I really be sure? Tharin is right that I can't remember. But, oh God, it breaks my heart to see him so upset.

"I love you," I say simply, tears falling down my cheeks. "I realize that now. I really do."

His eyes flicker with emotion. "And yet you are here with him."

"We came to get some stident fungus," Adin says, gesturing to a green substance in his hands, "to help Kate remember. We did not plan to meet with Ryker."

"You are lying," Tharin shouts. "Clearly you all have been conspiring against me."

"I would never do that, Tharin," Adin pleads. "I do not

believe Kate would either, despite what my brother says," he adds, giving Ryker a hard look.

There is a noise of marching in the distance, and dozens of defenders suddenly come flooding through the forest, led by Heldran.

"I saw you running into the forest, brother," Heldran says. He notices Ryker, and his eyes widen. "What the hell?"

Tharin turns to the defenders. "Detain these three people for treason and murder," Tharin commands, eyes hard as he looks at me.

"No, Tharin, *please*," I whisper. But it's too late, hands are already grabbing for us. Adin doesn't even fight, he just looks at Tharin with hopeless eyes. Ryker thrashes against the men to no avail. He's quickly overwhelmed, and we are marched from the forest.

I don't know how long I'm in the strange dark dungeon beneath the training grounds. Two days, maybe three. I sit alone in a small cell made of impenetrable black walls and a tiny hatch in the wall for food. I listen to the moans and cries of the other prisoners, men and women. I think non-stop of Isla and the look of betrayal in Tharin's eyes. I desperately try to grapple with my memories from ten years ago, but nothing —*nothing*—comes back to me.

I can't bring myself to believe I betrayed Tharin. The possibility sits heavily in my stomach. Alongside it sits the knowledge somebody tried to poison me back then and now. Who? None of it adds up. Surely Tharin must be asking himself the same questions?

I'm surprised when the black wall dissolves, and the tall white-haired female defender who's been guarding my cell appears with a long, golden dress in her hands.

"Get up," she instructs, the hate I've grown used to seeing clear in her eyes. "You are to wear this."

Fear clenches at my heart. Is it my execution dress? I stand upon wobbly legs. "Where am I going?"

"You will see. You must put your hair up, wear makeup." She throws the gown on the dirty ground along with a brush, clips, and some makeup and then walks out.

I sigh, thinking of my first day on the *Irresent* and the way I'd felt looking at the dress they'd supplied. This is worse, much worse. At least I had Isla with me then. I pull the jumpsuit and cape I've been wearing the past few days off, not even wanting to think about how much I must reek. There is a bucket of water here, but it hasn't been changed since I arrived. I pull the dress over me and rake my fingers through my greasy hair. The woman comes back in, grabs my elbow, and drags me out into a dark corridor. I see other figures there and realize both Adin and Ryker are being pulled down the corridor by defenders too.

Ryker turns to look at me over his shoulder. "Hello, Kate," he says. "It's like history repeating itself, isn't it? The Grand Sovran dragging his future wife to be executed. Except this time, it's his son doing the dragging. Maybe you'll get lucky like my mother did, and be saved at the eleventh hour?"

"Ryker, leave her be," Adin shouts from the front.

"You think this is all a joke," I spit at Ryker.

His handsome bearded face suddenly goes serious. "Do I? Do I think watching my people enslaved for over thirty years is a joke? Do I think watching my father being slaughtered is a joke?"

"And your mother and sister?" I can't help but reply.

He blinks. "I did not intend for them to die. I do not know how that happened. They were supposed to be taken to safety."

I look into his eyes. "Did I really send you that video on purpose?"

He drops his gaze from mine. "Of course not. One of my men intercepted it."

"Then why did you lie?" I cry.

"Because I knew what it would do to Tharin to think you had deceived him."

"And now he is executing her," Adin shouts at his brother. "You must tell him the truth, Ryker. I have told you again and again to drop your foolish desire for power and revenge. You cannot have this woman's blood on your hands. Haven't enough women died for your cause?"

Ryker's face hardens. "Haven't enough Fostinians died and been enslaved for the Skarsdonian cause? Let Tharin know what it is to lose the love of his life. Let him learn the valuable lesson I did." Then he turns from me and doesn't say another word.

Tharin

I can hardly breath when I see Kate brought into the grand hall with Adin and Ryker. She is wearing the dress I chose for her three days ago when I thought we would be attending this banquet as Pledged and Prime. How oblivious I was then to what would befall us. Her hair is swept up, exposing her soft, graceful neck, and her lips are painted red.

Her full, treacherous lips.

She looks confused. I imagine she was when she saw the dress brought in for her. Had she forgotten about the banquet as quickly as she forgot her words of love? This is the perfect chance to show my allies that I can do what must be done. A grand spectacle to reveal I will not tolerate any treachery, even from those I love. I should have listened to my men all along. She is not to be trusted. It's the same with Adin. All these years, I marveled at the loyalty he was able to show me despite my role in his brother's death. Now I know why. He was colluding with Ryker all this time.

I look at Ryker now. What joy I will take in killing him. Kate can watch as I tear the skin from his back and expose his ribs, each one to be broken by my fingers. I drag my eyes away from his vicious grin and look down at my fingers, flexing them in anticipation. At least the path laid out for me is clear now. The path of a future Skarsdonian Grand Sovran. We are not meant to love. It makes us soft.

My father always has always said the same, even in front of my mother. Their marriage was one of convenience for him, a chance to showcase his power over Fostinia. Of course, he was enraptured by her beauty. But the main reason he stopped her last-minute execution was he realized the advantages of such a partnership and how it would look to the rest of the planet. All eyes were on him as a young Grand Sovran, and he wanted to make his mark.

I think of what my father said to me earlier when I visited him. "Stay strong. Do what you must. Do not be blinded by love. Isla will be enough."

I look at Isla now, walking down the aisle to the table before us. Her cheeks are streaked with tears, and she refuses to allow me near her, clutching Castian or Kate's friend, Charlotte. But she will understand with time, just as I eventually understood all the actions my father took. She looks like a warrior priestess in her armor, her long dark hair down, her brown eyes fierce.

"Are you ready for this, brother?" Remus asks me.

"More ready than ever," I say.

Kiah, who sits on my other side, glances at Kate. "And you are still convinced this is the best plan for her?"

"Yes," I reply firmly.

"What of the child?" Kiah asks. "Will she not miss her mother?"

"Isla will be fine," I say firmly.

"Tharin is right," Heldran says. "She is better off without the treacherous and disloyal influence."

"It can be difficult for a child without its mother," Kiah says, frowning as he regards his own child among the faces below. I slam my fist onto the table. The room goes quiet, and Kate raises her gaze to meet mine. Her eyes are sad and desperate, and it makes my whole being want to go to her and hold her. But that is part of her power, her deceitful power. I glare at her, and she flinches, turning away. "You will not convince me otherwise, brother," I say. "My mind is made up."

Remus looks at the tables before us. "Everyone is seated. It is time to begin."

I stand up, my anger and resolve strengthening within me as I survey the room. "It is with great pleasure that we gather here today to form an alliance that will secure the future of Skarsdon."

Kate

I try to hold my tears back, but they fall anyway. I see the agony in Tharin's eyes, in his posture. He's like a quivering bow ready to be shot into the air. Still, he maintains his composure and delivers his speech beautifully, finding Isla's face among the crowds as he does. My heart stabs with pain as I look at her. She can't see me from where she is. I'm too high up with my pretty dress and angry guards. She's been

251

crying, I can see that, but like her father, she is trying to hold on to her composure.

I just hope she doesn't have to watch me die.

"And now," Tharin says, his eyes still on Isla, "to the future."

Castian, who is standing beside Isla, gently puts his hand on her shoulder. She peers up at him and then walks up to the stage, armor clinking. I see Charlotte among the people below, her face pale and drawn. What does she think of all this? What do the other human women think?

When Isla gets to Tharin, he places his hand on her shoulder. She tenses and scowls up at him. *That's my girl.*

"True Skarsdonian warrior blood runs through this child," Tharin says. He pauses, eyes finally catching on me. They are so cold. "Unique fortified blood that will ensure her place in history. Like all her fellow Sacred children, she will be taught by the planet's best scribes and trained by its best warrior. That's me, by the way," he adds with a charming smile, and the men in the room laugh. Many of the woman remain silent. It brings joy to my heart even in this awful hour that my fellow humans are standing by me in spirit.

"Why am I doing all this?" Tharin continues. "I am doing it because investment in our future is crucial. And part of that is ensuring the people I make alliances with are good, honest, *loyal* people." His eyes drill into mine. "Hence this feast today, in honor of our best, most *trusted* allies. Now let us drink to our future together."

The whole room cheers, the sound so defeating it makes my ears ring. I can see it's going to get quite raucous in here and notice with relief that Castian is taking Isla's hand and leading her out. The other Sacred children are also led out by their scribes. I don't want Isla around these drunken men. At least I can trust Castian will keep her safe.

As the noise dies down, Tharin addresses the audience

again. "It is also important to weed out those who are not honest and not good, even if it weighs very heavily on our hearts to do so."

I almost stop breathing. I know he's talking about me. Adin too.

"As is the Skarsdonian way," he continues, "the two rebel brothers, Adin and Ryker, will be executed as the sun sets, their ribs pulled from their bodies."

My stomach turns over. Is this the fate that awaits me too?

"Oooh, sounds perfect," Ryker shouts out sarcastically. "I've been feeling pretty tense lately, so a good rib stretch will be ideal." The defenders either side of him squeeze his arms behind his back, and he flinches. Adin doesn't react, just looks sadly ahead of him. I don't believe he directly betrayed Tharin. I think he took the chance to meet with his brother and check on him. He just looks too upset by it all.

"Now as for my Pledged," Tharin says bitterly, turning his hard gaze to me. "The most deceitful of all." His voice cracks slightly, finally showing some emotion, and I want to run to him and wrap my arms around him.

"What are you doing, Tharin?" Charlotte shouts out. "You *know* Kate wouldn't do this to you."

"Yes!" Louisa adds. "Why aren't you holding a trial, like she taught you?"

"She taught me nothing but disloyalty and pain," Tharin says in a firm voice.

"But Ryker is lying, Tharin," I shout out. "He admitted it. He's lying about the video just to hurt you. Charlotte is right. I would *never* be disloyal to you. Please, for Isla's sake."

This only seems to give him new resolve. "As for my Pledged," he repeats to the audience, "she will be taken back to the Earth she so loves. A transporter vessel is awaiting her now." A murmur of surprise rings out among the men around the hall. Clearly, they were all baying for my execution. I ought to feel relief. But what about Isla?

"Now take her away," Tharin shouts, turning away so people can't see the emotion on his face.

The defenders grab at me, but I battle against them. "Don't do this, Tharin," I shout. "Don't take me from Isla." But he doesn't even look at me. I try to kick at the defenders and bite them as I'm pulled away, but it's no use. They are too strong. "No, Tharin, no! Please talk to Ryker, please! He was lying. And what about the herlecian? What about my memories of someone giving me purple petals? Something's not right. Surely you can see that?"

But all he gives me is the back of his head until I'm dragged away.

TWENTY-THREE

Tharin

It is torture to maintain my composure as Kate is dragged away. Her words echo inside my mind. Is Ryker lying? No. All the evidence was there before my eyes, the three of them conspiring in the forest. All the doubts of the past few years and whispers have all just been proven to be true. I allow more pemelonian to be poured for me and try to join in with the laughter and the revelry, even allowing the frisky human woman Kiah bedded with her Prime's permission to sit upon my lap and whisper in my ear.

But all I think about is Kate.

"Oh, don't look so sad," she says in her Italian accent. "She betrayed you, the slut."

I shove her away and gulp down more pemelonian. The woman is right though. Kate did betray me. But if she is right, why does sending Kate away feel so wrong?

I look out of the vast window towards the landing strip where she is being taken right now. Soon, she will be gone. No human ship would ever be able to bring her back to

Obrothea. The pain of it is crippling. I press my finger into the scar that has reopened on my palm.

"Brother, are you well?" Kiah asks.

"I am very well," I lie, continuing to rub at the wound on my palm. Kiah's eyes drop to it, and I hide my hand beneath the table. I continue to drink, my eyes on Adin and Ryker, who have been made to stand and watch from the galleries above as the sun falls low upon the horizon outside, counting the moments until their death. I cannot help but feel pain at the thought of watching Adin die too. For so long, he has been at my side, as a protector, a brother…a friend. That makes it all worse. As for Ryker, the only regret I have is that I didn't check for his pulse myself ten years ago. At least I can guarantee his death now. That will just leave my brother Ethos to deal with, and the Mad Prince, of course. I am sure there will be many more enemies to come over the years as well.

Good, it will be something to focus my mind on.

It has occurred to me that maybe Ethos was not behind the attempt on my life. Maybe it was Kate all along, as he said? Heldran has suggested it too. I tell myself it might be true, a salve to ease the pain of her betrayal. But how would that explain the attempt on her life? Now and ten years ago?

"The sun will soon set," Remus says, interrupting my thoughts. "I think it is time we made our way outside."

"We are ready," I shout and peer up at the balconies above towards where Adin and Ryker stand. "I hope you two are as well," I add with a wicked smile as cheers ring out around me.

I go to stand up and then pause. There is a commotion at the front of the hall. Suddenly, the walls disappear and people dressed in furs and leather armor flood into the great hall.

Fostinian rebels here for their leaders.

I reach for my sword, and those around me do the same.

There are at least fifty of the filthy savages, green eyes searching the hall for the betraying brothers. My defenders begin fighting them as Ryker and Adin are pulled away from the balconies above by their guards. I jump over the table, rushing through the crowds, swiping my sword out at the rebels as they try to come at me, relishing the chance to unleash all my fury on them.

"The upper galleries," I shout over to Persean and Heldran, who are fighting together nearby. They nod and follow me towards the stairs. As we get to the top, Ryker and Adin are already there. The axes in their hands gleam with the blood of their guards. Behind them stand three Fostinians. A woman with a blunt black fringe, a young man with a mullet, and an older man with long black plaits that hang down his back. I recognize him as my mother's brother, the man who cared for Ryker and Adin growing up.

"Let us past please," Ryker says. "I would rather not kill you all."

"I *would* rather kill you," I say. "In fact, I will take great pleasure in killing the man who murdered my mother and sister."

Ryker sighs. "Why do you rush in headfirst and believe the whispers around you, Tharin? You didn't take the time to truly investigate their deaths, instantly blaming it on the invasion. Have you ever wondered if the explosion was an inside job?"

"I will not listen to you."

Another sigh. "Then it looks like I will have to kill you after all." Ryker raises his axe above his head, but before I have the chance to stop him, because stop him I will, Persean scoots in front of me, shoving Ryker away. Ryker stumbles but regains his balance, then he wields his axe to the side, bringing it crushing into Persean's neck. A guttural scream rings out as my old friend's blood splashes into my eyes, blinding me for a moment. I am fighting blind now, trying to wipe the blood from my eyes with one hand as I raise my sword with another. I hear shouts, screams, the tumbling of men downstairs and the gnashing of blades.

"She did not send me the video by the way, you fool," Ryker whispers into my ear. "I lied." I go to grab him, but he disappears down the stairs with the other men as my vision returns.

"They are escaping," Heldran shouts.

I realize then that I don't care. All I care about is Kate. Ryker lied about the video. How could I have not seen he would do that? My rage mists my mind, like the layers of fog upon our beds. My sister once warned me that my empathy was problematic, that my judgement could become clouded by emotion. She said the day I control it is the day I would become the great leader I was meant to be.

"Gather more men," I shout at Heldran. "Follow them!"

Heldran frowns. "Will you not come with us?" The realization dawns on him then. "Please do not tell me you are going after Kate."

"Would you have not done the same for Liva?" I say, referring to his great love.

He sighs, shaking his head. "Go."

I run from the room, heading outside, anger curling inside me like a fist.

Find Kate.

Kate

I'm crying so much that I can hardly see. Squashed in front of a huge defender on a tuskian moving at terrifying speed, I try to struggle out of the grip he has on me, but he is unmovable.

I even bite him. While I feel him flinch, he does nothing, his loyalty to Tharin so strong he is able to endure the pain. I look over my shoulder, the sphere-like palace where my daughter is being held is beginning to disappear from view behind a mountain. I didn't even get a chance to say goodbye to her. It's an impossible situation. What can I do against these giants? How can I ever *hope* to return to her?

Tharin has destroyed me. Completely destroyed me.

I stop fighting and sink against the defender's hard armor, looking out as the golden mountains sweep past us. Ahead, a gold-hued lake appears, and I imagine stepping into it and not stopping until the water laps above my head. As I think that, I notice something glowing by the lake. Something that glows a luminous green.

The stident fungus.

I didn't get the chance to take it after Tharin found me and Adin with Ryker in the forest. If I remember who pressed those petals into my palm, at least I might be able to get a message to Tharin to warn him. Somebody is clearly trying their best to sabotage him. I look up at the huge defender.

"We may have our strength," I remember Tharin telling me, *"but you women have your wits."*

I point towards the lake. "Is that Ryker?" I suddenly shout. "Has he escaped?"

The defender follows my gaze, obviously not wanting to miss this chance to please his master. He kicks his foot against the tuskian's bulk, and it changes direction, heading towards the lake. I ready myself as we approach the lake, holding on as tightly as I can. Just as I predicted, the tuskian rears up when it sees the water. Tharin once told me how they hate water, and now I can see it is true. Thank God, because my plan relies on it. The defender's arm shoots off me as he scrambles to stay upright. I give him a shove with my elbow to help him along, and his giant form falls from the tuskian.

He's knocked as he hits the rock below, and I bite my lip, hoping he's okay. I can't worry too much about that. I have bigger fish to fry.

I carefully climb off the tuskian and run to the stident fungus. In the gloom, I see strange shapes swirling in the water and remember what Adin said about the lakes here being as dangerous as the forest at night. But I have to do this. I lean over the fungus. It glows so prettily under the three moons, undulating with luminosity. How much do I take? Adin picked a small ball of it, but he's always been a bit conservative. I scoop up a whole lot. He did say it was harmless, like mushrooms.

"Here goes," I whisper. I shove it all into my mouth, trying not to retch at its acrid taste. The memories come straight away, small jigsaw pieces of recollection clicking together in confusing ways.

Laughter as Tharin leans over me, dripping a warm pink liquid between my breasts.

Lights flashing in my bedroom. The sight of green eyes blinking down at me.

Tharin walking back and forth, reading from a book as I listen

My hand flat against his large chest, pushing him away.

The sound of his soft moans as I feel his tongue between my legs.

Tears on my face as I watch him walk away…

The memories come faster as more of the stident fungus slides down my throat, nauseating flashes that make me groan and double over. They assault me from all corners, a roar of emotions. Intense hatred. Unbelievable love. Pain and ecstasy. Laughter and tears, so many tears. Then Tharin's face, strong and sure, his green eyes filled with so much love I find I am crying and laughing now from the memory.

"Oh, Tharin," I whisper. "I really have always loved you."

And then there it is again, that memory of fingers pressing purple petals into my palm. I squeeze my eyes shut. "Focus, Kate, focus," I whisper. Yes, there it is. A large hand oscillating with color. "Their face," I hiss. "You need to see their face."

But then the image is gone as quickly as it came. I let out a cry of frustration, striding up and down the banks of the lake as the tuskian watches. Another memory assaults me. I'm at a doorway. It's night. I've just come back from recording the video in the communications area while Tharin sleeps, but for some reason, I'm frozen, fear pulsing in my heart as I watch two figures through frosted glass in a communal area. I can barely make them out. Their faces are indecipherable and blurry, but I can see one is dark haired, and the other has short golden hair.

"If you are right about Tharin having managed to seed her," a voice says, "then she is bound to be pregnant already. She *cannot* have this child. The combination of the enzymes in Tharin's seed and her secretions will create a child of such power that Tharin is sure to become the Grand Sovran when the time comes. I will not risk losing my rightful place. All our plans will unravel."

"But murder? Must we really *murder?*" the dark-haired man replies.

"A few for the sake of many, remember? And she is just one human."

"Two if a child is growing within her."

"A child who will seal Tharin's ascension," the other man hisses back. "Imagine it, a defender in charge. It will be worse than my father being in charge, a guarantee blood will continue to be spilt and people will continue to be enslaved. Only I can bring peace to Obrothea now." The man's voice softens. "Especially if I have a scribe like you at my side. Now go while Tharin sleeps. Tell her you want to chat, as you did the other night. Give her the herlecian. Tell her it is a Skarsdonian delicacy. It is so sweet tasting she will not know how dangerous it is. You told me yourself how she has enjoyed tasting our food. It is what must be done, and she trusts you, Castian."

Castian? He's been involved all along? Another terrifying thought comes to me then. He's with Isla right this very minute.

"Oh God, no!" I shout out. I need to get back to the palace but how? I peer towards the tuskian. Looks like I'm about to get a crash course in riding these beasts.

Tharin

I run out of the Globe Palace and call for my tuskian. As I do, I hear a thunderous noise in the distance. Is it my imagination, or is that a tuskian approaching the palace? As it draws closer, I cannot believe my eyes. Kate is riding it, and she looks glorious. Her raven hair is flying up behind her, her arms strong as she holds the tuskian's reins.

I run to her. "Kate, I got it all wrong, I—"

"It doesn't matter. We can talk about your stupidity later. Where's Isla?"

I frown. "She is safe with Castian."

"No, she is not safe with him."

She must know about the incursion. "Do not fear, Ryker's men are outnumbered, and I have been told all the children are secure in the library with their scribes."

She looks confused. "Ryker's men?" As she says that, a Fostinian stumbles down the stairs. He's chased by Kiah, who lops his head off in front of us.

"Oh God," Kate whispers, watching as the head rolls

down the stairs. "I–I see what you mean now. I didn't mean Isla is in danger from Ryker's men. I mean Castian is the one who gave me the herlecian blossoms."

"No, not Castian."

"Why not?" she says as she watches me from atop the tuskian. "He's a Fostinian. He has plenty of reason to want to ensure you Highborns don't get even more powerful. How about you finally trust me, Tharin?"

I look into her eyes. "I do trust you, Kate."

"You have a funny way of showing it."

I turn to Kiah to prove my point. "The library. We must get to Isla and Castian."

"The library was breeched," Kiah says. "That is why we have come out. If you are after Castian and Isla, I just saw them running to what I thought was safety in the forest."

Kate and I exchange a look. "Get on," she says to me, gesturing to the space behind her on the tuskian. "It'll be quicker if we head to the forest together." I snag my foot in the stirrup and swing up behind her, wrapping my arms around her and going to grab the reins.

"No," she says in firm voice. "I'm in control for once."

TWENTY-FOUR

Kate

As we approach the forest, we see two figures striding towards it beneath the bright three moons. One tall, one small. It's Castian with Isla. I steer the tuskian in their direction. As we draw closer, Tharin leaps off the moving beast, landing on the ground with precision and rushing towards them. Castian turns, his hand on Isla's shoulder, eyes widening as Tharin runs at him. He quickly removes a dagger from his cloak and raises it to Isla's neck.

Tharin freezes.

"Isla," I scream, jumping off the tuskian and going to Tharin. I can feel the anger in his trembling arm as I stand close to him. I want him to barrel towards Castian and knock the dagger from his hand, but I also know it could be fatal for Isla. One movement, and the dagger could be plunged into her tiny neck.

"Mommy?" she says, her voice trembling. "Why is Castian doing this?"

"I know why," I say, trying to keep my voice calm as I look into Castian's eyes.

"How can you possibly know why, Kate," Castian says, hand trembling as he holds the knife against my daughter's skin.

"Haven't I too been ripped from my home? And Isla as well?" I say.

Castian shakes his head. "No, that is different."

"Is it?" I ask. "The skills I offer may not be as sophisticated as those you offer, but they are skills all the same, a way for the Skarsdonians to improve their lives and the lives of their children…by ripping others' futures away. It is a savage, immoral, brutal way of doing things. Do you really want to copy them?" I ask, eying the dagger.

"We must do what must be done to bring a better future," Castian says in a shaky voice. "A few sacrifices for the survival of many. We must bring an end to the brutal Skarsdonian ways, and if that means stopping their most powerful asset, then so be it."

"Is it though?" I ask gently. "Surely things can change. Look at Tharin now. He could have rushed at you with all his might and thunder just now. And what about Isla? Do you really think she is going to make Skarsdonians more dangerous, more invincible? Have you considered she might make them more…well, more human?"

Castian frowns slightly.

"I know you have grown to care for Isla in the time you have spent with her," I say, taking a step towards him. "Do you really wish to harm her?"

"No, that is why I'm taking her to our people, the Fostinians," Castian says.

I feel a sense of relief. He was never going to hurt her. "What if I come with you?" I suggest. Castian opens his mouth to say something, but a voice sounds out behind us. We all turn to see Heldran, Remus, and Kiah striding over, several defenders behind them.

266

"Good, you found Castian," Remus shouts. "I will kill him now if you wish, Tharin."

Confusion crosses Castian's face. "Remus, I don't understand."

I look between them and it hits me. The other man in my memory from ten years ago was Remus. I have seen all along how close they are. Who else could draw Castian into his plans?

"You're the one behind all this," I say to Remus.

"What *are* you talking about?" Remus says with a laugh.

"I remembered a conversation I overheard ten years ago," I say. "You and Castian were talking about poisoning me. You wanted me out of the picture, my unborn child too, so Tharin would be weakened. *You* wanted to be the Grand Sovran."

Tharin looks at his brother in shock. "Is she right, brother?"

"Tharin, this is getting ridiculous now," Heldran says. "Your love is blinding you."

"No," Kiah whispers, a look of shock on his face. "She is right. I remember now seeing you gather herlecian blossoms before you left for Earth ten years ago, Remus. It all makes sense. You wanted to take them onto the ship with you, just in case you needed them."

Remus is quiet for a moment and then sighs. "Maybe it is good to finally be honest."

Tharin's face falls, and my heart goes out to him. So much betrayal from all sides of his family. No wonder he suspected me.

"You know I love you, brother," Remus continues, "but a defender cannot be Grand Sovran."

"But a murderous and deceptive sage can?" Tharin hisses.

"Come on, you know deep down inside I am right," Remus says. "You have never wanted this power. I saw your face when our father declared you were the new heir after our mother and sister were buried. I had hoped, of course, that our father would take the sensible option and see a scribe would be better. Ethos was out of the question, the deranged fool, but I was perfect."

"What about our sister?" Tharin says. "Thesera was alive then and—" His face suddenly drops, the colors beneath his skin darker then I have ever seen them. "Ryker didn't intercept Kate's video," he says in a low, strained voice. "You saw her record it, and you sent it to him. You *wanted* Ryker to invade Skarsdon. You wanted a smokescreen so you could arrange for our sister to die, and pave the way for you to take power when the time came."

Castian's mouth drops open. Clearly, he knew nothing of this. Isla catches my eye, peering at the dagger that is now hanging by his side. She narrows her eyes, and I know that look. It's the one that comes before she's about to be mischievous. I shake my head. I don't want her doing anything risky or too dangerous, but it's too late. She is way too much like her father, her *real* father. As I watch in horror, she grabs the dagger.

"Daddy!" she shouts.

She throws the dagger to Tharin. He catches it and runs at Remus with the dagger held aloft. I run forward, pulling Isla into my arms and taking her to safety a few meters away. Tharin throws himself onto Remus. They scuffle, Remus punching Tharin in the face as Tharin scrabbles to pin him down with one arm as he raises his dagger.

"You killed our sister for nothing but greed," Tharin shouts into his face. "And what of our mother? Why take her life?"

Remus's eyes glass over. "That wasn't meant to happen. She was not meant to be in the library with Thesera. Of course, the server I tasked with drawing Thesera to the library at the opportune time was punished for her mistake of letting my mother accompany her."

Tharin lets out a roar and looks helplessly up at the three moons. "What a fool I have been. It has been you all along, not Ethos. Every step of the way, you've tried to squeeze the support and power away from me. Tried to take my love and my child away, as you took my mother and sister. All for your empty ambitions." He shakes his head. "I will have to kill you now."

"Now, brother, do not let your emotions take over," Remus quickly says, eying the dagger in Tharin's hands. "Remember what Father always says, a few for the many. You have said yourself what a great leader I would make."

Tharin suddenly goes very still and looks back down at his brother, face so tormented I want to go to him and hold him.

"You have tried to destroy everything for nothing," I shout out. "You say you did all this for the greater good, but the truth is, you did it for you and your hunger for power."

"Kate is right," Tharin says. "And now I will take that hunger away."

He raises the dagger even higher.

"You will not kill your brother," Remus says.

"You are no brother of mine," Tharin says and plunges the dagger into Remus's heart.

TWENTY-FIVE

Kate

I stroke Isla's head as she sleeps, still not quite able to leave her side. I know Tharin waits for me outside. He insisted the defenders he has assigned to protect us leave so we could have some time alone. I'm not sure I can face Tharin though. I feel such a dizzying mixture of emotions. Anger that he so easily mistrusted me and misread a situation. Fear he's capable of doing it again, that he could remove me from my daughter again. But love and sympathy too. He's been played for a fool, his love for me used to his disadvantage by two evil men intent on driving us apart and destroying everything we've created together.

I'm also still reeling from the horror of learning Remus was responsible for his sister's and mother's deaths. But he has paid the ultimate price at Tharin's hand. He is dead and for that, I'm relieved even though it was difficult to watch. I think I could have killed Remus myself if I had to. He tried to poison me and my unborn child. What if he had succeeded? It's helped me understand Tharin and his species' drive for battle. When you're protecting your home and people, you will do anything.

And Castian, what of the role he played? It's clear he loved Remus. I saw it in the way the scribe reacted to his death earlier. He threw himself on top of Remus's body and wept. Did Remus love him back? I'm really not sure a man like Remus could love. He'd used Castian's feelings for him, twisted Castian into supporting his plan to wipe the two heirs above him away so he could be Grand Sovran one day.

At least Tharin listened to me when I begged him not to kill Castian and instead imprison him. He *had* been dragged from his home and no doubt seen people he loved die. He loved Remus, clearly, but he also wanted a new world where people were not taken as slaves. Could we blame him? When I was first taken, if I'd had the chance to ruin the men who'd kidnapped me without risking Isla's life, I would have taken it.

What about now, what chances will I take now? The vessel waiting to take me back to Earth might still be on that landing strip right now. Would Tharin let me leave with Isla? I think so. He seems so defeated.

I peer out of the window towards the three moons. What a surreal, stunning sight they make. They are the stuff of dreams. I've been too scared to pursue my dreams because of what happened to my mother. And what of love? Am I too scared to pursue that too? Apart from those nights I spent with Tharin ten years ago, I've been so ruled by fear since my mother died. Those nights are slowly coming back to me as the hours unfold. I really did rediscover my sense of adventure as I fell for him on that ship above Earth. Maybe I need to be more Skarsdonian in my ways. More like Isla. Brave. Fearless. Willing to grab life and make the most of it like she grabbed that dagger?

And maybe Tharin needs to be more human and learn life is not a game of war and strategy?

I leave the room to go and find my warrior alien. Tharin is standing by the window, looking out towards the three moons, gorgeous face drawn. I take a moment to study him. His huge form, the muscles that bulge and flex in his back. His long golden hair. He represents all I fear and love. Adventure. Risk taking. Otherworldly beauty.

I walk over to him, and he turns. Emotions flood his eyes. I can see he wants to pull me into his arms, but I think he knows I'm still hurt by what he did. He battles his desire, and it makes me love him even more.

"Is she asleep?" he asks.

"Yes."

Tharin nods. "She will have a long journey ahead of her tomorrow, you both will, so it will be good for her to rest."

"Journey?"

His jaw flexes. "The vessel that was to take you to Earth will remain here until the morning for you and Isla." He sighs. "I know it is what you want, Kate, and I cannot stand in your way." His eyes fill with pain. "How can I after what I have done to you? Now you will have the freedom you so desire."

I look out towards the landing strip. So there I have it, the chance for freedom.

"Freedom," I whisper. "What *is* freedom? My mother once told me freedom is not worth having if it does not include the freedom to risk mistakes. Freedom is love. Freedom is the courage to take a leap of faith. She should have done that by leaving that commune and making her own way in life. Maybe she would be alive now if she hadn't been so afraid to start a new adventure, just me and her."

"And maybe my mother and sister would still be alive if I hadn't been so afraid."

I look at him in shock. "You? Afraid?"

He sinks down onto the chair behind him, putting his head in his hands. "I was not sure about Ethos's experiments with you human women. My gut screamed it was wrong, but I didn't fight back. I was too afraid of disappointing my father. If I had pressed my case, maybe I would have stayed in Skarsdon and been able to protect my mother and sister." He peers up at me, eyes sad. "I have been afraid to love. I was taught it is a weakness, but now I see refusing to love is a weakness. The truth is, I would give everything up for you, Kate. I would even give my own freedom up."

I go to him and kneel before him, taking his hands in mine. His touch sends shivers down my spine, and the way his sad, green gaze sinks into mine makes my breath quicken. "I don't know what I want right now, but I do know I need time."

"Time on Earth?"

I frown. "Not yet. I don't want to be hurried."

"So you will stay…for a while?"

I nod. "For a while."

"And us?"

I reach up and stroke his face. "You're a damn fool, but I love you. And I really, really want to kiss you right now." His face erupts into a smile, and he scoops me up into his arms. Our lips collide as he stands, takes me to our room, and lays me on the bed of mists. I look at him as I have so many times before—not just these past few days but ten years ago too, all those memories now surging back. He stands tall and other-worldly against the three moons in the window beyond.

"Undress," I command. He does as I ask, unlocking his shoulder armor to reveal more of his muscled chest beneath skin that oscillates with desire. I sigh, taking him all in, this beautiful god-like figure. My Pledged. My future king. The love of my life.

I put my hand out to him. "I need you inside me this instant."

He inclines his head to me. "As you wish." He comes to the bed, spreads my legs with his palms, and sinks himself into me. I look out towards the three moons again and smile. This is only the beginning of our story.

EPILOGUE

SIX MONTHS LATER

Charlotte

Seriously, I don't think I've ever seen a hotter couple than Kate and Tharin. Look at them up there, waving at the crowds. That's king and queen material right there, and I should know, considering I've spent the last ten years observing the British royal family do their thing.

Kate catches my eye, and I blow her a kiss. She looks so cute in that golden dress of hers, her growing tummy all round and compact. Honestly, that girl is lucky. I bet if I ever fall pregnant, I'll look like the tuskian they're sitting on as they ride through the streets of Skarsdon celebrating the peace Tharin has negotiated with his brother, Ethos. Not that I plan to get pregnant any time soon. Hopefully, this witch vibe won't run out of steam.

I watch as Tharin places his hands on Kate's stomach and kisses her cheek. He really is wrapped around her little finger. This huge beast of a man is on his knees for a little human woman. Isla spots me in the crowds. I can't help but laugh whenever I see her in her little suit of armor. I mean, she rocks it, for sure, but she's so tiny. She notices Henry, who's standing beside me, and beckons him to join her.

"Can I?" Henry asks Helena.

"Only if I can," my sister replies, clearly missing her years in the spotlight. I watch as they run towards the tuskian. I would join them, but I'm about to go on a hunting expedition into the forest…again. It's all I've been doing the past six months. There have been more sightings of Ryker and his Fostinian crew. I thank my lucky stars they failed when they stormed the Globe Palace six month ago. I'm not exactly a big fan of the Skarsdonians, but at least they have *some* manners. The Fostinian race seems a little—how shall I put this?—rough around the edges. I saw the way they stormed into the palace, roaring like boars with their dark hair and furs. I'm not sure my experience on the vessel coming from Earth would have been the same if they had taken over Skarsdon and been the ones to kidnap us.

Now it's up to me to me to shoot the most hated Fostinian of all with my bow and arrow. Turns out it's tradition here— and gosh, do they take their traditions seriously—that if a well-regarded warrior is murdered, their partner must be the one to kill that murderer. Sadly, as Helena's Pledged, Persean, was one of Ryker's victims when he stormed the palace, the tradition has fallen to her. Except this is a woman who faints at the sight of blood. So they're insisting a human woman kill their most wanted rebel.

So yet again, I've offered to do something for my sister. I guess it's gotten me out of the Globe Palace the past few weeks. I've been allowed to roam the amazing Fostinian forest with two annoying Skarsdonian defenders as my guides. Oh look, there they are now at the edge of the forest, beckoning for me to join them. I sigh and go over to them.

"Hey, Crabbe and Goyle," I say as I greet them. It's my own private little joke. Of course, they've never read the

Harry Potter books so have no idea they're being compared to Draco's brainless henchmen. They grunt in response and give me the suspicious side-eye they always give me. They do, after all, think I'm a witch, which is just as well, since they both eye my cleavage sometimes. I honestly think if they weren't convinced I was a human witch, they'd be throwing me into the undergrowth and sharing my virginity between them.

We step into the forest, and I take in the scene before me. The strange purple trees with branches that pulse and contort with color all still awe me. The pink-carpeted ground below has small creatures I can't even begin to imagine squirming beneath. This place is as far from a British royal estate as you can get. We walk in silence for over an hour. I try to ignore the huge defender behind me, who I'm convinced is staring at my butt. I'm starting to wonder how long this witch act will really last.

A branch cracks nearby. We all stop, and one of the defenders dives behind a nearby fallen trunk, pulling me with him as the other joins us. The trunk is covered in pink glowing moss that smells sickly sweet. I keep my bow upright, my focus honed as I peer over the fallen trunk. This happens a number of times each day, so I can pretty much guarantee it's just going to be one of the forest's strange creatures. But I have to *pretend* to think it's Ryker.

There's another cracking noise, and suddenly a figure appears between the trees in the distance. My heartbeat accelerates. That's no forest animal.

It's the rebel, Ryker. I hold my breath. He's even more magnificent in the flesh, at least seven foot tall, maybe taller, with muscles that ripple and skin that oscillates with color. Though he wears a hood to shroud his face, I see strands of his long brown hair as he treads carefully through the dark forest. The outcast brother. The disgraced war hero. The heartless killer. I look at the two defenders to my side. I've been told I need confirmation. They both quickly nod, and I pull back the arrow, watching it quiver slightly.

I can't believe we've finally found him.

Slowly, slowly...

Ryker suddenly turns and looks straight at me. I can hardly breath. That face. He's a *Wuthering Heights* Heathcliff and a sultry barbarian all wrapped up in one. Those green eyes stare out from pale, filthy skin and elaborate tattoos trawl down his mammoth chest. Everything inside me screams, *Don't kill him!*

So I do what I did when my royal brother-in-law took us hunting.

I purposefully miss the kill shot and aim for his shoulder instead.

You can read more of Charlotte and Ryker's story in
Seized by the Rebel Barbarian from Amazon

ABOUT THE AUTHOR

Trinity Blaise has published a bunch of books in other genres, many of which have become Kindle bestsellers (like, #1 of the entire chart kinda bestsellers). She is now publishing sci-fi romance series under this pen name because, well, super steamy + trad publishers = shocked faces. Check out her website for more information!

www.trinityblaise.com

Printed in Great Britain
by Amazon